BLOOD RELAY

A Novel

Devon Mihesuah

I0823649

BANTAM
NEW YORK

Bantam Books
An imprint of Random House
A division of Penguin Random House LLC
1745 Broadway, New York, NY 10019
randomhousebooks.com
penguinrandomhouse.com

A Bantam Books Trade Paperback Original

Copyright © 2026 by Devon Mihesuah

Penguin Random House values and supports copyright. Copyright fuels creativity, encourages diverse voices, promotes free speech, and creates a vibrant culture. Thank you for buying an authorized edition of this book and for complying with copyright laws by not reproducing, scanning, or distributing any part of it in any form without permission. You are supporting writers and allowing Penguin Random House to continue to publish books for every reader. Please note that no part of this book may be used or reproduced in any manner for the purpose of training artificial intelligence technologies or systems.

BANTAM & B colophon is a registered trademark of Penguin Random House LLC.

ISBN 978-0-593-98382-9
Ebook ISBN 978-0-593-98383-6

Printed in the United States of America

1st Printing

BOOK TEAM: Production editor: Jennifer Rodriguez • Managing editor: Saige Francis • Production manager: Jane Haas Sankner • Copy editor: Melissa Churchill • Proofreaders: Chuck Thompson, Amy Harned, Claire Maby

Book design by Caroline Cunningham

Title page background art: MarekPhotoDesign.com/Adobe Stock

The authorized representative in the EU for product safety and compliance is Penguin Random House Ireland, Morrison Chambers, 32 Nassau Street, Dublin D02 YH68, Ireland. https://eu-contact.penguin.ie

BLOOD RELAY

To Dr. Taylor Dunagan

Welcome to the family

In each family, a story is playing itself out, and each family's story embodies its hope and despair.

—Auguste Napier

BLOOD RELAY

PROLOGUE

Dels Billy rolled up the window and plugged her iPhone cord into the dash. The Jonas Brothers' song "Sucker" blasted the cab.

Lee looked out his window and asked, "Is that Rhonda?"

"Yeah. I dunno who that is with her and I don't care."

They listened to the Jonas Brothers for a minute, then Lee said, "Those guys."

"Yeah. And so?"

He shrugged. "Just sayin'."

"Who would you rather listen to?"

"Um. Luke Bryan."

Dels sighed. "Well, he's okay. But we'll go with what I got for now."

As she hit I-40, Santana's "Aqua Marine" began.

"How's your knee?" he asked.

"It throbs and so does my head."

After the Santana song, Metallica's "Enter Sandman" started. Dels tapped her fingers on the steering wheel. "I still think there's nothing wrong with playing Black Sabbath's 'Paranoid' and Led Zeppelin's 'Rock and Roll' during the relays."

Lee laughed. "The music would drown out the announcers."

They said nothing else for almost eight minutes.

Pink Floyd's David Gilmour was in his last solo of "Comfortably Numb" when the truck gave a small sputter. Dels sat up straight.

"You feel that?" she asked Lee.

"Feel what?"

"Hmm. Nothing, I guess."

"So what about that Crow girl?" Lee asked. "She's tall like you. But we got better horses."

"Yarda is awesome," she said. "She's a good rider."

Joan Jett's "I Love Rock 'N Roll" was only at the halfway point when the truck sputtered again. Noticeably this time. Dels looked to her dash. "Gas is three-quarters full. Maybe water's in the tank. No engine light. Probably water."

"You think I can ride this summer?" Lee asked.

"You love the horses and they love you," Dels said. She kept looking at her dashboard. "I think that you—"

The engine skipped again.

"Fumes! Holy shit, Dels," Lee yelped as he rolled down his window.

Gomer barked from the back seat.

Dels fought to keep control of the steering wheel.

She gasped.

"What?" Lee squeaked.

She looked into the right side-view mirror. "Trailer's got a flat!"

The truck pulled harder to the right. She gripped the wheel.

"There!" Lee yelled. "There's an exit."

"That truck stop is closed," she panted.

"Doesn't matter."

"Okay. Okay. I think I can get in there," Dels said. She leaned forward, her hands still tight around the wheel. "Oh my God. We're losing power."

The truck stammered.

"The gate's open," Lee said.

Dels could see the outline of two dented gates in the growing darkness. She fought with the wheel to turn the truck toward the entrance.

They passed the gates, kept going another half minute, and as soon as Joan stopped singing the truck died in an old eighteen-wheeler parking spot. Dels popped the hood.

"Lee, check on Issi. Make sure the fumes didn't make her sick. And give her some water."

She reached for the controls by the radio. "No flashers. The electrical system's dead."

"I'll get her out," Lee said. "I need to find a post to tie her to."

Dels looked at her phone, then opened the door. "Gomer. Here." The dog hopped onto the middle console, into Dels's lap, then out the door. She held the phone to her ear, praying he would pick up. "Come on, Bake. Answer."

Headlights illuminated the cab's interior through Dels's window.

"Truck's coming," Lee yelled.

Dels squinted into the light, jumped out, and opened the hood. Smoke billowed out.

Issi whinnied and her hooves clicked on the broken concrete.

Lee said, "I hope that's another team."

"It's not," Dels responded. Her voice had risen an octave.

Gomer barked over the sound of the truck engine.

The mystery truck slowly rolled toward her, then the lights turned off.

"Hey," Lee greeted. "We need some help."

Dels could make out a jumble of shapes in the darkness, then Lee's high-pitched scream was cut off.

One of the shapes came toward Dels. She turned to run as she screamed, "No!"

A few minutes later the other truck's engine revved and its headlights briefly illuminated Dels's empty cab before fading along with the engine's growl as it made its way out the exit and back onto I-40.

1

When Perry Antelope and Sophia Burns entered the victim's garage, a lanky female officer with false eyelashes and rosy pink blush stepped forward. "Detectives," she greeted, passing them the logbook. "Sign in, please."

Tarps covered the floor and two layers of painter's plastic hung from the ceiling with duct tape, protecting the otherwise orderly garage. The man—Perry checked her notes, Nathaniel McGee—sat slumped in a camping chair, its drink holder clutching a Coke whose ice hadn't yet melted. Perry and her husband, Troy, owned half a dozen of those chairs. Nathaniel sat on a blue one, the exact color Perry had chosen when she and Troy had taken the kids camping last weekend.

Sophia sighed. "Suicide?"

"A regrettable resolution for a fixable problem," Perry replied. "At least cleanup will be somewhat easy."

Despite the man's efforts to ensure a tidy death, Perry saw what looked like raw hamburger on the garage ceiling lightbulb and on the painter's plastic that gently undulated in the breeze. Blood droplets and other particles dotted the iPhone that lay on the garage floor six feet from the body.

Sophia pushed her short, wavy hair behind her ears and exhaled.

"You can step out for a minute," Perry said quietly.

When Sophia had been a patrol officer, she had seen a variety of grim injuries and corpses in various stages of decomposition, but Perry recalled that Sophia almost fainted at the first autopsy they attended together when they became partners six months ago. Sophia had turned white at the sight of their first call as a team—a woman had been found decapitated. She had stared without blinking for a full minute at the headless torso. Perry thought the six-foot, 175-pound former NCAA Division 1 shotput winner would falter, but after a minute, she was crouching over the woman for a closer look.

Sophia took two more deep breaths, then pulled herself together. "I'm good. I've seen worse."

Perry patted her on thc back.

A red Mercedes GLS SUV pulled up in front of the driveway, with 2 Shadows's "Mad God" blasting so loud Perry could hear it through the car's rolled-up windows. Perry knew of the Goth band because of her daughter, Olyve. How the heck did the chief medical examiner know about them?

"How're you, Melinda?" Perry asked when the woman finally reached them.

"Was about to have second dessert with Milt." Melinda smirked. "After cake, if you know what I mean."

Perry chuckled. "What do we have here?"

"You tell me." Melinda gave the body a quick perusal. "Well. Did you inspect him?"

"I did," Perry responded.

The two looked at each other, and Perry could tell Melinda was thinking the same thing she was.

"Thoughtful prep work," Perry said. She brushed away stray

hairs that had come loose from her bun and stuck to the sweat on her face.

Melinda nodded in agreement. "This style of offing helps a bit. That suicide a few years ago—you know, the woman who killed her fourteen cats then slit her wrists in the bathtub? The tub helped."

"I do remember that." Perry had been one of the first on the scene. Cleaning up the physical carnage was one thing—a specialized cleaning service could deal with the tissue and stains. The survivors' emotional chaos would take much longer. Now, through the kitchen door, she could hear the man's wife wailing.

"No suicide note," Sophia said.

The rest of the forensics team pulled up in a white van. The crime scene supervisor, Sarita Bianchi, emerged from the driver's side, followed by her three colleagues carrying bags of various sizes.

After the forensics team pulled on their gloves, Perry and Sophia rounded the corner of the house to find a distraught bald man standing with a trio of police officers. "I want to talk to him," said Perry.

The bald man was dressed in loose-fitting black Adidas running pants and a T-shirt with a Gandalf figure wearing a robe and tall wizard hat and holding a football. The letters underneath read FANTASY FOOTBALL. His head was down and he kept sniffing, like a man who was trying to hide the reality that he was crying. He refused a Kleenex.

She approached the sniffing man.

"Hello," she said. "I'm Detective Perry Antelope, Oklahoma City police. And your name?"

She moved the bottom of her black blazer to the side so he could see her shield attached to her belt. Perry knew the man was upset, but he could cry later at home.

"Jason Lyndon."

"What is your connection to the deceased?"

She sensed rather than heard Sophia approach. The taller woman stood to her right, a step behind her. Perry did not acknowledge her.

The handsome man let out a shaky breath. "I'm his attorney."

"How did you hear about his death?"

"He contacted me."

Perry thought about that. If you were going to kill yourself, contacting your attorney would make sense if you had a will.

"May I see your phone?"

"Sure." He scrolled to the message, then handed it to her.

J—I need you to make sure that Jahneen and the kids get everything. I have been depressed for some time now and don't know what else to do. I trust you and thx. Nate.

"Sir, do you mind if I take screenshots and send them to my phone?"

"No. Go right ahead." He shuffled his feet, and when he dropped his gaze, Perry glanced at Sophia and gave a quick nod toward him.

While Perry's thumbs flew over the screen, Sophia asked him, "Do you come over here often?"

"Yeah, we do barbecues and the kids play. I've known Nate a long time."

Perry finished with his phone and handed it back. She asked, "What did you do after you got this message?"

"I immediately called the police. I had showered and was drying off when I got the text, so I read it, called the police, and hurried over."

He motioned to his bright red 2024 BMW iX xDrive50. Perry could not remember every car model, but she prided herself on knowing most of them. This one probably cost Jason close to ninety thousand dollars.

"Where do you live?"

"Apple Valley." The wealthy neighborhood was about fifteen minutes away. "I banged on the garage side door when I realized it was locked. Then I went to the front door. Was about to hop the fence when the police came and told me to stop. Then Jahneen and the kids drove up. I guess they were at their oldest kid's soccer tournament. Jahneen opened the garage door with the remote."

Sophia took out her phone.

Jason watched her as he kept talking. "I ran in first and found him, so I was able to keep Jahneen and the kids away."

"Good for you." Perry knew that seeing their father in this state would permanently traumatize the children.

He rubbed his hands over his face. "What else was I supposed to do?" He cried loudly.

She did not respond.

It seemed he expected an answer. He glared at Perry and clenched his fists. "It wasn't my fault. Nate did it right after he texted me," he said, his voice growing louder. "If I had known what he was going to do, I would have been here to stop it. I was *not* a part of this."

Perry stood straighter and twitched the fingers of her right hand. She felt the outline of her Glock in her holster. She glanced to Sophia, who also registered the man's agitation.

Jason took a few deep breaths, then leaned back on his car. "Okay. Okay. I'm okay," he repeated.

"All right." She kept her eyes on Jason. "How did you arrive here before the police?"

The yard became silent. The only sounds were the muffled cries of Nathaniel's wife and a dog barking in the distance.

"What do you mean?"

"Well, Mr. Lyndon, according to Google Maps, your home is a seventeen-minute drive away from here. But the police station is right around the corner. It would take three minutes max for them to get here."

Jason's mouth stayed open but he said nothing.

"Answer the question."

"Well, that can't be right."

"There was no soccer tournament today, but there is one tomorrow," Sophia added. She had assumed her ready stance—legs apart and hands clasped in front of her. "I wonder why Mrs. McGee dressed up her son in a soccer uniform."

The other officers took a step closer.

Jason Lyndon began to sweat.

Perry saw Melinda out of the corner of her left eye.

"Mr. McGee has a head wound," Perry said.

"Of course he does!" Jason yelped. "He shot himself."

"This particular wound is on the crown of his head."

Melinda added, "Under all that hair is a depression."

Jason's hands clenched. Perry continued, "You know, if you had used a shotgun, his head would have blown apart and we wouldn't have known about that. And if you had aimed it, say, straight at his throat, we might not have noticed the ligature marks around his neck."

"When you strangle someone," Melinda said, "the vessels in their eyes rupture. Like what we see here."

The officers stepped closer.

"Officer Jimmison," Sophia said, "please secure Mrs. McGee."

The officer hurried into the house.

Perry continued. "And let's not forget that if a person used a rifle or shotgun to shoot themselves, they would not have one arm draped casually on the armrest. And the weapon's trigger probably would be facing the ceiling, not toward the floor as we see in this case."

Jason's eyes rounded and he hunched over as if he might vomit. Instead, he turned and bolted off the driveway and onto the grass. Sophia leapt forward as if pushing from starting blocks. In a move that would make Zaire Franklin applaud, she stayed low to the ground, and as she wrapped her arms around the surprised Lyndon she used her strong shoulders to drive him forward and down until he face-planted into unmown dandelions. The other officers had followed and within seconds Jason Lyndon was cuffed.

Perry was grinning as she said, "This has got to be one of the stupidest murder plots ever."

Perry backed into her driveway and parked outside the garage. She wanted to expend some energy before Troy came home.

After changing into shorts and a T-shirt, she went to the garage, where her family kept all their shoes on shelves that lined the south wall.

She retrieved her Boker training knife from the top tool drawer, removed it from its sheath, and faced the tennis ball that dangled from a string attached to the ceiling. The yellow ball was a formidable opponent.

She started slow but warmed up quickly. Soon sweat ran down her face and soaked her clothing. Then she heard the door leading to the laundry room open and braced herself.

"I don't understand why you feel you need to do that." Troy Antelope stood in the doorway, his arms folded across his broad chest as he observed his wife attempting to slice the tennis ball. His hair was plaited into two long braids that fell down his back. The light behind him outlined his tall, lean yoga body. Since his football days ended, he had given up heavy lifting in favor of running, swimming, and more repetitions of lighter weights. She did not have to see his face to know his dark eyebrows would be scrunched in annoyance.

The knife she held was not the same as the Merlin throwing knife that she used on the vertical oak log with a red bull's-eye painted on the bark. Troy helped her set up the heavy log after she had hit a sapling oak at the back of their property so many times that the tree trunk finally broke in half five feet from the ground.

After fighting the tennis ball, she planned to use the training knife on her expensive BOB. She also pounded the Body Opponent Bag with her fists and feet. She liked BOB more than their Everlast bag because BOB had a face.

"Told you," she panted. "I need to work on my timing and speed."

"Olyve's basket is right over the garage door, Perry." He nodded toward the driveway. "We can play one-on-one. You can work on your footwork shooting hoops."

"It's not the same thing."

"We can go to the track and do sprints."

"I hate sprints. So do you."

"Why do you need a knife? You have a gun. Four guns, actually." He paused for effect. "That I know of."

Perry did not respond.

"Not counting the shotgun," he continued. "When are you gonna be in a knife fight?"

Perry kept swiping at the swinging ball with quick, short horizontal moves.

"Knife fighting is no joke, Perry," he persisted. "People who know how to knife fight know the best way to fight is to not get into one."

"Thank you, sensei."

"You need to watch Tommy Lee Jones teach Benicio del Toro in *The Hunted*."

"Saw it."

"I don't mean watch it to learn how to knife fight. I mean watch it to see what can happen to you."

"I get it."

Perry had watched the movie several times and she knew

how devastating knife wounds could be. After all, she was a homicide detective.

Perry had also earned her red belt in tae kwon do, but a hamstring tear prevented her from earning her black belt. By the time she healed, police academy training dominated her time and she never returned to the dojang. Still, during the four years that she trained, her Korean sahyun also offered courses in the use of Okinawan nunchucks and knife fighting four times a week. She had attended every one of those classes. In her spare time, she learned to flip butterfly knives and to walk a pen through her fingers. Those skills had greatly impressed Troy, but she had never needed to use a knife except to cut food.

Perry was not foolish enough to think that she could prevail easily in a knife confrontation. She knew that if she were to get into such an altercation, things could go sideways before she could blink.

Her husband droned on and said the same thing he always did when he found her with her knives: "Knife fighting is vicious. It takes skill and concentration. Even people who know how to use a knife get cut, and they spend years getting every possible move down. A random swing by someone who just picked up a knife for the first time can do damage. Flailing around could cut your throat. The best fight is no fight."

"I know," Perry said as she continued to dance around the ball. "You should write a poem about it."

He ignored that last statement. "And they don't fight a swinging ball. A knife fight means the other person also has a knife."

She had heard this before. "Same concept as with the heavy bag, Troy."

"Basics are good, but you need an opponent."

"Go get the other rubber knife over there and spar with me, then."

Troy plowed on. "What you're doing is like shooting at a

target. That ball and a silhouette target doesn't cut or shoot back."

She panted, but mainly from anger. Once she had warmed up and found a rhythm, it took some effort to stop. Troy's incessant lectures caused her to move faster. She hated when he watched her.

"Are you listening?" he asked.

Perry stopped and pushed stray strands behind her ears. "What?"

"When do detectives use knives?"

"They don't. But you never know when you'll be glad you have one."

"Have you ever been in need of a knife?"

"That chicken you cooked the other night wasn't exactly tender."

He did not respond.

"Just doing fundamentals," she said. "Fundamental movements. You have to master those before you can be successful at anything. Tennis, boxing, lifting weights, shooting pool, martial arts, writing, golf, math, cooking. Troy, everything depends on foundations. I'm just doing the basics."

Troy didn't move. Perry knew an argument was imminent. Still, she admired her husband as he stood in the garage doorway, his long braids moving in the breeze of the box fan.

"The best thing you can do is keep your distance."

"Close the door," she said. "You're letting the cool air out."

Troy stood watching his wife another minute, then said, "You're tired."

"Thanks for noticing."

"You need an early dinner, then sleep."

"Where are the kids?"

"Olyve has to backwash after the pool closes. She won't be home until after nine. Nico is spending the night at Sean's. I'll have food ready in twenty-five minutes." Troy shut the door.

"Love you," she yelled.

He opened the door and looked at her, then smiled and shut the door again.

That had been their MO since they met twenty-one years ago when Troy started his PhD program at Oklahoma State in Stillwater and Perry began her first year as a patrol officer. She had earned her degree in criminal justice from Eastern Oklahoma. She had no interest in advanced degrees, but she was interested in law enforcement. She met Troy one morning while both were running the bleacher steps of Stillwater High School. When they encountered each other at the bottom of one of the stairs, Perry was instantly smitten with the tall Comanche man with a thick ponytail that reached his waist. She smiled, then pointed up. The two raced to the top. By the time Perry reached the landing, she realized she was only two steps ahead. She had run cross country all four years of high school and two years in college and was surprised he kept pace with her. Both of them fell onto their backs, feet on the lower step, and gasped, hoping they would not vomit. Perry sat up. Troy recovered and leaned against the vertical pole railing.

"You want breakfast?" she asked.

"Pancakes and hashbrowns," he answered.

They met at Granny's Kitchen, where they introduced themselves in the parking lot, and after breakfast they agreed to have dinner together the next night. Perry invited Troy to her apartment, and since that time they had not been apart except for school and work. They married after eight months. After Troy earned his PhD and got a tenure-track position at the University of Oklahoma in Norman, Perry secured a job with the Oklahoma City Police Department. Six years later Troy got tenure and Perry became a detective.

It had been an easy twenty years with everything they both wanted falling into place. Olyve and Nico. No health problems except for the near-fatal head wound she'd sustained in the line of duty. Despite all the positives, her job was the long-running stressor between them. Troy was ready for Perry to retire despite her sustained rebuttals that she liked her job. She knew that she was not the only law enforcement officer who argued with their partner about their potentially dangerous career choice. Perry had been in the business for twenty-one years, fourteen as a detective, and had seen plenty of separations and divorces. As far as she could tell, her forty-one-year-old partner, Sophia, and her lineman husband, Mike, got along. To date, she had never heard Sophia mention an argument with him. Sophia had twenty years' experience as a police officer in Las Vegas and only a few months as a detective in Oklahoma. Prior to her career in law enforcement, she had thrown the shot put at the University of Oregon and after qualifying for the Olympics her junior year tore her rotator cuff in a freak accident while warming up. After graduation she taught high school math and coached track. Perry found Sophia to be cool-headed, street-smart, and a woman of few words. She was physically strong and her height and build commanded respect. They meshed well.

She'd decided to move to the backyard and confront BOB when her phone chirped.

"We got a dead man and a possible kidnapping," Sophia said on the other end. "Deputy Chief Loretta Dickinson wants us to take a look even though it's out of our jurisdiction. It appears the victims were Natives."

Their supervisor sometimes called them about cases outside of their jurisdiction because the victims were Indians and somehow had a connection to Oklahoma City.

"A Choctaw woman rode in a horse relay race in the city today, and now she's missing."

2

"What's a horse relay?" Sophia asked.

Perry and Sophia were speeding east on I-40. They passed farms and ranchlands, expanses of forests and occasional homes. The flat landscape allowed an unfettered view of the lightning that flashed along the southwestern horizon.

"Indian horse relay," Perry corrected. "A sport in which one rider switches horses twice around a half-mile track. One horse per lap. They jump off one horse and leap onto another. They have helpers who hold the horses waiting to run and catch the ones who've finished. It's dangerous and batshit crazy. They paint their horses and usually wear regalia. Women do it too."

"Sounds like something I'd like."

Perry reiterated the details of their new case. "The missing racer had left for home before the rest of the team—and when the team passed one of the rest stops, they found her truck and trailer parked there, empty. Her horse had been tied to a rail, but she was gone, and the man who had been with her was dead."

"An abandoned rest stop," Sophia said after a thoughtful silence. "I guess that means no lights."

"Correct," Perry answered. "Oklahoma used to have lots of rest stops, but they're expensive to maintain and they're prime spots for all manner of unsavory activities. Policing those spots is difficult."

"Not enough of us."

"I always wondered about truckers," Perry said. "You have to drive all day without letting your attention waver. Seems exhausting."

"Three hours of driving is my limit," Sophia said.

"You got me beat. I start squirming after two. You got a rain poncho in your pack?"

"I do. Sky's looking funky."

Perry sighed. "I've got two paintball ponchos and a waterproof parka in mine too. But I hope we don't need them. I don't want rain to wipe out any tracks that might be around here."

"Do they exercise?" Sophia asked.

"Who?"

"Truck drivers."

"Some do. Some have weights or bikes in their cabs. Some rest stops have short walking trails. But for the most part, probably not."

They thought about that for a few minutes.

Perry ran up behind a white Mercedes in the passing lane whose driver seemed oblivious to her lights and sirens. She could not go around because of an eighteen-wheeler in the right lane.

"Move it," Perry said. She flipped her lights a few times, then sounded two short siren yelps.

"Must be texting," Sophia said.

The Mercedes finally accelerated and moved in front of the truck.

"Thank goodness," Perry said.

Perry shot past. Her headlights lit up a sign ahead that read ENTERING SEMINOLE NATION OF OKLAHOMA.

"Seminole Nation," Sophia said.

"Yup. Their land and their jurisdiction."

"Will they work with us?"

"I hope so."

"Not easy to eat good food, I guess," Sophia said.

"Who? Seminoles?"

"No. Truckers."

Red and blue lights flashed in the distance off the road to their right. Perry slowed.

As they drew closer, Sophia said, "This way is blocked."

Two highway patrol cars were parked nose-to-nose, lights on, across the exit ramp. A fire truck flashed lights farther up the exit road.

"That's the exit anyway," Perry said. She kept going. "Here's the entry."

Perry drove up the ramp and stopped even with the two patrol cars parked on either side of the entry road. She recognized the Oklahoma patrol officer with a blond crew cut and a nametag reading EVANS. Perry rolled down her window and took the logbook he passed her to sign in. "Hey, Earl."

"Perry." The husky officer leaned down and shone his light at Sophia. He nodded. "A kid's unconscious and a woman's missing. Her truck is the one with the hood up."

"I heard the male was deceased," Perry said.

"Not as of about three minutes ago. Bad shape, though. And he's actually a teenager. He's in the grass."

She and Sophia assessed the scene as they moved down the lane. Counting the four that blocked the entrance and exit, there were eight highway patrol vehicles. The three in the parking lot were the black vehicles of the Seminole Nation, with white siding, POLICE in large black letters, and the label LIGHT-

HORSE above the gas tank. All the Five Tribes—Cherokees, Choctaws, Chickasaws, Muskogee-Creeks, and Seminoles—historically utilized Lighthorsemen. Among the Choctaws, Lighthorsemen rode through the Choctaw Nation with permission to punish law violators. They were not utilized as much after the Civil War because of the creation of sheriffs and deputy sheriffs. The Five Tribes now refer to some of their tribal police officers as the Lighthorse. A male patrol officer stood next to a short woman who gestured toward the open area of dirt and overgrown grass, and two more Seminole Nation officers knelt in the grass. Beyond stood a forest.

"The boy's not dead." Perry turned off the engine and lights. "Good to know."

"We'll see," Sophia responded. "Whatever we need to do, we have to do it fast. Storm's coming this way."

An ambulance with full sirens and lights moved past them, and Perry's heart began to thud. The paramedics exited and Perry and Sophia hurried to follow them toward a young Native man lying supine.

One paramedic shone the beam of her penlight on the young man, illuminating his injuries. Blood flowed from his left ear, both nostrils, and left eye. His bruised and bloody left temple appeared to have taken the brunt of whatever had assailed him. His eyes were closed. Perry thought he looked about sixteen, the same age as her daughter, Olyve. She sighed. The second paramedic slowly took a knee and inspected the victim's torso.

"He's alive," the tribal officer said in a baritone voice.

"Shallow breathing." The female paramedic opened her bag and pulled out an oxygen mask and a blood pressure cuff.

"So the Seminole Nation is on it," Perry said to the young officer. The man was short, dark, and handsome. He turned to greet her and Perry was surprised to see that he appeared to be a teenager.

Well, they take them if they're at least twenty-one, she thought. She blinked. If that was the case, she had him by nineteen years.

"We try to be." He pointed at the wounded man on the ground and swallowed. "But you're welcome to join the party."

"Don't want to step on toes," she replied.

"Osceola Tiger," he said as an introduction. His gloved hands were bloody and he did not extend them for a shake.

"Good to meet you," Perry said.

And she meant it. This officer had a powerful name. Osceola was the revered Seminole leader who refused to be removed to Indian Territory in the 1830s. He maintained that fight until he was deceived in 1837 and arrived at Fort Peyton under a flag of truce for peace talks. True to form, the United States government officials arrested him and, ultimately, Osceola died at Fort Moultrie, South Carolina. The official report said he perished from malaria or possibly an infection. The powers that be decapitated Osceola and buried him without his head.

"My partner is Sophia Burns and I'm Perry Antelope," she answered. "Oklahoma City homicide. I'm Choctaw, but my husband is Comanche, hence the last name. We got this call because the victims are all probably Choctaw and I often get those even if they're a bit out of my usual radius."

"Very good," Osceola said, removing his gloves, then reaching for his phone to exchange numbers. "I have a feeling this situation will require multiple hands."

Perry saw bobbing lights in the trees beyond the barbed wire fence. Lightning shot across the sky and thunder boomed, closer this time. One light was moving erratically in the darkness.

"What's going on out there?" Perry asked.

Another officer stepped forward. "Looking for the woman," he said. "Mickey Payne," he added as a way of introducing himself.

Perry and Sophia both shook hands. Payne introduced his partner across the way as Lopez.

"The woman driving that truck is missing and we got people looking in that tall grass and the trees," Mickey Payne said. "Her friends are over there." He pointed to the trailers where four horses stood drinking water from buckets and two officers spoke to two men and a woman. A dog with flowing reddish hair sat in front of them. The unique canine had fancy ears with tufts, a bushy yellow tail, weirdly long legs and snout, and an elongated body. Like a cross between a fox, Red River hog, and red-maned wolf.

The white horse drank, then touched noses with the canine. The other three horses also pricked their ears. Perry took in the diamond shapes on the thin brown horse's legs. The decorative paint had faded, probably because they had been hosed down, but the shapes were unmistakable. Perry loved to ride horses and for a moment visualized herself on the tall chestnut one with the braided mane.

Horizontal lightning flashed again like a strobe light.

Perry went to the truck and surveyed the inside. Payne followed. "The friends were driving past and saw her truck and trailer so they pulled in to investigate. There was no one in the truck and the woman didn't answer her phone. Neither did that kid," he said.

The key fob was in the cup holder. An iPhone lay on the seat. A fanny pack that could do double duty as a purse was next to a purple pack in the back seat. A gray Adidas bag lay next to it. A dog bed for a medium-sized canine was in the middle.

"You don't mind if we talk to them?" she asked.

Officer Payne took a small step back. "Of course not."

"Thanks." Perry touched Sophia's arm and motioned with her head to follow. This was a perfect opportunity for the young officers to learn a thing or two.

Perry and Sophia approached the group and introduced themselves.

Perry turned to the woman first. She was short in a Big Lebowski El Duderino T-shirt. "Your name?"

"I'm Vera Spring," she panted. Perry thought she might hyperventilate. The distraught woman held out her hand. Perry took it and her eyes widened at the strong, callused grip. "We came from the relays. At Crutcho Creek Park."

"The rodeo grounds?"

Vera nodded. "Yes."

Perry turned to the two young men. "And you two?"

"Sealy Billy," said the tall young man with thick dark curls that reminded Perry of her husband's hair when he cut it short after a trash pile burn went awry. Embers had latched on to one of Troy's braids and singed it off to his shoulder.

"My cousin's missing," Sealy said. He kept panning the dark area where the lights bobbed. He lifted his CHAHTA RIDERS T-shirt to his nose and wiped it.

The second man also wiped his nose with his team shirt and put his hand on his forehead. "Benny Durant. I'm one of the riders." Unlike Sealy, Benny focused directly on Perry. At five feet five inches, he stood as tall as her nose but acted taller. Benny's tangled hair reached his shoulders.

Then she heard a voice in the darkness. "Dels! Dels!" the voice screamed.

"Who's out there?" she asked.

"Bake Folsom," Vera answered. "He's searching for Dels. They're together." Obviously, Dels was the missing female.

A male Oklahoma Highway Patrol officer climbed over the barbed wire and strode on his long legs toward the screamer. Perry assessed the three T-shirt-clad people in front of her and decided to question Sealy.

"Come with me, Mr. Billy. Ms. Spring, please go with Officer Tiger. Mr. Durant, you stay here with Officer Payne." Perry turned to Officer Lopez. "Officer Lopez," Perry said. The woman cocked her head. "It's best if you assist with retrieving the man who's still out searching for his friend."

"Will do."

Perry led Sealy Billy to her cruiser. Sophia followed. Perry stopped by the driver's side door and pulled the small notepad and pen from her jacket pocket.

"Tell me what happened."

Sealy sighed, then stood straight and took a deep breath. "We were at the relays until about nine forty-five. Dels and Lee left before us because Dels hurt her leg jumping off Worf. We told her to go ahead so she could get home. When we drove past here, we saw her truck and trailer so we swung by to check, but she and Lee were gone. We scouted for them and I found Lee by the fence, but Dels is still out there and . . ."

"Okay, Mr. Billy. Slow down. Who is Dels?"

"Dels. Delphine Adele Billy—you know, two Dels. She's a rider. She won today. And she's my cousin."

"And Worf is her horse?"

"Yes. The tall chestnut."

Sealy Billy had blood on his hands, likely from touching the wounded man who was now on a stretcher. When he realized the young man was heading for the back of the ambulance, Sealy turned suddenly and sprinted to the gurney. On the back of his team shirt was the slogan I WANNA RUN FAST.

Sophia chased him, but the female paramedic straight-armed Sealy in the chest.

"We'll take it from here, hon," she told Sealy. "He'll go to OU Health first."

"Mr. Billy," Sophia said, "that's a level one trauma center. They'll take care of him."

"Lee?" Sealy's voice sounded shrill.

"Mr. Billy, he's unconscious." Sophia took him by the arm.

"Come with me." She guided him back to Perry. "What's Lee's last name?"

"Robinson."

"Is he related to anyone here?"

"No. He's our apprentice. He's just a kid."

Perry thought that an interesting thing to say considering that Sealy Billy appeared to be nineteen himself.

They watched as the large male paramedic closed the ambulance doors on the injured Lee Robinson. The man waddled to the driver's door and struggled to climb into his seat. As the vehicle started down the exit ramp, an Oklahoma Highway patrol car moved in front to lead the way, its lights on. As soon as the ambulance hit the highway the sirens sounded, but the driver kept it at twenty miles per hour. They would have to make a U-turn across the median in order to head back to Oklahoma City.

"Why did Lee ride with Dels Billy?" Sophia asked.

Sealy shrugged. "So she wouldn't be by herself. It's not safe . . ." He trailed off. "It's several hours to her house and Lee was gonna spend the night there. It's got a lot of rooms. Bake would take him home in the morning. Dels shoulda waited and we all coulda driven home together."

Perry listened to the exchange. *Shoulda, coulda, woulda.* These relay riders were going to beat themselves up over this.

"Mr. Billy," Sophia began as she shuffled her feet. "It's not your fault."

You made him walk into that one, Sophia, Perry thought.

"Breakdowns happen to women and men," Perry interjected. "And bad things happen to both on the roads. Every day. All the time. You are not to blame and it's not the fault of Mr. Robinson. Or you."

Sealy sniffed.

"Mr. Billy," Perry continued.

He sniffled again. Perry had enough of that and reached for

her travel tissue pack from her jacket pocket. She pulled out two tissues and gave them to Sealy.

"Where do Dels's parents live?"

Sealy shook his head. "They're dead. Dels is an only child and she lives in the house."

Perry envisioned a child roaming a creaky empty home. "How old is she?"

"Twenty-four."

The same age as when I had Olyve, Perry thought.

"Do you have a picture of Dels?"

"Lots of them." He took his phone from his back pocket, opened the photo app, and held it up for her to view.

Perry and Sophia leaned in. Dels stared straight at the camera, her long, thick hair unbound and her face nearly makeup-free, though she did wear mascara. She had a wide face, strong jaw, and full lips. Her full black eyebrows and eyelids slanted a bit upward, as did the corners of her mouth. Perry thought her a woman who probably looked good all the time, even if she was covered in race track mud.

Sealy tapped another shot and they saw a close-up of a woman dressed in a purple sleeveless top and yellow basketball shorts lined in red. She expanded the picture and saw that the shorts had the Great Seal of the Choctaw Nation on the left side, mid-thigh. Her knee socks had a purple background with dozens of small Great Seals. Perry liked those. Dels wore yellow high-tops. Her long braid hung over one shoulder, the thin purple, red, yellow, and green ribbons hanging to her hips. The colors of the Choctaw Nation. A tattoo circled her right biceps. Dels stood in front of the lithe horse that was now tied to the rail drinking water. Perry thought the picture could be a poster.

"Is the horse in the picture that one over there by that dog?" Perry asked.

"Yes. That's Issi. Gomer's the dog."

"How tall is Dels?" Sophia asked.

Sealy raised his hand horizontally a few inches above his head. "About five-ten maybe. I'm five-eight." He scrutinized Sophia. "She's almost your big," he said to her.

Perry had not heard that expression since her grandfather was alive. *About your big. About his big. About her big.* Her grandfather also used *his* and *her* when he compared animals.

"Mr. Billy, please send me as many pictures as you think reflect what Dels normally looks like." She handed Sealy a business card. "I'll pass them to the other officers."

"I saw a tattoo," Sophia said.

"A circle of corn around her right biceps," a voice sounded behind Sealy. Vera Spring had been listening. She moved closer. Officer Tiger was on her heels. "The cobs are vertical and the kernels are different colors. They're connected by green husks. I have a clear picture of it." Vera kept her head down, scrolling through her own photographs. "I knew she was going to have it done and I thought it would look like shit. But it came out really well." She held up her phone.

Perry did not have any tattoos but she would consider getting this one. "Looks like gem corn but brighter. Please send that to me." She handed Vera her card and stood watching her until the shorter woman clicked at her phone and a few seconds later her phone dinged.

Sealy looked back into the dark. Distant lightning illuminated the trees. "God, where is she?"

Perry followed his gaze. "If she's out there, we'll find her. Did anyone take videos today? Of the races, before and after?"

"Yes. Dels and I had on head cams."

"Head cameras?" Perry asked, suddenly enthused.

"We've done that at several races this year. Dels wants to put together a documentary."

"Where are those videos?"

"Bake has them on micro SD cards."

"We need to see them. Do you live stream?"

"No. Too much cursing."

Perry started to laugh but caught herself. If this kid only knew her vile vocabulary he would blanch. She'd learned it all from her mother.

"Do you get video of the spectators?"

"Sometimes. We both do a quick pan of the arenas and sometimes the parking lots."

The ambulance lights and sirens roared past, heading west.

Perry turned to face the highway. Two cars, one pickup, and two eighteen-wheelers headed east. Three cars drove toward the city.

To Sophia she said, "We also need to find out if any drivers saw something as they went past."

"The missing woman is too old for an Amber Alert," Sophia said.

Perry shrugged. "I know that's for children, but we can use it to find out if anyone saw anything here. Call dispatch." Sophia nodded, then made the call. She watched as Officer Tiger did the same.

Officer Lopez brought Bake Folsom to where Perry and Sophia stood. The officer said, "I've been thinking. We should also go to the truck stop that's just three or four miles east. Talk to any drivers who passed here."

"Good idea," Perry said. "They'll probably be asleep; we'll have to knock on their cabs."

"I'll do it," Osceola Tiger said.

Lopez nodded. She held up a finger. "I can check the truck stops to the west. The Biscuit Hill Travel Plaza is five miles." She pointed to the west. "There are more stops as you get closer to Oklahoma City."

Perry nodded and turned her attention back to Bake Folsom, the man who had been yelling Dels's name. He appeared as distraught as the other team members. He wore the same wet and dirty team shirt, his dark hair damp and flat on his forehead. Perry wondered if he'd played high school football and still lifted weights. He looked like a smaller version of her husband, Troy, who had done the same thing at Haskell Indian Nations University in Lawrence, Kansas.

"Mr. Folsom, come with me." Perry guided him to a Seminole cruiser away from the others. "You know Dels Billy well, I am told."

"Yes. We live together." Like Sealy, he kept his eyes to the south.

"Where?"

"I have a place in McAlester, a few miles from Dels. But I usually stay at her house."

He took a deep breath and Perry thought he might cry. She gave him a few seconds.

"Please tell me what happened. Start with why Dels left before you did."

"Dels hurt her leg in the race. It's really hot and she didn't want to hang around while we got the horses ready. We live almost two hours away and she wanted to get home."

"Why didn't you go with her?"

"Well, uh, the process of getting our gear packed and the horses cooled down and fed goes faster when I help. And she had Lee with her."

Lee was a thin teenager. Perry wondered what Bake Folsom thought the young man could do if Dels got into trouble.

"Do you normally ride together to races?"

"Most of the time. But occasionally the team splits up and goes with someone different."

The hood was up, which would be the only reason that Dels would have pulled into this dark place. If they had to stop to pee they could have gone to a gas station.

"I know it's not that far from the track to this spot, but did Dels by chance call you or anyone else after she left?"

Bake sighed. "She did. But my phone was almost dead and

it was charging. I didn't check it until we were almost here. I saw that she called about ten minutes before we spotted her truck and trailer from the highway and drove in. We both have each other's location. Her phone's in the truck."

She also wondered why he wouldn't hear his phone even if it was charging.

Lightning lit the sky, but more to the east. The storm would pass them.

Perry assessed Bake Folsom as being maybe twenty-six. Now that he had run through the dirt, grass, and trees he had calmed a bit and seemed ready to think.

Sophia joined Perry but made sure not to crowd her and Bake. "You have any ideas about this?" Sophia asked.

He sniffed and kept his focus to the south, where lights continued to flit like fireflies in the darkness. So far he had not made eye contact with her.

"Nothing unusual happened. This isn't the Kentucky Derby. We don't make that much money and it makes no sense to go to this trouble to hurt Lee and take Dels. Dels and Benny each won two thousand dollars. That goes to pay everyone, vehicle maintenance, and vet bills."

Perry knew that snatching women often had nothing to do with money. "You didn't see anyone unusual hanging around the track? Maybe someone you've never seen before?"

"I always see new people," Bake said. "The stands are full. Every time. Some people who want to see the horses close-up stand around the fence. Sometimes we let them pet the horses. Those people are always excited. I mean, you can tell they're not weird or anything."

"How long have you known Dels Billy?" Perry asked.

"Almost six years."

"How long have you been together?"

"Three years last Sunday." He smiled.

“What do you do, Mr. Folsom?”

“I’m a landscape architect.”

Perry cocked her head. She imagined fountains, vine-covered rocks, and slender weeping willow branches flowing in the breeze.

Bake looked to the woods again, then said, “It’s not as fancy as it sounds. I design yards to be drought tolerant.”

Perry liked that. Her property in Oklahoma City was not large, but unlike her neighbors, she and Troy had opted for wildflowers in the front yard. Raised garden beds, wild garlic patches, and fruit trees occupied much of the back.

“Sounds like a timely job,” she said.

“It’s only going to get hotter and drier. I stay busy giving estimates to home and business owners concerned about their browning and increasingly crispy lawns, planter boxes, flowerbeds, and walkways. My latest gig was a redesign of the lawn around a golf course clubhouse.”

They stayed silent for a moment. The lightning flashed again, but even more distantly now. They heard voices in the parking lot.

“Sealy Billy said you have video of the races today.”

“I do. Dels and Sealy wore head cams. And Dels also put her cap on the dash to record conversations while driving. Same with Sealy. I went to her truck when we arrived and took the hat. It’s in Vera’s truck. Sealy’s should be in there too.”

“We need to see them.”

Bake nodded. “When?”

“As soon as we finish here.”

“Now what do we do?”

“Figure out how to find her. And we’re not going to stop until she’s back home, I assure you.”

3

Perry watched Bake return to Issi and Gomer. He put his arms around the horse's neck and hugged her for a moment, then sat on the broken concrete with Gomer in his lap. Vera went to the bed of her truck and removed two fold-out chairs, then set them next to Bake. He chose the blue chair, identical to the one Nathaniel McGee died in, and together the two stared out into the distance. She sighed. "Oh boy," she muttered to herself as she surveyed the parking area. Sophia walked over, small notebook in hand. She had removed her jacket and rolled up her sleeves. Perry appreciated that her partner did not make trite comments about the heat.

"We need to tell Dickinson we're going to stay with this case," Sophia said.

"We will. But not now."

Sophia pursed her lips. That meant Perry had no intention of calling their supervisor anytime soon.

"What are you thinking about him?" Sophia nodded toward Bake.

"He's not telling us something," Perry said.

"Like what?"

"Well, if I knew that then maybe all of us could go home."

Perry's eyes went to the entrance. A 1997 white Ford F-150 had pulled up the ramp and the driver was conversing with Officer Earl Evans, who still monitored the entrance. The truck rolled through and pulled up next to one of the Seminole cruisers.

"And who do we have here?" Sophia asked.

The door opened and out stepped a woman the same height as Perry but at least twenty pounds of muscle heavier. She wore cargo pants and a tight camo T-shirt.

"That is the Marine and Choctaw Lighthorseman Raquel Hunter." Perry smiled and put her hands on her hips. She had not seen Raquel for almost two years, since she had assisted the McAlester Lighthorsemen in tracking down a man who had killed three Choctaw women. Raquel dealt with many cases, but she poured her heart and soul into situations involving abused and murdered women and children. Perry was not at all surprised that Raquel would show up once she heard a female had been nabbed.

"Detective Antelope," Raquel greeted in her monotone voice.

"Halito, Nanulhtoka Hunter," Perry answered.

Hunter's presence surprised and pleased Perry. The stout Lighthorseman walked toward them with her thumbs through the belt loops of her pants, reminding Perry of Yul Brynner's *Westworld* Man in Black strut. Instead of her usual perfect Marine bun, she had the top of her long kinky black hair pulled back and the rest of it trailed behind her like a cape. She still looked as if she could barrel through a cinder-block wall. Perry knew from experience that Raquel would follow the law, although she would find every loophole and stretch every meaning in order to get what she wanted.

"I'm glad you're here," Perry added. "This is my partner, Sophia Burns."

The women shook hands.

"What're you doing in our neck of the woods?" Perry asked.

"I had three days off from work and spent the day in Oklahoma City picking up gear at Bass Pro Shop, Sports Authority, and the Brew Shop."

"You make beer? I didn't think you liked beer."

"I don't. I like wine and decided to try my hand at cultivating a vineyard. I have a half acre of grapes. Last year I got almost one hundred bottles of Pinot Noir."

"My goodness. You drink all that?"

Raquel shook her head. "Gifted some and sold some to a local liquor store."

"You wanna help?" Perry hoped so. Raquel had more experience than she did with abducted women and children.

"Missing woman. Seriously injured male. Yeah. Ryan's on call for the next ten days, so why not?"

"You're welcome here," Osceola Tiger said.

Raquel shifted her attention to the young Seminole. "I appreciate that."

Perry was glad to hear that Raquel and Ryan the firefighter were still together. At dinner one evening Raquel had told Perry that they were happy staying close to home and had talked about the beauty of Oklahoma: more shoreline than Minnesota, beautiful forests, fast-moving water, fish-filled streams and lakes, fall colors, bears, deer, and turkeys. They sometimes ventured to Colorado or Missouri, and once to Glacier National Park, but their jobs and financial situations prevented extensive traveling.

Raquel scanned the scene.

Perry still wondered if Raquel was a Freedman descendant. At first glance, Raquel appeared Black. Full lips that Perry envied. Perfect posture like a dancer. Smooth skin and enviably thick hair. Then, with a turn of her head, Raquel morphed into a Native woman. Almost like a mosaic of the best pieces of a puzzle. Raquel had served as a Marine, which meant she had survived prejudice against women in a branch of the military that many thought best reserved for men.

She also wondered about Raquel's status as a citizen of the Choctaw Nation. If she was a Freedman descendant with family on the Freedman Roll, she probably did not have full tribal citizenship. But if she had documented Choctaw blood on the Dawes Roll, then perhaps she was enrolled. Perry did not intend to ask. Maybe Raquel would bring it up. Regardless, Perry knew this woman was not someone to mess with.

"And so?" Raquel asked Perry. She stood with her arms crossed behind her back. She looked relaxed yet dangerous.

Raquel listened without comment as Perry told her the details. Then she walked to Dels's trailer, looked inside, once again resting her thumbs in her belt loops. She turned in a circle again and looked around her, taking in the vehicles, the people, and the light flow of trucks and cars on the highway.

Then she looked back to the vehicles. "You say the missing woman pulled in here because the truck broke down."

"That's our theory," Sophia said.

"Why's the trailer tire flat?"

"What?" Perry leaned down to look. "We missed this." She rubbed her chin. "A flat *and* engine trouble."

Osceola Tiger shone his light on the tire. "A screw. Slow leak."

"Where's the screw?" Raquel asked.

"Right smack in the middle of where the rubber hits the road."

Vera stood and moved closer to listen to the conversation. "My trailer had a flat too," she added.

Raquel's eyebrows rose.

"When?" Perry asked.

"Back at the fairgrounds," Vera answered. "And Benny's Hummer had one as well. That's why Dels and Lee left. We stayed to change tires."

Perry and Sophia looked at each other. This was not what Bake had told them. When Perry turned her gaze to Raquel, the shorter woman was staring at her.

"Nails or screws?" Sophia asked.

"Neither," Vera answered. "There were punctures on the inside. I mean, where you can't see them."

"Let's see the tires," Perry said.

Vera entered the trailer and rolled the tire out. Sophia held the light while Perry and Raquel inspected the flat. Officers Tiger and Lopez leaned in to look.

Raquel pointed to a hole on the inside of the tire. "Here," she said. "Like you said. On the inside. Ice pick, probably."

"Here's another," Perry said, her index finger pointing to a hole two inches from the first.

"Two jabs," Raquel said. "Let's look at the other one."

An inspection of the Hummer tire revealed two holes like the ones in Vera's tire. Both holes were on the inside.

"This is why Ms. Billy's tire has a screw," Perry said.

"It needed to take longer to go flat," Raquel added.

"Ah," Sophia said. "So she'd get down the road a bit."

Perry turned to Vera. "Did anyone else who parked near you have flats?"

"No. And we asked."

Raquel scrutinized the driver's side of Dels Billy's truck. She cocked her head.

"What?" Perry asked.

Raquel walked to the fuel tank cover. "What's this down the side? It's shiny. Looks like oil."

Osceola Tiger shone his light. He leaned in and sniffed. "Smells like olive oil."

"Double whammy," Raquel said. "Someone wanted her to stop down the road. Right here. A slow tire leak and oil in the tank would take a bit of time."

"We need prints from this truck," Perry said. "And the area around the tires that were flattened. If someone poked holes in them, maybe they put one hand on the bumper, the back panel or something. Sophia, you and I can do the trailers and the Hummer, but Dels's truck and trailer need a thorough scrutiny."

"I can do the Hummer," Osceola said.

"Good. Kit's in my trunk." She tossed Sophia her keys.

"And a puncture would take just a few seconds, especially if you moved the ice pick around," Sophia said before moving to Perry's vehicle.

"Unless the tire is self-sealing," Perry said.

"They're not," Vera said. "I mean, my trailer tires aren't."

"Mine aren't either," Benny said.

"Does anyone have the name of the race host?" Perry asked. "Who is your contact?"

"I got it," Vera said as she consulted her phone. "Name's Cody Ryder. With a *y*." She gave Perry the number.

She wondered if Cody Ryder was his given name. She visualized a tall, fancy-mustachioed cowboy wearing a hat, jeans, boots, and Western shirt with snaps instead of buttons.

"Excuse me." She walked away from the riders and dialed the number.

A deep voice answered after the second ring. "This is Cody."

Sure enough, his voice sounded like Slim Pickens's.

"Mr. Ryder, my name is Detective Perry Antelope. I'm sorry to bother you so late." She looked at the time. Her phone said 2:03. "Er, I mean early, but there has been an incident involving one of the horse relay teams."

"I don't sleep much—I keep the scanner on. Was waiting to hear about it. What happened?"

"A rider was abducted from a truck stop and another was assaulted. It's crucial that you get to the rodeo grounds and make certain no one enters the space where the competitors were parked. Or the barn. And I need a list of the names and numbers of all the vendors and teams."

"I got all that information right here."

"Great." She added, "Please make sure not to dispose of the trash."

"No problem. I'll have a few workers guard the place."

"This is time-sensitive, as you might imagine."

"I live just a few miles from the grounds. I'll be there soon."

"Thank you, Mr. Ryder. We'll talk again soon." She clicked off, then motioned with her head to Sophia, who came over.

"We need two officers out there now to help him," Perry said.

Sophia held up her phone. "Already called it in."

"Well done, partner." Perry considered Dels's truck. "This appears to have been planned," she said. "The tires. Her tank. There was some thought put into this."

Perry looked to where Bake stood by the horses. He quickly looked away from her gaze. "If this was a plot, then the perps might have assumed she had a formidable boyfriend with her," Perry said.

"That's true," Raquel agreed as she scrutinized Bake. "But it doesn't matter. If there were two or more perps it wouldn't be difficult to do what they did here, especially if the victims had no weapons."

Perry turned to Vera. "Did Dels carry a weapon? Mace, gun? Do any of you?"

"Dels keeps a baseball bat by the bed and in her back seat," Vera said. "Plus a tire iron and pepper spray. She doesn't carry a gun, but I do. So does Bake. We have permits. I mean, Dels can shoot, she just doesn't travel with one." She sighed and looked regretful.

But you weren't with her, Perry thought. She knew that Vera thought the same thing.

"So the perp or perps counted on her breaking down around here," Sophia speculated. "And they knew she was with a guy. They just didn't plan on it being Lee."

"If that is what they thought, then they probably were armed," Perry said. "Ms. Spring, we need to look at where your team parked at the fairgrounds." Perry looked at her watch. "It's now 2:07. Sun will be useful about 6:45. We don't need all of you. These horses need to get home. Forensics will look closer at Ms. Billy's truck and trailer. They need to be towed in."

"I have two spare tires," Vera said. "I'll take Gomer, Issi, Xena, and Worf. Jezie will have to go with you, Bake. Is that okay?"

"Yeah. Take Gomer home and I'll get him tomorrow."

"What does Issi mean?" Sophia asked.

"Deer," Perry, Vera, and Raquel said at the same time.

Perry wanted to get them moving. "Ms. Spring, you and Mr. Billy take your truck and horses home. Mr. Folsom and Mr. Durant will meet us at the fairgrounds in the morning." She turned to the two men and loudly asked, "How far is it to your homes?"

"We all live around a hundred and twenty miles away, but in different places," Benny answered. "I mean, Bake and I are about four miles apart."

"Do you have another vehicle besides that Hummer?" Sophia asked. "You already used your spare."

"No."

"Get a hotel room," Sophia suggested.

Perry knew they would not do that.

Benny shook his head. "We'll go back to the fairgrounds. I can stop at Discount Tires when we're done at the racetrack. That's where I got these."

"You'd have to park at a different spot," Perry said.

Bake nodded. "I want to stick around anyway," he said. He looked to the trees again and saw the lights bobbing. "And it's just four hours or so before the sun comes up. We can get some food at that McDonald's and park by the concession area. There's water for Jezie."

"All right," Perry said. "I'll call dispatch and tell them you're coming and for Cody Ryder to let you in." Then she turned to Vera and Sealy. "Okay, Ms. Spring and Mr. Billy, you can go, but call us if you think of anything."

Sealy nodded. Sophia and Perry watched them begin to load the horses.

Perry turned to the Seminole officers. "Well, there's plenty for all of us to do."

Osceola Tiger put his hands on his hips and chewed his bottom lip. "This is true. How about we come here tomorrow and go through the area again. I can get a few more to help. That'll free you up to look at the rodeo grounds. The Oklahoma Patrol will keep this closed."

"That sounds good." Then she addressed the racers. "Detective Burns, Officer Hunter, and I will contact you soon. Don't go anyplace besides your homes. You have our numbers."

Vera sniffed and then slapped Sealy on the back. "Let's go."

As Perry, Sophia, and Raquel watched Xena's swishing tail disappear into Vera's trailer, Perry asked, "Why was Dels Billy targeted?"

"That's the question," Raquel answered.

"Someone went to a lot of trouble to get her," Sophia said. Lightning flashed in the far northeast and thunder boomed six seconds later. "Did someone spot her at the race and then decide they were going to take her?"

"I wonder if we can get footage of the audience," Osceola said.

"Sealy says they have videos of the races and that he pans the audience. But it might not be enough."

Perry took out her phone and called Cody. He answered immediately. "Detective." She could hear music. He was driving. Good.

"Hello, Mr. Ryder. This is Detective Antelope. Sorry to bother you once again." Actually, she was not sorry. "Is there footage of the audience? Did any video of the races also take in the people in the stands, around the track, in the food area?"

She put him on speaker. "No, we don't take videos, but a lot of people in the audience do. And the teams take videos and we also take pictures of the winners. In front of the stands. You can see a lot of the audience in those, but the winners are usually in the same spot. They stand pretty much in front of the middle of the stands so you wouldn't be able to see anyone on the edges, or those who stand by the fences, or the back stretch of the track."

"Can you send me the photos you do have?"

"Well, I don't have them. The woman who manages our social media posts those. I can ask her in a few hours."

Perry thought a moment. "I received the contact information for all the teams, so maybe they have footage we can use. Another thing. I need you to send out a message. Let me write that out for you and I'll text it so you can pass it on."

"All right."

"Let me know if you hear anything and tell your photo person to send those to me as soon as possible."

"I will. Uh, who is missing? If this happened at the old rest stop, then the only team going that direction is the Chahta Riders."

Perry hesitated.

"Vera Spring?" he asked. "Dels Billy? I know the team members except for the youngest one."

Perry knew Dels's parents were deceased and they had just

spoken to her first cousin, Sealy. Still, she was not going to tell him. "Sir, right now we aren't releasing that information."

"It's Dels Billy, right? You don't have to say it. We can't let anything happen to her."

Something already did happen to her, Perry thought. She started to click off but Cody said, "That lovely young lady has had a hard time. I looked her up about a year ago when I first watched her race. She lost her parents."

The music continued. Perry waited.

"My family came to Indian Territory in the 1880s. They settled on Choctaw lands. I'm not proud of it, but that's how they got their property by Coal Creek. They ended up selling and I reaped the benefits. I know about the missing and murdered women problem. I mean, none of the women deserved any of that."

Perry appreciated the concern, but all of this sounded like a land acknowledgment. As in "We acknowledge that we are on the traditional lands of tribes X, Y, or Z, but we have no intention of giving it back to you and we're not going anywhere."

"All right. Well . . ."

"And I will do everything I can to find Miss Billy and to catch who hurt the other person."

"Thank you, Mr. Ryder. We will be at the rodeo grounds shortly."

They turned their heads to see the bright headlights of two tow trucks. They watched as an officer pointed to the wounded truck and trailer. The big tow vehicles slowly made their way around the curved entry.

"Ms. Spring and Mr. Billy, you should go home and tend to the horses. Mr. Durant and Mr. Folsom, you two go on to the fairgrounds. We'll see you soon."

Benny stood watching her for a few seconds, then turned to leave.

Perry watched him walk away. "I'd like to go home and shower. Maybe sleep just for an hour or two, no more. We can't waste time on this one. If this is trafficking, then Dels Billy could be a long way from here by now. Officer Hunter?"

"Yes, ma'am," Raquel answered. She sounded almost bored.

"Care to join us at the track?"

"Wouldn't miss it."

"It's only thirty minutes away. Less without traffic."

"I'll be there," Raquel said. "Right now I'm going to get my spotlight and walk this area." She turned and headed for her vehicle.

"I'm going to do what I can here," Osceola Tiger said.

Vera drove past with Sealy in the passenger seat, with the horses in the trailer.

Perry sighed. "It's going to be a long day."

"And even longer for them," Osceola said as he watched Benny Durant and Bake Folsom follow Vera out the exit.

4

Perry and Sophia remained at the rest stop with the Lighthorsemen and Raquel until 3:15 A.M., walking the entrance and exit drives, combing the cracked parking lot, and walking through the grass. They found nothing of use.

No trucker or anyone else who heard the Amber Alert had responded to the call for witness reports. The Seminole Lighthorseman who visited the casino also did not find anyone who had witnessed suspicious behavior at the Love's Truck Stop on U.S. Rte. 377 off I-40, or at Biscuit Hill Travel Plaza off Valley View Road, or at the Grand Travel Plaza next to Highway Drive. Whoever assaulted the riders did it quickly and stealthily.

Perry knew she would have chigger bites on her ankles by sunrise and by noon she would have to refrain from scratching her crotch. The little fuckers latched on to clothes, then slowly made their way behind waistbands, bra straps, and underwear elastics. In the summertime at home, she only worked in the garden after spraying with Chigg Away, then patting herself with a sock filled with sulfur powder.

"Hopefully we'll catch a break at the race site," Sophia said after they made their way to the interstate. Perry had cranked the air conditioner and Sophia leaned back, eyes closed, sleeves rolled up.

Perry was sweaty and wanted a shower. She settled for cleaning her face with body wipes she kept in the back seat. She offered the pack to Sophia.

"I really need a wet towel."

"True. I'd settle for cold water out of a hose." Perry looked in the rearview mirror. "Raquel's right behind us." She sighed. "I could crash right now."

Sophia set her seat back a bit farther. "Yeah."

"Don't get too comfortable," Perry said.

"I could sleep sitting or even standing."

"I need to call Troy."

"Kind of early for me to call Mike. I'll wait awhile."

"Troy won't mind since he gets up at four. He lifts weights, then writes before he goes in to teach."

"What is he teaching this summer?"

"Indigenous poetry. It's a short course, just a month. It's his first time back in the classroom since Covid. He decided he likes online courses, but he only taught one class in spring, so he has to make that up in summer and the chair says he needs to teach in person. OU's quiet in summer so it's not too bad."

"Are there a lot of people who take poetry classes?"

"He's got twenty-three."

"Wow. The only class like that I took was a literature course and we read *Moby-Dick, The Sun Also Rises,* and *Death of a Salesman.*"

"Exciting stuff." Perry clicked Troy's number. "Hi, hon," she said.

"Where are you?"

"Heading home for a shower."

"Why were you there so long?"

Perry sighed, partly from physical fatigue and partly because it was shaping up to be a stressful case. Troy always asked this question.

"It's complicated. Many people involved and there's a missing woman. Time is crucial."

Troy did not respond.

"Sophia is with me and Lighthorse Raquel Hunter is following in her truck."

"Raquel Hunter? You mean that Choctaw officer I met at dinner after y'all caught that guy?"

"The very one."

"She's a little ball of big firepower."

"No kidding."

"How long is this going to take?"

"I have no idea. How're the kids?"

"Olyve had another late night at the pool. Two guards called in sick so she had to sit on the stand more than usual."

"As long as she drinks enough water and stays under the umbrella she'll be fine."

"True. But she's pissed because it's putting a crimp in her swimming schedule. Workouts are optional the first part of summer, but the rest of the team is getting two-a-days and the double-shift guarding wears her out."

"She'll get paybacks from the other guards. Olyve knew that might happen when she decided to take the job."

"At least she's making money."

"What about Nico?"

"We're gonna run a couple of miles when he wakes up. It's too hot to do more. He finished *Where the Red Fern Grows*. He was pretty upset so I let him play *Minecraft* last night."

"Dead animal stories. I hate those."

"You should come home and sleep, Perry."

Perry tried to squelch a yawn. "I'll be there shortly. Sophia is telling me jokes." She looked at her partner, who seemed to be asleep.

"All right. Love you. Bye."

Perry called Raquel to notify her of their plans, then dropped Sophia off at the precinct lot. "So, I'll be back here at five-thirty. Not much time, I know."

"It's not," Sophia said with a yawn. "But I'll be here."

After showers, power naps, and eating as much as they could at such an early hour, the two detectives reached the rodeo grounds at six A.M. Two police cruisers parked at the entrance and a third was parked at the gate on the backstretch of the track. A maroon Chevy dually sat in front of a closed food stand and a tall cowboy, wearing the exact clothes that Perry had predicted Cody Ryder would choose, leaned on the tailgate with a cigarette in his left hand and an insulated coffee mug in his right.

Beyond the big truck, Bake Folsom and Benny Durant stood next to Benny's Hummer.

Perry drove to the left side of the Hummer. Raquel stopped several lengths behind Perry.

"Let's get to it before we fall asleep," Perry said.

Sophia yawned. "I already did that."

The morning sun raised the temperature to a humid eighty-three degrees. Perry put on her favorite visor with an alien face on the band. She got it from the UFO Museum when her family visited Roswell, New Mexico, two years prior, and it had a wider brim than other visors.

Perry and Sophia wore their regular slacks, but because of the heat Perry had opted to change into a navy golf shirt, like the ones she kept in her trunk in case of long days. She also wore her cross-body bag, which held Kleenex, sunscreen, and a camera. Sophia wore another light oxford button-down shirt with the sleeves rolled up. Raquel had changed into a gray tank top and piled her long hair into a bun with a claw clip. Beadwork adorned the rim of her light blue visor.

"You sleep any?" Perry asked her.

"Shower and two solid hours. My cousin's guest room has a powerful fan and blackout shades."

"Sounds nice."

"It is. I made sure that 'Enter Sandman' was my alarm music."

Bake Folsom wore the same jeans and T-shirt with the Great Seal of the Choctaw Nation that he'd been wearing the night before. Benny Durant had on nylon shorts and had changed into an old Choctaw Commemorative Trail of Tears Walk T-shirt that was a size too large. Perry got that same shirt when she and Troy did the Skullyville walk before their kids were born.

She nodded to Bake and Benny, then turned to greet Cody Ryder. "Mr. Ryder, I presume."

"That's me," he said, dropping his cigarette and grinding it with his boot.

"Thank you for being here."

Perry introduced Sophia first, and when she gestured to Raquel, Cody looked her up and down, clearly liking what he saw. After letting go of Sophia's hand he enthusiastically clasped Raquel's and held on a few beats longer than he should have. She let go and gave him a look that caused him to clear his throat and glance away.

Perry could already feel sweat on her forehead under her visor. *This is indeed going to be a long day,* she thought.

"Mr. Ryder, we really appreciate you coming here and watching the grounds," Perry said. "Now that we're here, you should feel free to leave."

"I do need to get home to feed the animals."

"Just let me know if there's anyone else who was involved in the races that I should know about."

"Will do." He gave them a smile, winked at Raquel, then got into his truck and drove out the gate.

Sophia went to dismiss the other officers who had been here before them.

Perry turned to Bake and Benny. Benny stood inside the barn tying Jezie in the shade while Bake filled a bucket with water. "Y'all get any sleep?"

Benny shook his head.

"I tried," Bake said.

"Where is Dels?" Benny sniffed and wiped his nose with a wad of Kleenex he pulled from his jeans pocket.

"We'll find out," Perry said.

"Where'd everyone park yesterday?" Sophia asked Bake.

Dels's partner stood with his arms crossed over his chest and kept his eyes down. "Over this way."

He led them to a fenced area that encompassed the barn, the six-horse hot walker, and a parking area used by racers and rodeo participants.

Bake motioned to the open space. "Right there. Dels pulled up so her trailer was even with the edge of the barn." He pointed to the southeast corner. "Right, Benny?"

Benny looked up and thought a moment. "Yeah. And the front of her truck should be about . . ." He walked twenty feet and stopped. "Here." He looked at the ground behind him. "Here. But, I mean, twenty feet to my left. You can see where her fold-up chair left holes in the ground. The rubber things came off the bottoms of the legs and that made the metal push into the dirt."

"Let's see," Bake said, pointing with both hands to the general area around the four holes in the earth. "Vera parked next to Dels. The trailers were almost even."

"That's right," Benny agreed. "Vera's trailer is a little longer, but yeah. About even. And five feet apart. You can see where Worf shit right before he was loaded." The group turned their attention to a pile of road apples.

"And your Hummer?" Sophia asked.

"Dels's truck was parked between Vera's truck and my Hummer. Even with Vera's trailer," Benny answered. "Four or five feet apart. But still parallel."

"All facing the same direction," Raquel repeated.

"Yes," Benny said. "The sun went behind the barn around seven-thirty and we were in shade."

"Are there cameras?" Perry asked. "I don't see any."

"No," Benny answered. "Teams had asked for cameras last year but they still haven't put any up."

"Did you move the vehicles at all over the three days?"

Benny scratched his head. "Yeah. Vera left the trailer and went to get ice and stuff from Subway yesterday around noon. Dels, Bake, and I slept at the hotel. And we'd take turns showering and watching the horses and vehicles during the day."

"So some of you slept here?" Raquel asked.

"Yes. We never leave the animals here alone."

"You didn't like the fair food?" Sophia asked.

"Oh yeah," Benny said. "But it gets old. Even the fry bread with beans and cheese."

Perry looked at the ground, not sure yet what she was looking for. "And Vera backed in when she returned?"

Both men nodded.

"All right. You two go in the barn where there's shade. We're gonna look around."

Perry, Raquel, and Sophia walked the circumference of the area, each circling from a different direction. They crossed paths and ended up where they started.

"Well," Sophia said with a sigh. "Horse, tire, and human tracks everyplace. Horse crap too. Not surprising."

"Indeed," Perry said. "Follow me." She walked to the four holes in the dirt that marked where Dels's chair had sat, then strode past and stood where she believed the middle of the front bumper had been. She walked slowly, as if heading for the driver's door of Dels's truck and the passenger side of Vera's. She looked from side to side for another two paces, then stopped and looked left.

"This is where the fuel filler neck would be."

Perry squatted and inspected the dirt. The night had been calm. No wind or rain. She zeroed in on an area of about one square foot. The dirt was Oklahoma red. But what made this spot of interest was the light sprinkling of white particles the size of sugar grains. She took several photos, then took out her pen and circled the area.

"Raquel, come here. What do you see?"

"Looks like sugar."

"It does. And what else?"

"It looks like it's, well, oily."

"Oil and sugar."

"Someone put both in her gas tank."

Perry took a small vial from her bag and scooped a sample.

"Now to the tire." Perry took five steps forward. "This is where Dels's trailer wheel was."

Sophia crouched next to Perry. She considered the dirt. "I don't see anything," she said. "Just the tire tread when she pulled left to go home last night. Right?"

"Let me see," Raquel said. She squatted and inspected the ground, her hand hovering over the dirt like a conjurer. Then, brushing the dirt aside, she plucked a three-inch screw from the soil, held it up, and smiled.

"Whoa," Sophia said.

"Looks like the screw in Dels's tire," Perry observed. "Let's look at Vera's spot."

They went through the same routine in Vera's and Benny's parking spots. There was no sugar, no oil spots, and no screws or nails.

"None of this is surprising, Perry," Sophia said. "The people who took Dels Billy set it up here."

"The people?" Perry asked.

"Yeah. How could one person have wounded that kid and taken a five-foot-ten woman? She had to be a heck of an athlete to jump off and on horses."

"At least two people sounds about right," Raquel agreed. "One person might have distracted the team while the other sabotaged the vehicles." She paused to think. "Although a strong, thoughtful man could have done it."

"A strong man would have been noticed," Sophia countered. "Women might not be."

"A man might not be noticed if he's part of the team," Perry added quietly.

"What?" Sophia replied. "Now what are you thinking?"

"Just considering several theories."

Sophia put her hands on her hips. "Who?"

Perry shrugged. "There's got to be a motive. The question is, who stands to gain from taking Dels Billy and trying to kill a teenager?"

Raquel said nothing as she listened. Sophia frowned so intently that her eyebrows almost merged.

"Just pay attention to everything these guys say," she said before calling over Bake and Benny and advising them to stop three feet from where Sophia had marked the spot where Vera's trailer bumper had sat. "When y'all are racing and are on the track, does anyone stay here with your vehicles and the horses that aren't running?"

"Yes," Bake answered. "There's always someone around here. Another team was next to us and they had a lot of family come from Montana. We watch out for each other."

Perry thought a moment. "So, all the team's vehicles were parked close together. And none of you noticed a flat until right before you packed to leave, correct?"

"Yes," Bake quickly answered.

"So the tires were punctured by someone shortly before that time."

Bake shrugged. "I guess."

Perry looked at Bake and cocked her head.

"Did you see or talk to anyone before leaving? That is, did anyone come into the staging area who shouldn't have been there?"

"No one is allowed back there except racers and their families. But there was a white lady who came by to see Sealy."

"Girlfriend?" Sophia asked.

"I've never seen her before. I think her name is Rhonda." Bake turned to Benny. "What's Rhonda's last name?"

Benny's eyebrows rose. "No idea. But Sealy told me she works at Trophy's Bar and Grill at the Choctaw Casino. She's a bartender."

Perry and Troy had been to the casino several times on their way to Choctaw tribal events.

"How did the perps know Dels Billy would leave first?" Sophia asked.

"Good question," Raquel admitted.

Perry held up a finger. "Hold that thought. All right, gentlemen. Show us what's in the barn."

They followed Bake and Benny into the dim coolness. Jezie's ears pricked as she watched them.

"Ah, that's better," Sophia said.

"Six stalls on either side," Bake said.

Perry entered the first. Straw and several piles of manure covered the dirt floor. The feed box was empty. "Why does this wall go all the way to the ceiling but on the other side it's half wall and half grille?" she asked.

"Socialized horses can go in the stalls with grilles," Bake explained. "Some horses are less comfortable around ones they don't know. And they might get aggressive if they know there's feed in another stall."

"Ah, makes sense," Sophia said.

"No cameras in here either," Perry repeated.

"Right," said Benny. "This place is empty most of the time. Horses are in the stalls where there's shade before the races. After the races they're in the hot box on the walker to cool down. Cows and pigs stay in here when it's county fair time. There's nothing worth much in here. We always bring our own gear and tools."

After Perry assessed that there was nothing of use in the barn, she said, "Mr. Folsom, I brought my laptop. We can watch the videos Dels and Sealy made. Let's do that in here where it's comfortable."

5

"Set the scene for us," Perry said to Bake and Benny. She, Sophia, and Raquel stood in the corner of the stall with the least amount of horse shit. Perry brought Troy's eighteen-inch laptop and propped it on a feeder so all five of them could watch.

Bake inserted the SD card with Dels's head-cam footage. "The camera is attached to her cap," he began. "This is before her race." Everyone moved closer to watch.

At the announcer's booth, a Native man removed his black cowboy hat and told the audience to stand for the national anthem. Hundreds of spectators stood to the right of Dels, some along the fence line, many with food or drink in their left hands and their right hands over their hearts. The usual formalities one sees at rodeos commenced—the national anthem, the recitation of "I Am the Flag," the parade of Junior Patriots, and Miss Oklahoma riding a brown mare and waving like an automaton.

To the right was a tall Native woman with a red-painted

forehead and a thick horizontal black stripe that covered both cheekbones and eyes.

Benny offered commentary: "That's Yarda Red Plume from the Running Bison Ranch out of East Glacier. Blackfeet. Dels doesn't wear face paint because Choctaw women didn't wear it. I don't know the history of Blackfeet face decoration, but Yarda's not trying to look flashy for the audience. She does it for herself."

Perry appreciated Benny saying that.

During the national anthem, Yarda stood with her hands at her sides, eyes focused on the clouds.

Benny continued, "Check out Yarda now. How do you generate enthusiasm when the race sponsors asked all of us to dress 'more Indian' and 'yell more war whoops'?"

The drum group started playing the "Victory Song," which Perry always liked hearing. She wondered how many in the crowd knew what that song represented. This was the anniversary of Custer's demise at Little Bighorn and the song was created to honor the Natives who fought him.

After the pageantry ended, they heard a click.

"Dels has a bad habit of clicking her teeth together and biting her lip when she feels anxious," Bake said. "One misstep and she'll have a split lip and black stitches sticking out from her smile for ten days." He paused a second, then added, "She's done that twice."

He still did not look at either detective, or at Raquel. Perry wondered if he might be autistic.

Benny added, "Everyone gets hurt at some point. Vera's our team handler and got four broken toes several years ago. She switched to steel-toed work boots. A human foot doesn't stand a chance when stepped on by a twelve-hundred-pound animal."

In the video, they heard Vera say, "Damn dust."

"I need Visine," yelled a female voice off camera.

"That's from the South Dakota Red Sky team camped next to us," Bake said.

"I have some, Cheena," Dels shouted back. "Look in my purple pack. It's on my chair."

"Thanks, Dels," came the reply. "I owe you."

Dels answered, "You do."

Bake said, "A rider blinded by dust or a dirt clod could become disoriented and fall off their mount."

They watched from Dels's view as she and the other female riders made their way to the staging area while the seven men tried to control their horses at the starting line.

"Why are they dressed like that?" Sophia asked.

Bake paused the video so he could zoom in on the riders. "Riders in the men's mile race chose clothing and face paint that represent their team colors and tribes. You see Benny there second to the end. He doesn't wear the usual colorful shorts, breechcloth, headband, long socks, braids, and ribbon shirt. Some paint their skin."

Benny interjected, "I look different because our Nation is not a Plains tribe. We weren't nomadic. We didn't follow bison herds, didn't live in tipis, and no Choctaw leader or warrior wore an eagle feather headdress. Riders in the chief race wear war paint and headdresses."

Perry felt mesmerized by what she was seeing and hearing, although she disliked the unsteady camera. It reminded her of the *Blair Witch Project*, which had made her feel seasick.

Bake added, "You know, Dels's mother loved Indian kitsch and had Cher's album *Half-Breed* on a bookshelf. Dels hated that Cher wore a full headdress for the back cover, but her mother said, 'I'm aware that no woman of any tribe wore a headdress, honey. What makes it funny is that Cher is Armenian, not Cherokee.' I don't think it's funny."

No one commented.

Benny said to the women, "I dress the same as our historic

police force, the Lighthorsemen. They wore long pants, low-heeled boots, buttoned-up shirt, neck scarf, and sack coat. No pistol and carbine for the races." He snickered. "I think I should carry those. Anyway, the Lighthorsemen of the past rode with saddles, but all relay riders ride bareback." Benny hit play and leaned in between Perry and Raquel to watch himself talk to his horse Jezie. She had blue diamonds painted on her legs.

"What do the diamonds mean?" Sophia asked.

"Signifies the eastern diamondback rattlesnake. We admire its venom and fearless nature."

The horses twirled and whinnied. There was no starting gate, just a chaotic milling around of excited animals until all the racers were more or less in a line. The sweaty horses flung their heads and behaved like children about to be set loose on an Easter egg hunt. An Appaloosa kicked its back feet, narrowly missing a buckskin.

The starter dropped the red flag.

A tall, thin rider kicked his chestnut thoroughbred to the front. Right behind ran an Appaloosa with red and blue handprints on her rump and ribbons streaming from her tail.

Benny narrated: "I don't like how Miles Old Bear from the South Dakota team is using a switch." He pointed to a brightly painted man astride a black, shiny horse with matching colors on its rump and neck. "It's not necessary."

They watched as Benny and Jezie ran a slow first stretch but gained speed at the curve, passing the Iowa and South Dakota horses, then maintained their pace down the backstretch. Jezie made her way to the second spot around the last curve, then passed a white horse before the line, winning the two-thousand-dollar purse for the Chahta Riders.

Dels's camera followed the racers and their sweaty horses as they loped a cool-down lap. Dels slapped her right thigh, yelled "Tushpa!," and the picture quickly shifted to the large paint

Worf, who stood with his ears pricked, nostrils flaring, and front feet stamping. Sealy Billy, also wearing a head cam, held the reins as Worf whinnied and pulled back on the lead.

Sophia asked, "Sealy Billy is also filming this at the same time?"

"Yes," Bake said.

He hiccupped and Benny put a hand on his shoulder. "It's okay, dude."

They returned to the video. Dels quickly glanced at Benny as he led Jezie to the hot walker.

Benny said to the detectives, "The temperature was ninety-seven degrees and I had on too many clothes."

On the video, Dels shouted, "You could always dress like a half-clad stickball player!"

Benny laughed and yelled back, "Good luck."

A dog barked twice and the camera focused on the strange dog Gomer where he stood tied to her truck. As they watched, Bake said, "Not supposed to have dogs at the relays, but no one complains about Gomer. He weighs only twenty pounds. That makes him easy to carry and hide from race hosts if necessary. Gomer's pretty calm and the horses like him as much as our companion goats, Speed Racer and Trixie."

"Leg up!" Dels yelled as she rushed to the side of her eleven-hundred-pound horse. Another handler, the tall, rangy sixteen-year-old Lee Robinson, cupped his hands for her to step in.

The camera caught only Worf's ribs as they heard Lee say, "Come on, I got you."

The picture showed Dels's hand on Worf's mane and then they saw the horse trailers over Worf's shoulder as Lee lifted and Dels used the mane to pull herself up. The camera settled a bit after Dels stilled and took the reins from Sealy. She looked down at Sealy, who kept one hand on the leather straps below the horse's chin.

Bennie explained to the detectives, "Dels could have mounted the horse herself by pulling upward using Worf's mane as she jumped. She didn't do that now because she had to save her energy for the transitions after each lap. Also, Worf is tall and tends to spin when someone tries to hop on him. We wanted her to start with Worf because he's hard to jump on and he's the best first leg horse. We thought he'd stay out in front and her other two horses would keep her there."

The jiggling picture told the women that Sealy had struggled to keep the big animal calm.

"I got him," Dels said to Sealy.

"Don't let him act up," Sealy answered. "He's being a butt."

Worf bucked. Dels slapped his neck. "Stop it!" she yelled.

The horse flicked an ear and huffed.

"Leave that attitude here," she continued. "None of that on the track."

From Dels's perspective atop the tall horse, the view ahead looked chaotic. Dozens of people and horses were moving in front of the stadium stands on the front stretch.

Bake stopped the video. "Indian horse relays are not like other horse races," he said. "The track is four furlongs instead of the eight furlongs of a classic horse race or the ten furlongs of the Kentucky Derby, Belmont Stakes, and Preakness Stakes. Each rider races a horse around the track, then jumps off and onto another horse, runs a lap, then transitions onto a third horse. Each team's mugger grabs the reins of the incoming horse and hopefully keeps it from slamming into another horse or running away riderless. The handlers calm the horses waiting to run. The rider has to dismount one horse and then jump onto the next without falling and getting trampled. They have to get on the horse without making it flip out and buck them off. All of this happens at breakneck speed."

Bake paused, apparently remembering the race. He pointed to the screen.

"That's our team between the teams in bright blue and red. Sealy's the mugger. Vera's holding Xena, the white one. I've got Issi. This won't start until all six teams are at their assigned places. You see them spacing out over the length of the bleachers."

Bake tapped play and the camera went back to the five other horses at the starting point, cavorting, turning circles, and swinging their heads. The camera moved to face down the track.

He stopped the video again and said, "Men usually make the transition faster than women can. The Siksika rider Cody Big Tobacco can vault onto his horses like he's playing leapfrog. But plenty of male riders lose races because they can't mount their horses. Women who play sports—basketball, especially—have a jumping ability. Still, timing and agility, or lack of it, make or break the race regardless of gender."

"Taller riders have an advantage, right?" Sophia asked.

"In theory, yes. All the horses in the race stand on the average about sixteen hands, which means their backs are approximately sixty-one inches, or a bit over five feet. Dels is five-ten and Yarda Red Plume is six feet tall. She played basketball at Gonzaga. Yarda *should* be able to jump off and on and sprint away.

"But a lot of things go wrong in those transitions. Despite their strength and long legs, both women have had more than their share of tweaked ankles and shin splints from repeated landings during the off-season when they practice transitioning from horse to horse in their barns. Horses can flip their heads, kick, bolt, or freeze, resulting in a storm of concussions, breaks, sprains, and blood. Or maybe there's no transition at all if the second- or third-leg horse gets away from their handlers and decides to book it back to the barn. That always pisses off everyone, but you can't blame the horse.

"So here's the race from Dels's view. It's going to be all over the place because of the horses' gaits and she'll be jumping."

The video showed the homestretch of the track. The anthill of horses, handlers, and muggers shuffled around next to the stands, where they would watch the first-lap horses and riders streak past, then wait for them to complete the lap.

Bake turned down the volume and said, "After the first transition the horses that just completed their lap and the horses that waited, but wanted to run, will pull their handlers closer to the other teams. It never fails that some horses will pull the handlers onto the track or break free and take off."

Benny added, "Notice how the horses are really impatient at the line. The starter is taking a really long time for some reason."

When he dropped the red flag, Bake turned up the volume. Amid yelps and feminine trilling, the horses took only seconds to transition from prancing to running.

The crowd roared.

A couple of horses in front of Dels seemed heedless of each other. The brightly painted buckskin veered into the quarter horse–Appaloosa mix mare. The mare's rider, the petite teenager Cheena Red Sky, dressed in red Adidas shorts, a yellow tank top, bison hide leggings, and a Ukraine babushka scarf as a headband, screamed as her left knee collided with the buckskin's shoulder.

"Holy shit," Dels exclaimed as she leaned onto Worf's neck.

The video calmed a bit because Worf had a fairly smooth gait. Still, the up-and-down motion was getting to Perry. She wished she had a Dramamine. As they rounded the turn into the back stretch, Worf pulled away from a reddish-brown quarter horse mare.

"That was Yarda's horse Aphrodite," Benny said. "That mare washed out of the professional races but does well in the shorter relays."

"I've never seen anything like this," Sophia said. "It looks like pandemonium, but everyone knows where to go. It's truly amazing."

The whistles, horns, and shrieks from the stands made Perry realize that her heart was racing right along with the horses. *What a batshit-crazy thing they're doing. I wonder if I could do it.*

"It is amazing," Bake said as he muted the sound. "No one's gonna become monetarily wealthy in the relay business, but the cultural meaning doesn't have a dollar amount attached. This is *our* sport. Northern tribes started it. Shoshone-Bannocks were doing this over a hundred years ago, but all of us who ride take great pride in it." His eyes went back to the screen showing the empty track in front of the lead rider, Dels. "Pretendians. You know those non-Natives who claim to be Indians for profit? Those fuckers have contaminated academia, literature, movies, and TV."

Perry saw his jaw clench. Then he said, "Those race-shifting frauds can't take Indian horse relays away from us. They can go ride fucking ostriches."

Perry thought that a somewhat random thing to say, but she appreciated his meaning. Troy encountered more than his share of race shifters in the Ivory Tower.

Bake turned up the sound.

Dels's eyes were on the track, but the edges of the camera frame still caught the excited audience. Everyone in the stands stood in an attempt to see the sleek horses and crazy humans who participated in the dangerous sport. Perry knew that some people probably came to horse relays for the same reason they watched NASCAR. Accidents are exciting to watch.

Dels and Worf barreled toward Vera Spring, who held the reins of the towering white mare Xena with bright blue eastern diamondback rattlesnake diamonds painted on her legs and along her sides. The statuesque horse stood out like a beacon among the darker animals.

Xena grew closer as Worf powered his way toward the crowd of humans and second-leg horses. Dels screamed "WHOA!" before he ran into the mugger Sealy.

They saw in a blur the picture jerk around as Dels dropped three feet to land in the dirt. The horses snorted and some whinnied. They saw the legs of a person on the ground before Dels rushed toward Xena.

Sophia gasped when the picture showed Dels's hands on the horse's mane. Dels grunted and the picture quickly rose up to look over the horse's ears.

"That was a great mount," Bake said.

They heard Vera scream, "Lookin' good! Yarda's right behind you. Her new mustang can hustle."

Dels did not answer nor did she look behind her.

"No pressure or anything!" Vera added.

They saw Dels's left hand pull the reins hard to the left to encourage the horse away from the commotion at the same time that she yelled, "Tushpa!"

"What does *tushpa* mean?" Sophia asked.

" 'Hurry,' " the other four said in unison.

The other horses and people fell away so they were only looking at the track. Dels was in the lead.

"Sorry, Xena," they heard Dels pant. The horse didn't even flick an ear.

Xena fell into a rhythmic run, but the camera rose and fell more than when Dels was riding Worf. Perry wondered if she wore padded bicycle pants under her shorts. Dels looked back to see Yarda five lengths behind.

The second leg proved uneventful, and Xena remained the front-runner. Dels looked ahead and everyone saw Issi in the distance standing calmly with Bake.

Dels commanded Xena to slow and guided her to where Sealy stood waving his arms, then jumped from Xena's back. The camera shot dropped with her as she hit the dirt.

"Shit fuck damn," Dels yelped.

Bake looked at the women. "She says that when she's injured. Right there is when she hurt her knee."

"Jee-bus!" Dels continued to complain. "Oh shit fuck damn."

Perry snorted at the outburst. The detectives were riveted.

The video revealed that Dels hopped to Issi. She made a loud noise that sounded like "Aaargh!" as she jumped.

Now atop Issi, Dels shouted, "Tushpa!" Then she added, "Don't be my meniscus. Don't be my ACL," after they made it to the backstretch.

Bake said, "Issi's the fastest horse. Faster than Worf. But she's got shark-fin withers and even a short ride really hurts without a saddle." He answered Perry's unspoken query by saying, "Wearing padded bike shorts helps, but she still complains because she has to walk bow-legged for a few days after a race. We've tried bulking Issi up with NickerDoodles and vegetable oil, but she's just gonna stay thin. She's got a great personality and looks. Long, lean, and ready to sprint."

Dels looked back and saw Yarda behind her. The Blackfeet rode a stout buckskin gelding with stripes painted across its nose and feathers braided into his mane. Perry knew that traditionally, warriors would use eagle or hawk feathers. Considering that Yarda could damage the feathers when she pulled on the mane, they were probably mainly turkey feathers or maybe plastic. The horse had a nice stride, but after Dels looked back twice more, it seemed clear that Yarda's horse would remain six lengths behind Issi.

A riderless mustang with handprints of various colors along its neck and rump moved ahead of Issi.

Benny said, "Like I mentioned, horses get away."

Fans in the stands yelled as Dels crossed the line. Issi slowed to a gallop as she kept going around the turn, then the camera bobbed up and down as Issi trotted the curve. Perry grimaced at the thought of being on that horse bareback. Dels reined Issi around to meet Bake, who had moved along the rail to avoid the incoming traffic from the opposite direction, then watched the last riders finish.

Dels looked down. Bake's face filled the screen. "Yup, yup," Bake said as he took the reins. "Most excellent."

"Yeah," Dels muttered. She slowly slid off Issi. Her camera pointed to the dirt track as they spoke.

"You hurt?" Bake asked. "Why're you limping?"

"Landed wrong getting off Xena."

"There's frozen peas in the chest. You gotta ice that knee," Bake said over his shoulder. He clicked a few times and Issi followed him to the middle of the straightaway for the team photo. Dels kept looking at Bake's back, but Perry thought she was probably admiring his ass.

Perry looked at Bake standing here now in the empty barn. He looked like he was about to sob.

"Good race," came a female voice. Dels looked to her right. The tall Blackfeet Yarda held out her hand and the young women shook.

"Hurt your leg, I see," Yarda said.

"Yeah," Dels responded, then faced the barn again. "Could've been worse."

"You got that right. Cheena's knee might be dislocated. Okay, well, we're taking off," Yarda said. "We don't have anyone in the finals of the men's relay so we want to get down the road."

"We don't have anyone either."

Bake stopped the video to say, "We only have four horses. Benny still can't jump so we invest in his race and the ladies' relay. Sometimes they're called the maidens' race. Not every venue has female relay races. Usually they just have women ride one lap. Dels, Yarda, and other women have protested, and we're behind them. There should be relays like the men's, but the sport still doesn't have enough female riders."

He restarted the video, which showed Dels turning her head and stepping close to Yarda so they could hug. Then Yarda slapped Dels on the arm.

"I expect to see you there, sister," Yarda said. "Be careful."

"Always am," Dels said.

Yarda stopped and turned. She looked to the barn, then to Dels. "Bake's cute. Seems smart."

"I know," Dels said.

Perry looked at Bake. He stared at the screen and said nothing.

"Whenever you find a smart guy," Yarda said, "hang on to him."

Dels laughed. "I'm trying."

Dels limped to the starting line, where her team had gathered for the requisite winner's photo. Bake came to her side.

The video feed showed the dirt. They heard Bake whisper, "Don't even think about jumping." Then, "Let me help."

In a flash, Dels was atop Issi. Perry knew that Bake had put his hands on her hips and lifted her.

The next clear shot showed Dels looking down at Bake. He winked.

The camera feed went upside down when Dels took her hat off for the team picture. They heard the photographer prompt them with, "Say commodity cheese!"

The screen went black.

"Is that it?" Sophia asked.

"Shouldn't be," Bake said. "Dels put the camera on her dashboard to catch her conversation with Lee. Hang on." He played with the phone, then said, "Here we go."

6

They saw Dels behind the wheel and Lee Robinson in the passenger seat. They watched as the pair discussed Rhonda, and Perry wondered what Dels had against her. Their banter about music and Dels's easy way with the young Lee made her smile. Both seemed earnest and she wondered how the teenager was faring. When Dels asked about the sputter, Perry could detect a slight movement, as if the truck had run over a branch.

All five gasped when Lee yelled, "Fumes!" They watched Dels try to hold the truck steady as it pulled to her right. Sophia put a hand on her chest as they all witnessed Dels and Lee make their way up the ramp to the truck stop. When Dels tried to call Bake and said his name, he stiffened and closed his eyes. Perry started to put a comforting hand on his arm, but she was curious as to how he would react to the rest of the video.

They listened to the arriving vehicle as it drew nearer. Lee yelled, "Truck's coming."

"Now we know it's a truck," Raquel said.

Gomer barked, Lee yelled something indecipherable, Dels

screamed "No!," and the other truck's engine roared, then retreated.

Then nothing was visible on the dark screen except for occasional flashes of distant lightning, and they heard only Issi's hooves tapping on the cement and Gomer's whines.

Bake's shoulders drooped, then he seemed to melt. His knees buckled and he slowly sat on the barn floor. Benny knelt next to him.

The three women remained riveted on the computer screen.

"So," Sophia said. "The truck driver did not speak." Then she verbalized what they all were thinking. "And Dels didn't turn her hat around."

Perry wished Sophia had not said that. She looked down at the distraught Bake. "Mr. Folsom, you said that Sealy also recorded."

"He did. And he also recorded in the truck with Vera."

Perry thought a moment. "All right. We need to review the video we just watched again and it needs to go to the crime scene unit to see if they can figure out that truck."

"Let's see what Sealy recorded."

Bake stood slowly. He switched out the SD card, then said, "All right. Here it is."

They all gathered around and watched the relays and interactions from Sealy Billy's perspective. He had almost everything that Dels did except from different angles. Whereas Dels had her eyes on the ground for the most part after the race, Sealy kept his head up and captured more of what was around him.

One segment caused Bake to hiccup again.

Sealy walked behind Issi, trailing Bake and Dels on their way to the barn after the photos were completed.

Sealy got close, almost next to them, clearly trying to record what they said.

They watched as Dels started to dismount Issi, but Bake put a hand on her thigh.

"No," he said. "Let's ride to the barn." Bake jumped up on Issi behind Dels. They heard him say in a low tone, "I think that when we get home we'll take a nice long shower. Then I'll help you dry off. And then we'll eat the pasta that I'll make and we'll—"

"How're you feeling, Dels?" Vera interrupted as she trotted alongside them.

Perry was annoyed that Vera had interjected herself into a sweet moment, but obviously Vera was unaware of their conversation.

The video jogged along until they arrived at the barn. Sealy moved ahead of Issi, then swung back to look at Dels.

"I'll live," Dels said. "You're my role model, Vera."

Sealy recorded Bake slowly dismounting, his hands caressing Dels's waist and then her thigh as he slid off Issi.

Perry was captivated by Bake and Dels. She almost didn't notice that Bake gasped and let out a sob that few men would allow women to hear. She motioned to Benny, who stopped the video.

"You okay?" Perry counted on Bake's machismo to get him through this so she could see the remainder of the video.

"Fine," he muttered. She knew he was not okay.

Perry nodded to Benny.

"You need to sit," Bake said through the computer screen. "I'll get Lee to deal with Issi."

Sealy recorded Dels as she landed with a plop in a camping chair and propped her right leg on an empty ice chest. She reached into another chest and pulled out a bag of frozen peas that she draped over her knee.

"Ice bath?" Benny asked.

"Hell no," Dels snapped. She poured water from her bottle onto her towel and gave her face and neck a once-over. She removed her red high-tops and poured water over her feet.

"My leg feels like it got run over," she said to Gomer, who sat at Dels's side, butterfly ears pricked. He cocked his head as if he understood every word.

"That'll feel better after a week or so," Vera said.

"One hopes," Dels muttered. "I dread the thought of wearing a brace. Hey, Cheena!" she yelled.

"What?" came a shout from the other side of the team vehicles. If Cheena had hurt her leg, she would not stand up either.

"You okay?"

"No! But I will be."

"Want some ice?"

"Got some."

"Drugs?"

"Sure!"

"Sorry. Don't have any."

"You're a turd, Billy!"

Dels laughed.

"You know I'll take care of that," Bake said as he moved into the frame. He nodded toward her knee. One could infer that he was looking at something else.

"Stop it," Dels laughed.

Bake took two long steps, then leaned down to kiss her. "You'll get through this. And I'll be right there with you." He gave her another quick peck on the forehead.

Bake sat on the floor of the shitty barn and let out a cry. Jezie whinnied. The others kept watching the video.

"And a job well done," said a female voice from the front of Dels's truck.

The video suddenly stopped.

"What happened?" Sophia asked.

"I don't know. Sealy turned it off."

Perry nibbled her bottom lip.

"Would Sealy have recorded inside the vehicle with Vera Spring?" she asked Bake.

"He was supposed to," Bake said, his head on his crossed arms. Perry wondered if he was looking at a horse turd.

Sophia had had enough; she grabbed him under an armpit and forced him to stand.

"Come on. You need to keep it together," she said in a calm, motherly tone. Perry thought that Sophia could scramble an egg without breaking the shell.

Bake straightened. He looked as if he had been on a three-day bender. Perry still wondered about him. "Part of our script includes candid moments, conversations," he said. "What we're really like. You know."

Perry considered if Bake acting romantic was just for the camera or the real deal.

Bake lurched to the laptop and clicked on the keyboard. The video fast-forwarded.

"Yeah. Here's where Sealy started filming."

They all leaned in.

Perry's phone vibrated in her back pocket. The caller ID showed her captain's name. "Stop the video please," she commanded. Then she hurried out of the barn.

"Perry," Deputy Chief Loretta Dickinson said as Perry picked up. "A body was found about twenty minutes ago by the mountain bike trails northeast of Lake Stanley Draper. An officer responded. I just found out. Female. Early twenties."

Perry's stomach dropped. She turned to face the track.

"Anything else?"

"Obvious foul play. You need to stop what you're doing with the horse riders and get on this."

She closed her eyes. "Ma'am, this might have a connection to the missing Choctaw woman."

Dickinson did not reply for a few seconds. "Indeed. Get moving and let me know."

After disconnecting, Perry returned to the barn. She motioned with her head for Raquel and Sophia to follow her to her cruiser.

Perry whispered, "A dead woman at the mountain bike trails next to Lake Stanley Draper. Early twenties, maybe. Sophia and I are going."

Raquel's expression did not change.

"I'll let you know." Perry didn't have to say any more.

"I want to follow up with questions here," Raquel said. "If it is her or isn't . . . well." She trailed off. "Regardless."

"I know. We're taking the SD cards."

She returned to the stall and said to Benny and Bake, "Detective Burns and I are being called to another situation. Officer Hunter will stay. There are a few more things she needs to ask you."

"Where you going?" Bake asked, eyes wide.

"We have to pick up results from the forensics team," she lied. If she said anything else, she knew that Bake and Benny would follow her. Then she added, "It's another case. Mr. Folsom, I need to take those SD cards."

"But we have video of four races on those," Benny interjected. "We can't lose them."

Perry held up a hand. "Don't worry. You'll get them back." *Maybe*.

Bake grimaced and started to turn off Perry's laptop.

"Hang on," she said. "Where exactly is this video stopped so I can easily start watching again?"

Bake pointed to the time along the bar at the bottom. Perry nodded and he turned it off. She had to charge the laptop so it wouldn't die.

"All right, gentlemen," Raquel interjected like a choir director. "Walk me through the events of yesterday again."

Perry and Sophia took that opportunity to disappear into the cruiser.

7

The bike trails north of Lake Stanley Draper wound through the woods, challenging riders with varying levels of difficulty, loose dirt, and distances. The elevation of the trails was modest, although even seasoned bikers with technical experience on mountain trails could hone their skills on the red and yellow loops.

Perry and her family fished often at nearby Lake Stanley Draper. The sixty-two-year-old man-made lake, which was actually a reservoir, covered almost three thousand acres with thirty-nine miles of shoreline and was stocked with largemouth, white, and spotted bass; white crappie; channel, flathead, and blue catfish; and bluegill.

She and her husband had also biked the trails. Last time they rode twenty-eight miles. Perry was not crazy about mountain biking, but they started early on a cool March morning and were rewarded with only a few other riders and the sight of a herd of white-tailed deer and several turkey hens and their young ones.

"Lakes are good places to dispose of bodies," Sophia said as Perry drove toward the parking lot off South Post Road.

Perry nodded. She often wondered what one would find at the bottom of drained lakes and ponds. Surely bodies in barrels, like those discovered in the water-depleted Lake Mead.

This lake had a history.

In 1988, a couple was found buried at the shoreline. A female marina security guard was shot and killed in 1994. In December 1996, marina workers found a University of Oklahoma ballet student dead by the shore, raped and shot in the head. In 2010, a man who had been shot to death was also deposited at the water's edge. A year later, a man stabbed his pregnant wife twenty-nine times and left her near the bike trails, where riders found her a month later.

"What if this is Dels Billy?" Sophia asked.

"It might be," Perry said. She gripped the wheel tighter. "And if it's not, we'll also find out what happened to this person."

A flock of turkey hens ran across the road.

Perry slowed, then said, "Fuck it."

"I beg your pardon?" Perry often busted out with cursing but this outburst surprised her.

"What? No. Not 'fuck it.' *Fvkit.*" She spelled it. "The words sound the same. That's my tribe's word for turkey."

She was not smiling, so Sophia realized that this was no time to joke, but it might be good to keep talking.

"Turkeys are odd," she said.

"They are. They seem goofy, but they're smart. And they have incredible eyesight. Sneaking up on them is almost impossible."

"What a name."

"Several years ago conservative Choctaws tried to change the name to *akak chaha,* which means 'big chicken.' Not everyone liked that name change and protesters began wearing T-shirts with a turkey on the front and *Fvkit* below the image. I have one. And a matching coffee cup."

Sophia could not help but snicker. If she were not so exhausted, she could have kept a straight face.

Perry turned off the lights. "Chahta anumpa doesn't always have names for animals that translate neatly into English. Crows, for example, are called *fala* and a raven is *fala chito,* meaning 'big crow.' Like Dels's horse, Issi. That means 'deer,' but the Choctaw word for horse is *issoba,* meaning 'like a deer.' Did you notice that Dels yelled 'whoa' at Worf to get him to stop? The Choctaw word for 'stop' is *issa,* which could confuse the horse Issi if Dels yelled issa. The racers have to be consistent with their commands."

Sophia took off her sunglasses and wiped the lenses with a Kleenex. "Issi was thinner and smaller than the other horses. I can see why she chose that name."

"Well, that and it's two syllables and the horse responds to it."

They saw several patrol cars ahead of them in the distance. Perry slowed as they reached a bottleneck of patrol cars and fire trucks on the side of the road, finally stopping behind a black Oklahoma City Crown Victoria Police Interceptor. The parking lot was blocked with tape. Inside the lot were an ambulance, one truck, an old green van with a bike rack on top, and a Honda Civic with a rack mounted via the trailer hitch.

Two paramedics stood next to a tall officer who spoke with two women. Both wore riding shorts and expensive-looking neon bike tops. One woman's short brown hair stuck up, as if she had run her hands through it after removing her helmet. The other had a blond braid that fell over her shoulder and two full-arm sleeves of tattoos. Her friend held up the hem of her bike shirt to wipe her eyes.

"I guess those are the ones who found her," Sophia mused.

When they reached the group, Perry greeted the tall officer, who brought them up to speed.

"These ladies"—he nodded his head at the two women—"had just started their ride this morning when they discovered the victim."

"We appreciate your call," Perry said. "Hang tight. We need to see something." Meaning, they had to see if it was Dels Billy.

Perry followed Sophia, both of them eager to see if it was Dels but also dreading finding out that it was. The two observing officers stood in the middle of the trail.

"I hope they didn't step on tracks," Perry muttered.

Sophia scrutinized the dirt. She crouched at one spot. "Heel mark," she said. "I wonder if there are any cameras on the trail."

Perry turned and stepped into the brush so as not to walk on the dirt. "I'll get some flags. Stay there. Take pictures," she said over her shoulder.

She hustled to her trunk and pulled out a bundle of small white flags attached to metal wire posts. Returning to where Sophia stood, she stuck a flag into the ground four inches from the track and took pictures of the area. Sarita and her forensics team would make casts if they deemed these viable clues.

Perry could see a Converse high-top sticking out onto the trail. She walked along the edge of the trail to the yellow tape and onto the scene, then froze. The perp had made no attempt to hide this body. The woman had been tossed into the brush, limbs akimbo. Her blue T-shirt with Billy Idol on the front was unstained, but her tight jeans were dirty around the knees. The shirt had risen up—possibly when she had been deposited here—revealing a large tattoo of a turtle on her ribs. Each of the thirteen scutes that made up the top of the reptile's shell was a different color. Perry thought that getting that tattoo on her rib cage must have been painful. There was also a dark tattoo around her left wrist. Perry couldn't tell what it was supposed to be.

"See any footprints?" she asked the officers.

"You can see the bike tracks," one officer responded. "And there are prints where the rider got off and approached the body. But from where we are standing at least, we can't see if there are tracks in the brush."

"Yeah," the other agreed. "We walked along the edge of the trail, and you can see a few partial footprints. They're not from running shoes. I put three stones on the side of the trail to mark where I saw them. I didn't have flags with me."

"Good," Perry said, relieved.

"No trail cams?" Sophia asked.

"No. And none in the parking area."

Perry turned her attention to the body. The knees looked as if she had been crawling in the dirt. She wore her long dark hair parted in the middle. What Perry initially thought were tattoos on her wrist were actually three inches of colorful braided bracelets. Perry had a few of those.

The dead woman's mouth was slightly open and her head tilted to the right. Her eyes were closed. She seemed to be sleeping. A deep laceration across her neck might have been the cause of death, but that would be up to Medical Examiner Melinda Batters to decide.

"That's not Dels Billy," Sophia said.

"No, it isn't." Perry stared at the dead girl's face. "Dels is five-ten at least and this girl is maybe five-three."

"Are you going to call Dickinson?"

"No. Let's see what these bikers know."

"Do you want me to call Raquel?" Sophia asked as they slowly made their way back to the parking lot.

Perry kept her head down, still looking for clues.

"No. Let's get all we can here. I don't want to interrupt whatever she's got going with Bake and Benny."

Perry straightened as they reached the bike riders. She took out her small pad and pen. "What are your names?"

"I'm Louise Grant," said the one with the braid. Perry could see now that the woman's tattoos extended far beyond her arms. They covered her neck and stopped under her chin.

"Ciara Johnson," the shorthaired one said. A shiny red stone adorned the top of her right nostril.

Both had been crying. Louise had her arms wrapped around herself as if she were cold.

"How did you find her?" When speaking with other officers, Perry would say "the body" or "the deceased," but seeing how distraught these two were she thought it best to soften the language.

Ciara turned and pointed to the trail behind her that opened to the south. Yellow police tape stretched across the dirt path, and two officers stood peering into the trees. "We hadn't gone very far. Just right there. I was in front and saw her leg sticking out of the bushes under the trees. Louise hadn't even changed gears yet."

"And you called 911?"

"Hell yes," Ciara said.

"Did either of you touch her?"

"I did," Louise said. "I hoped it was a mannequin, you know? I jiggled her foot. But I could see that it was a real person. She's messed up."

"Did you walk around the body?"

"No." Louise sniffed. "Most of her is in the bushes. Off the trail."

Ciara put her arm around her. "It's okay," she whispered.

"And then you rode back here, or walked your bikes?"

"I turned my bike around and then yelled for Ciara to turn around."

"All right," Perry said. "Ladies, please stay here. You can sit in your vehicle but don't leave yet. An officer here is going to talk to you some more." He nodded.

Sophia said to Perry out of earshot, “Not Dels. I don’t know if that’s good or bad.”

Perry had her hands on her hips as she looked back down the bike trail. “Bad for this woman. She is somebody, and I want to know who did this to her.”

8

After Melinda Batters arrived and Perry briefed Sarita and her forensics team about the situation, she and Sophia left to find food.

Perry called Raquel from the car to tell her about the woman at the bike park.

"She was Native," Raquel repeated.

"Yes."

"Damn."

"Did you get any more information out of Folsom and Durant?"

"Not really. It's clear that both are upset, although Bake Folsom . . ." She trailed off. "I don't know about him."

"People handle stress in different ways," Perry said in hopes that Raquel would elaborate.

"I told them to go home."

"Sophia and I are going to eat something. Do you want to meet?"

"Nah, I found a taco truck nearby."

"That sounds good."

"Call if you hear anything else."

"Will do."

Perry turned to Sophia. "I'm starving," she said. "I think. It might be exhaustion."

Sophia swallowed the last of her water and shook the empty bottle. "I second that."

"How does a burrito sound?"

"I'll eat liver and onions at this point," she said.

"Eeeesh."

Sophia snickered. "I'm so tired I wouldn't be able to taste it."

"Oh, yes, you would," Perry countered. "Burritos it is."

Inspired by Raquel's mention of a taco truck, Perry drove to a nearby taco place and ordered two iced teas, two large chicken chipotle burritos, four tacos, and two chalupas.

She drove around until they located a park shaded by tall trees.

"You know the taco and chalupa are redundant, right?" Sophia said. "One item is flat and the other is curved but with the same ingredients."

"I know. I like the chalupas because they're like little crunchy pizzas. The tacos aren't shaped like a pizza."

Sophia laughed and rubbed her forehead. "I really am too sleepy to eat."

"You need to. There's hot sauce in the bag."

Sophia took out a red-hot sauce packet and squeezed it over the end of her burrito, then took a large bite. "You know," she mumbled, "this burrito is also basically the same thing as a taco except with a soft wrapping."

"That's what I like about you, Sophia. You're a deep thinker."

They sat eating in the parking lot of an empty playground. It was too hot for a child to play on the equipment. Perry recalled when she was six years old and slid down a metal slide.

It was a scorching August afternoon. The metal burned the back of her legs and her bottom where her underwear rode up. She grimaced and focused on a taco.

"Let's watch Vera and Sealy in the truck," Perry said. "Maybe that'll wake us up." Sophia retrieved the computer bag from the back seat and set the laptop on her knees.

She found where they'd left off and turned up the volume. The scene showed Vera at the wheel and Sealy in the passenger seat. Sealy leaned forward and pressed the radio buttons so fast that Vera gave him a death glare.

"How can you tell what you're hearing?" Vera asked. "You switch channels too fast."

"I can tell in a second what song it is."

Benny's Hummer headlights shone in Vera's side mirror and lit her face. "I never understood the appeal of that gas-guzzling Hummer," she said. "The air conditioner goes out and the engine runs after Benny turns it off. A sustained pain in the ass."

"I think it's cool," Sealy countered.

A booming bass sounded.

"What was that?" Vera asked.

Sealy rolled down his window. "Thunder. Hey, lookit." He pointed to the south. The sky lit up and illuminated the cab.

"Wow. Let's get home."

The two kept bickering as they changed the stations, until a series of men screaming religious phrases assaulted their ears.

"Why do people listen to this?" Vera asked.

"Oklahoma, baby." Sealy laughed.

Vera switched it again until Lynyrd Skynyrd's "Simple Man" filled the car.

"There you go," she said. "Something meaningful."

They listened a moment, then Vera said, "Dels needs to see a doctor. A sports doctor. Not Indian Health Service."

"She was walking," Sealy countered.

"Dels is tough, Sealy, but knee injuries have a way of sneaking up on you. She might have torn cartilage or trashed her ACL."

"She can wear a brace."

"Don't be a dick, Sealy. She's your cousin."

"We choose our friends, not our family."

Vera sighed. "You two need to get along. That allotment belongs to her and your father."

Sealy suddenly looked directly into the camera and reached forward, then the video went black.

Perry and Sophia kept gazing at the dark screen.

Sophia said, "He realized what he said and turned it off."

"He certainly did," Perry agreed.

"Who does he not want to hear that?"

Perry slowed her chewing. "Dels and the rest of his team, for sure. But—"

Her phone buzzed. She did not recognize the caller.

"Detective Antelope," she greeted.

"Detective, this is Dr. Blake. I'm treating Lee Robinson, the young man who was assaulted at the rest stop."

Perry swallowed and put her on speakerphone. "Yes, Doctor. How is he?" Perry hoped for good news.

"The same, but he did wake briefly."

"He's awake? Can we come over and speak with him?"

"Unfortunately, no. It was just a short period of consciousness."

She wondered why the doctor was calling just to tell her that.

"All right."

"A nurse and I heard him say something when we took out the ventilator. It doesn't make sense, but I was told to call if he said anything."

"Yes, yes. Go on."

"He is very weak, you understand. He struggled just to whisper."

Perry glanced at Sophia, huffed, then asked, "What did he say?"

"That a shampe hit him in the head. That's all."

"Shampe?" Perry's mouth fell open. Surely, the physician did not mean a *shampe*.

"He said it twice," the doctor said.

"Well," Perry said. "If he wakes up again, can someone use their phone and record what he says? This is important."

"I can't promise anything. Sometimes patients just wake up and start speaking. But I assure you, I heard him say that."

"I believe you. Thank you for calling. And please call again if need be."

Dr. Blake disconnected.

Perry stared at her phone. She felt Sophia's eyes on her.

"What's a sham-pee?"

Perry sighed. "Shampes are among the many entities in the Choctaw supernatural lexicon. They are huge, hairy, smelly beasts that followed the tribe on our removal trail from the Southeast to Indian Territory. They were probably the inspiration for the Bigfoot creature."

"He was attacked by Bigfoot?"

Perry picked up her drink and took a sip. She held it like a microphone.

"We have a lot of weird entities and deities," Perry continued. "There's the evil shapeshifting great-horned owls called opas. Kashehotapolo, the Deer Man. Ohoyochisba, the Corn Goddess who brought Choctaws the gift of corn. Shampes are probably the most well-known."

Now Sophia's eyebrows were raised. She remained quiet.

"Most tribal cultures include supernatural beings that help explain natural phenomena and teach life lessons. Many Natives, including traditionalist Choctaws, believe that hearing an owl hoot is a harbinger of something bad. But you can't generalize tribal beliefs. Other tribes view owls as mere messengers. I heard that Hopis see white owls as good luck. And some northern tribes view snowy owls as spirits of people who just died and haven't gone to the next world. Some Southwestern tribes have taboos against interacting with reptiles, while others, like Choctaws, used the pattern of the eastern diamondback rattlesnake on their decor because they admire the serpent's bravery. You saw that on the horses."

Sophia took a few slow swallows of her tea. Finally she said, "If Lee Robinson thought a shampe assaulted him, then he has knowledge of the creature and believes in it."

Perry was impressed that Sophia did not laugh or say something dismissive. Her gaze returned to the playground slide. She knew people who claimed to have seen them.

"Are we supposed to be looking for a different kind of perp?" Sophia prodded.

"What? Of course not. That's not possible." Perry pushed her head back against the headrest and snickered.

"He saw a big hairy person," Sophia reasoned. "It was dark."

"He hallucinated." The two women stayed silent a moment. Perry said, "Vera mentioned an allotment. A disagreement. Now that is something to look into."

Sophia cocked her head. "All right. These are just kids. Basically. How could they have orchestrated the truck and tire sabotaging?"

Perry ignored the question and said, "I want to talk to Vera again." Vera struck her as a thoughtful person who would stay awake mulling over the events. She would tell them something new.

"You think she knows about a shampe?"

"I would bet that she does know about shampes, but I doubt if she knows about any one in particular. I'm not concerned about a shampe. I am about an allotment."

"I'll call," Sophia said. "Drink the rest of your tea. You'll get a headache if you get dehydrated."

"Thanks, Mom." Perry yawned. She and Sophia needed to rest.

"It's only been a few months, but I've been around plenty of your headaches. They're not pleasant for anyone." Sophia clicked Vera's number and she picked up after the first ring.

"Ms. Spring, this is Detective Burns and Detective Antelope is with me. We want to ask a few more questions."

"No problem. I've been wanting to talk to you. Have you heard anything?"

"We're still gathering information and you can trust that we'll put it together."

Perry thought that optimistic. The clock was ticking and they really did not have much to go on. Dels was reported missing a little more than twelve hours prior, and any number of things could have been done to her in just a few minutes or hours after her abduction. Perry felt a sense of urgency.

Sophia leaned forward a bit as she concentrated. "Tell us about the day," she said.

Vera recounted the events of Sunday and her recollections were essentially the same as everyone else's.

"Tell us about Dels."

Vera sniffed. "Smart girl. She lives by herself, you know. I mean, sometimes. Bake basically lives there with her but he has his own place. Dels attends Eastern Oklahoma State. Getting her degree in criminal justice."

"Oh yeah?" Perry asked. That had been Perry's major at Oklahoma State.

"How does the team get along?" Sophia asked.

Vera stayed quiet for a few seconds. "Well, we get along fine. I've known everyone for at least three years. Except Lee. He started coming around maybe a year and a half ago."

Sophia let Vera consider the question before she asked another.

"Do you know of anyone who might hold a grudge against the team?"

Vera laughed. "Everyone wants to win, but I can't imagine that anyone we know would want to hurt another rider. Or a horse."

"And all of you get along?" she asked again.

Vera paused again. Perry thought she might be annoyed. "Just a squabble here and there. It gets hot. We get hurt. You know. Sniping."

"Sniping?"

"Yeah. Being short with one another like we are with family."

"Does Dels argue with someone more than the others?" She hoped Vera would mention the allotment comments on the video.

"Um. Well, sometimes she and Sealy argue."

Perry asked, "Do they have disagreements? I mean, they're related so maybe they have family tiffs?"

"Probably. Yeah, they do. And especially since Sealy and his father want to sell the family allotment." *Bingo*.

Perry sat up straight. Sophia did not change expression.

"That's why they argue?" she asked.

"Yes. Sealy's father and Dels own it jointly. Dels doesn't want to sell."

Perry took a sip of her tea. "I know how that goes," she said in an effort to get Vera to keep talking. "Once that allotment is sold there's no getting it back."

"No kidding," Vera agreed. "Natives have lost too much land—we need to keep it. Sealy doesn't seem to understand that. His father wants to ask a fortune for it, because the people who want it think they'll strike it rich with oil like the Osages. The allotments around them have pump jacks, and Sealy told me a few months ago that one of them came through. But Dels doesn't care about that. It's her family home."

"Did Dels ever talk about getting a place in town?"

"Why would she do that? She can't keep her animals in a neighborhood backyard. Her place has a barn, a well, it's completely fenced, and it's not that far from a grocery store or school. The tribe helps with some maintenance. She keeps it up. And Bake helps."

"They're serious?"

Vera paused.

"Ms. Spring?" Perry prompted.

"Well. I'm not supposed to say anything, but well."

"What?"

"Dels and Bake got married a couple of weeks ago. I'm the only one who knows."

Perry's mouth fell open. Had she found a motive?

"Why doesn't anyone know?"

"For several reasons. They don't have much money and didn't want to spend it on a wedding."

Perry could understand that. She knew several couples who had eloped to avoid the complexity of a marriage ceremony that often included intrusive relatives, expensive clothing, and catered food.

"Another reason is that this allotment issue gets pretty heated sometimes. If Sealy and his dad find out that Bake could now have some of Dels's assets, it could get really ugly."

Perry put down her tea and rubbed her temples. Bake having access to whatever Dels owned provided motive from another direction.

"They plan to announce it after the World Championships

next month. For now, they want things to be as smooth as possible."

Perry needed to think about this, but she asked, "And they have always gotten along?"

"Oh yeah. He's nuts about her. She wants to finish school. It's nice that young people can get along so well. Neither one of them have parents, but they manage."

"What do you know about Sealy's father?"

"Line? He's a jerk."

"His name is Line?" Sophia asked.

"Yeah."

"Is that short for something?"

"I have no idea, but he thinks he's hot shit because he's a correctional security officer at the state pen."

"You mean Oklahoma State Penitentiary?" Sophia asked.

"Yeah. He's bossy by nature. And he's on the tribal gaming commission. You know we have eight casinos that bring in over two billion a year."

Perry suddenly felt a twinge of giddiness. She already knew that about the tribe's worth, but that statement was not what got her full attention.

"How long has Sealy's father been working in those positions?" she asked.

"The pen for, I don't know—maybe ten years. He started on the gaming commission about a year ago. I know that because Sealy told us that his dad got paid every time the commissioners have a meeting, even if it's just for a few minutes. Line is fascinated with the behind-the-scenes action at the casinos. All the cameras. He gets to see how people cheat. And the amount of money that comes through casinos to be laundered is incredible. You know the gambling industry is complicated, right? Rules, regulations, security, surveillance systems, all that money coming in. You just know some people are stealing."

Perry listened and agreed with everything Vera said. Casinos could be big trouble. All those involved with law enforcement knew that casinos increased crime, drunk driving, and bankruptcy. People became addicted to gambling and stayed all night in casinos drinking, smoking, and mindlessly spending their money until they ran out. True, the revenue stream could be impressive and many tribal members found employment at the casinos and resorts. Tourists often came to gamble, then went to tribal lands and spent more money at restaurants, travel plazas, and golf courses. But all too often, the promised fair payouts to tribal members never materialized and despite the tribal casinos bringing in hundreds of millions—and sometimes billions—of dollars, some tribal citizens still lived in poverty while others thrived. The disconnects between the top and bottom economic rungs in some tribes could not be more obvious. So far, there had been no solution to the intertribal economic disparities.

"Thank you, Ms. Spring," Sophia said. "Try to stay available. We might have more questions."

"I'll have my phone with me." The call ended.

"Well now," Sophia said.

"Which part?"

"We know why Sealy clicked off the video," Sophia said.

"Maybe."

"And now there's motive," Sophia added. "I know you had thoughts about Bake, but I couldn't see him as a culprit. I'm curious. What do you think about him? He seemed adequately distraught, but now I wonder if he's a part of this situation. Could he want Dels's land?"

"Normally, if one spouse goes missing, I would be all over the other one. But in this case, if Dels dies Bake won't inherit her allotment. He might get a few assets, but as far as I know, the land would belong to Line Billy."

Perry called Raquel again. "I want to know more about Line," she said to Sophia while the phone was ringing.

"You think he's that interesting?"

Raquel answered before Perry could respond.

"Halito, Raquel."

"Halito, Perry. Where are you?"

Perry liked that Raquel did not waste time with small talk.

"Took inspiration from you and got burritos. We're by a park trying to stay awake. Hey, do you have access to Choctaw records? I mean, who owns allotments?"

"Sort of. I can find out whose ancestors had allotments. I have a subscription to Ancestry.com and all the fixings, like Newspapers.com."

"I want to know about Dels Billy, Sealy Billy, and his father, Line Billy."

Raquel was silent for a few seconds before speaking. "Possible resources on or under the land?"

"Yep. I'm just curious." Perry tried to sound casual.

"Now I am too. Give me a few hours—I just need to get on a computer. I'll find a library."

Raquel clicked off.

9

"We've been awake for at least thirty-two hours with just that half-hour nap, partner," Perry said. "I'm getting dizzy. And caffeine will just make it worse. I'll puke."

Sophia continued to stare out the window, her half-eaten burrito and tacos in her lap.

Perry slowly turned her head to face her. "Sophia?"

Sophia's eyes were red. "Yeah?"

"I say we go home and sleep. We both need a shower. I'll call Sealy and tell him we'll come to his house tomorrow."

"Yeah," she repeated as if on autopilot.

Perry recognized that Sophia had hit a wall. She was inches from it herself. She called Sealy to let him know when they would arrive and for him to be there and then she drove Sophia back to the police station.

"Go take a hot shower, then sleep," Perry said as Sophia got out of the cruiser.

She nodded and opened the door to her unmarked silver Ford F-250.

"You can do it," she added. "Your house is just twenty minutes away."

"You keep telling yourself that too, partner."

"I can do it," Perry said. "Demand a backrub!"

Sophia gave her a thumbs-up.

Twenty minutes later Perry backed into her driveway but did not open the garage door. Troy had a class, then planned to attend a book signing for a poet friend hosted by Green Feather Book Company. Olyve was at work. Nico was at his friend's house down the street, as always in the summer. She sat for a few minutes watching squirrels chase one another around the base of the huge oak tree across the street. She had done this often—sat in her car and watched life. The echinacea and coreopsis that lined her sidewalk provided a blast of purple and yellow against the dried lawn that struggled to stay green. She and Troy had vowed to turn their yard into a rock-and-wildflower haven next year. She yawned and grabbed her pack, then got out of the car and went inside through the side door to the garage, where she discarded her shoes and entered the laundry room.

She made her way to the bedroom, where she deposited her gear and put her gun in the side table drawer before flopping onto the bed, arms outstretched. The Maine coon cats, Odin and Zeus, followed and lay down, a cat on either side of her. Perry thought she would only sleep a few minutes. Four and a half hours later, a chorus of crickets from her phone and Zeus pawing at her right ear jolted her awake. The clock by the bed read 6:57. She rose and went to the bathroom, where she splashed her face with cold water. She turned and saw that the two huge black-and-gray cats were watching her from where they sat side by side on the edge of the bathtub.

"You two." She smiled and gave each cat a kiss on the head.

Perry knew that she better take advantage of the spark of energy she felt. She hurried to the second bedroom, where she kept her clothes, followed by her feline friends. The attached bathroom was hers too. Perry realized nineteen years ago after the first week of living with Troy that a foundational aspect of a happy relationship would be separate bathrooms and an extra bedroom. For those times when one of them was sick, she could sleep in that bedroom, and it also came in handy when she returned home late or had to rise early.

She quickly changed into shorts, and as she did, her energy began to dissipate. Despite her lethargy, she needed to think and she could do that best when Troy was not around. He would not be home for another twenty minutes.

Perry moved to the back deck to greet her German short-haired pointer–Labrador retriever mix she had named after the heroine in the *Alien* movies, Ellen Ripley. "How're you doing, Rip?" she asked. The hyperactive, long-legged mutt wagged her tail and bobbed her head. Ripley was a photogenic dog who smiled like a dolphin. Perry held out a doggie dental stick. The dog snatched it and ran into her doghouse.

Perry took a Gatorade Glacier Freeze from the garage refrigerator, then went out the door leading to the backyard. She opened the bottle and took three gulps. Her foot tapped and her eyes scanned the trees for squirrels. She couldn't stay still.

"Ripley. Here."

The happy dog trotted over, tongue lolling. Perry took the leash from where it hung over the porch railing and the pair headed to the gate and the front yard.

"A run it is," she said to Ripley.

Perry sat on the front porch to retie her shoes. She watched her neighbor across the street weed whacking. The large man wore jeans, boots, a long-sleeved T-shirt, goggles, and gloves. An orange scarf served as a headband. The scarf trailed down his back, the Oklahoma State University Cowboys logo visible on one of the tails.

The whirling trimmer lines powered through the wayward

grass and weeds sticking up along the edges of the sidewalk and driveway. Perry could see the greenery scatter like shrapnel all around the man's legs. The trimmers hit a rock and the line snapped. Perry heard him curse as he dropped the whacker and looked down at it, hands on his hips. She had seen that happen to him before.

"Enough of this," she said to her companion. Ripley licked her face. "Let's go."

Perry stood and pulled Kleenex from the front pocket of her running shorts and blew her nose, then threw the wad into the geranium flowerpot. She would retrieve that later. She turned on the hose and soaked Ripley. She knew that coolness would not last long in this heat.

Her phone chirped for a FaceTime call. She answered. "Hey, Troy."

"Where are you?"

"Got home a while ago. Had to rest."

"You look like you're outside. You gonna run or what?"

"I need to."

"I guess I'll start dinner later."

"You go ahead and make it and eat."

"It's hot, Perr. You should wait until morning. And you need to tell me what happened today. Did you drink anything?"

"Gatorade, tea, Diet Rite."

Troy sighed loudly. "Shouldn't drink that diet stuff."

"It's one of the few diet drinks without aspartame. Besides, they don't make it anymore. I only have half a case left."

"Still. You need to drink more water."

Perry stood. There was no use in arguing with him. "Not going far. Runkeeper's on. I need to get in six miles today so I can hit forty for the week." She put in one of her yellow earbuds.

"You shouldn't wear earbuds when you run," Troy said.

She smiled. "I'm not listening to music. I'm listening to the new Harry Bosch novel and it's not loud." She opened her audiobook app and scrolled to the book in her library.

"I'll be back before dark." Perry started down the steps.

"Lots of clouds. It's gonna be dark early."

Perry sighed and blew him a kiss. "Keep the volume down," he said, then disconnected.

"It's hot, dude," she said to Ripley as they jogged along the shaded sidewalk. "We'll go to the lake and you can jump in."

The lake was more of a large pond with a small dock, surrounded by a narrow trail that looped through the trees. Dog walkers thought the lake the perfect destination for their animals to wear themselves out. The county used to stock the lake with catfish, perch, and crappie, but too many people living outside the area continually took the fish, so the council stopped footing the bill for Dunn's Fish Farm.

Perry sped up and Ripley kept pace. She wondered if it had been a good idea to bring her dog. Her jog bra, shirt, and shorts were already soaked with sweat and Ripley was panting.

The pair took a left at the end of their street as usual, running against traffic as runners and walkers are supposed to do, then passed two streets. Most mornings Perry took advantage of the streetlights and ran those side roads, making a full circle in their cul-de-sacs. The two streets added at least a quarter mile to her tally.

They passed one of the two neighborhood parks. A family of four had a picnic dinner on the long wooden table. The father pushed his daughter on the swing while the mother cut a watermelon. Their young son stood on the bench watching.

A crow cawed from the tall cottonwood on the corner of the next road. Perry reached into her pocket and found two peanuts. She threw both, knowing that another crow observed from the tree across the street. The first landed and flew away with its treat, then the other followed suit but cracked the shell on the street as it watched Perry. She kept a bag of nuts by the back door specifically for the crows. She always had a couple of dog treats in her pockets, too, in case a dog came after her. She had made many canine friends after tossing them Milk-Bones.

The paved road stopped and now they were running on dirt, Perry's preferred surface for her knees and feet.

"Just another mile," she gasped. Ripley flicked an ear. She thought that one loop around the small lake would be enough. Running in heat always gave her a headache, but she was willing to have one in exchange for releasing the stress from the last twenty-four hours.

They crossed the old cement bridge. Every time Perry crossed, she stopped to see what people had dumped over the side. Through the years, she had seen tires, bags of mowed grass, branches, garbage, hides and body parts of poached deer, and once a dead dog with a collar and leash. She wondered when she might see a dead person. The year before Perry spotted a few pawpaws on a tree growing next to the water and she used the narrow, steep trail at the end of the parapet to make her way to the creek below.

The bridge's builder, William S. Visione, had written his name in the wet cement, along with the year it was built: 1916. Perry wondered when the county masterminds would pave the road and tear down the charming bridge. They had already changed the landscape by authorizing the use of machines that used a large arm to "trim" the trees. In actuality, the arms ripped the trees apart and caused the death of countless older growths, including the mulberry trees that Perry pilfered in spring to make jam.

The council had also approved the demolition of the local ancient barn. The owners had locked the gate to deter trespassers into the tall, gray, historic structure with a loft inhabited by bats and owls, but plenty of kids found it the ideal party palace. Two years before, a group of eighth graders fell through the loft and one broke her leg. The barn came down despite outcries from citizens who used it as a backdrop for high school senior pictures. Troy took some of the old lumber with the intention of making picture frames.

The two runners reached the far side of the lake, now murky from drought and heat. Perry let go of the leash; she knew Ripley would not run off. Instead, the dog sprinted toward the water, then took a leap and belly-flopped. Perry watched her friend paddle in random circles as she lapped the mossy water. She hoped the leptospirosis vaccine would fend off the bacteria.

The sun started to set behind the trees. It would be dark by the time Perry got home.

"Let's go!" she encouraged Ripley. The dog reluctantly emerged, shook, and returned to Perry's side. "Good girl. I'm thirsty. We'll stop at the park for water."

The pair completed their circle of the lake and once again hit the dirt road and began the two-mile jog home.

Perry was focused on the conversation between Harry Bosch and Mickey Haller on her audiobook when she heard an engine behind her. Ripley flicked her ears. Perry expected what sounded like a truck to pass her. It did, but slowly. The big engine quieted as it slowed, but it still sounded like the purr of a lion. Or a dragon. The dark windows of the silver F-250 that were well over the legal tint limit prevented her from seeing into the cab as it passed her. The truck was the same as Sophia's except for the tinted windows, black wheel-well covers, and black camper shell. And of course, Sophia's bullet-resistant windows and every other specialized feature necessary for law enforcement work.

Perry waved in thanks for the driver's slowing and not dusting her. Other drivers she encountered sped past, raising a tidal wave of dust that hung in the air like a dense fog, coating her hair and irritating her eyes. Some even had the audacity to wave, oblivious to what runners endured on back roads. Even more perplexing were the drivers who steered toward her, their hands turning the wheel in the same direction as their eyes. Those tended to be older drivers. She watched as the big truck rounded the corner and disappeared.

Dusk had settled and it would be dark in another twenty minutes. Perry thought that maybe she was remiss in not bringing the small light that clipped to her pocket. Perry knew the road, but many drivers did not see runners without reflective gear.

As the two ran the curve, Perry saw the bridge four hundred yards ahead. Her house was a mile from that. As Perry listened to Titus Welliver, she thought about what would be good the next morning for breakfast. She had to meet Sophia at eight, but she also needed to get gas. As she tried to remember how many eggs were in the basket on the kitchen counter, headlights appeared ahead of her. Had that truck done a U-turn? The distinctive truck engine roared.

Ripley's ears perked as they always did when a vehicle approached. The smart canine had learned that when a car was coming she should merge to the left of the white line or off the dirt. She was the perfect running companion. Perry was about two hundred yards from the bridge when the truck's engine revved.

A cold tingle moved across her back. The truck had super-duty LED C-ring lights on the outside of the regular headlights. Those were legal in Oklahoma as long as they didn't impede oncoming drivers, but combined with the headlights that were on the bright setting, Perry was almost blinded. She knew without much thought what the driver intended.

Perry sped up and glanced to the left, knowing that jumping off the shoulder was not a viable option. Both sides of the road were steep slopes covered with orange- and cantaloupe-sized rocks, most of them pointed. An attempt to run across that rocky area would result in a dislocated ankle, and a fall would be disastrous.

If she could reach the bridge, which was now a hundred and fifty yards ahead, she and Ripley could go down the steep trail to the creek. From there, they would cross the narrow stream under the bridge and then bushwhack through the trees uphill to the back of her neighbor's property.

"Come on!" Perry yelled as much to Ripley as to herself.

To the alarmed dog's credit, Ripley did not jump in front of Perry or stop in fear. In the heat, both were tired, sweaty, and having difficulty breathing, but fear coursed through Perry's veins and she pushed through. Her daughter, Olyve, ran a high school two hundred meters time of twenty-eight seconds—she would need a faster pace than that. An image of Allyson Felix flashed through her mind.

She blurted a laugh and hoped she would not cry.

The truck engine roared and its lights grew larger. The driver now had the truck hugging the white line of the shoulder with the intent of hitting her head-on. Perry gasped and moved her legs faster. Hearing the panic in Perry's panting, Ripley whined, understanding that something was amiss.

"Oh God, oh God, oh God," Perry gasped.

The headlights were closer and so was the bridge, but if she and her dog were to beat the truck, it would be by a hair.

Perry's legs burned and her old knee injury flared. She stared into the bright lights, then, when they were ten feet from the bridge, she started to scream "Fu—" when Ripley suddenly pulled the leash to the left and jerked Perry so hard she fell onto her side and slid down the trail.

She heard the engine roar past as she fell. Her body came to a sudden stop and her head hit something hard and unyielding. Her left thigh and the left side of her face burned from road rash and a stick punctured her right cheek. Worse, a shock of pain ran up her left arm from hitting her elbow on a rock. Ripley panted in her ear.

Perry looked back up the narrow trail and saw the rocks and tree roots she had hit sliding down the embankment. She hoped she had not broken anything. She knew from experience that sometimes the worst injuries did not hurt the most. Ripley licked her nose. The engine growled. The threat had not disappeared.

She rolled over and pushed up with her arms. She got her right leg underneath her, then pushed herself up to standing. She saw a bleeding gash on the outer part of her left thigh and skinned knees that looked like something a crashed biker received after sliding on pavement. And her ankle burned.

Ripley whined.

"We have to move," Perry whispered. The truck had backed up and was rolling to a stop above them. Ripley followed as Perry limped to the opposite side under the bridge. The dry creek bed made a sharp left turn. Through the gloaming, she spied a game trail that led up the hill and into the cedars.

Perry dreaded the trek through the unforgiving branches, but there was no choice.

"Tushpa!" Perry urged her dog.

Ripley ran ahead and pulled on the leash. The small assistance kept Perry moving upward. The murmur of the engine diminished, but that did not mean whoever was in the truck was not following her.

The pair followed the narrow trail for fifty feet. Perry sometimes bushwhacked while hunting for mushrooms and mulberries in springtime and pawpaws in fall. The latter trees thrived in the shade of the taller tree canopy. The difference between those gathering trips and now was that when she gathered she wore heavy hunting pants and she could see the branches. Now, the stiff, sharp cedars further lacerated Perry's injured legs. One caught her across the face and cut her right cheek. She stumbled and fell to her knees. Ripley turned and licked her nose again.

Perry laughed. "Oh my God. Movie moment."

She exhaled, then the tears started. She gasped and allowed herself a few seconds to cry. Ripley whined and raked the nails of her right front paw over Perry's forearm.

"Okay, okay."

Perry stood and listened for a few seconds. She heard nothing but her own panting. She reached for her phone, but it was not in her pocket. "Damn." She probably lost it when she rolled down the hill, but it was too dark to find it now.

They traversed the thick woods for another fifteen minutes until Ripley stopped at the barbed wire fence that separated the forest from the cow pasture behind her neighbors' homes. Perry lifted the bottom wire so Ripley could scoot underneath.

She let go of the leash and said, "Go."

Perry then took hold of the T-post and placed her left foot on the middle wire. She lifted her right leg over the top wire and carefully placed her foot on the middle line. Then she brought her other leg over and stepped off. Her left ankle continued to throb, and the long gash on her left thigh and the road rash on her knees felt tight.

She would have difficulty walking the next day.

The pair were just two hundred yards from her property. The multicolored lights woven through her neighbor's back porch lattice served as a beacon.

"Ripley, stop." Her dog obeyed.

What if the truck occupants were watching her through binoculars? She glanced around and didn't see movement, but that didn't mean anything. A person could watch her from the darkness of the woods or from the camouflage of the tall water plants along the stream that connected the neighbors' fishponds.

"Okay," she whispered. "Easy. Let's go." She sprinted to the corner of her neighbor's home and stopped. She still saw no movement.

"Ripley. Come!" She hurried to open the gate at the back of her property. "Ripley, in." She limped through the rows of tomato plants, then through the peppers and under the butternut squash arch. "Ripley. Kennel." She opened the kennel gate and Ripley ran in. Better to keep her in a controlled space than to let her run around and get underfoot.

She quickly moved past the chicken coop, then looked around to assess the yard, but the porch light was not on.

Perry limped to the water barrel at the corner of the walkout basement and crouched. Then she limped the twenty feet to the mudroom door, which she knew would be unlocked.

She went in and locked the door behind her. She hurried through the kitchen, turning the light off.

"Troy!" she yelled. He sat in his chair looking at his phone. No doubt looking at Instagram workout videos. Odin and Zeus lay across his elevated legs. Troy turned his head and did a classic double take. He flipped the footrest down, the two cats springing off him like Olympic divers as he stood.

"What the hell?" He looked her up and down. "What happened?"

"Where's Olyve?" Perry panted. She noted the delicious aroma of roasted chicken.

"Her room. She just got home. I was about to go look for you. You didn't answer your phone."

She turned to head down the hall.

"Perry, what the hell?" he asked again. "Did you fall?"

"Someone tried to run me down." She grimaced and leaned on the doorframe. "Fuck. Turn off the lights. Get Olyve. I lost my phone." She spoke rapid-fire. "Give me yours."

She did not wait for Troy to toss it to her. She limped to the recliner and grabbed it off the armrest, dragging the charge cord with it. The end popped out of the phone and boomeranged back onto the chair.

Troy stared at his wife for a few heartbeats, then called to their daughter. "Olyve! Now!"

He sprinted down the hall to meet his confused child. Zeus and Odin started to follow, but instead decided to dart into the guest room and under the bed.

"Turn off your light," he yelled from the distance as she entered their office.

"I'll call Sophia," she yelled. "I'm getting my weapon."

She kept a SIG Sauer under their bed and a Glock 19 in the office closet safe, along with a Remington 870 shotgun, an old Charter Arms Bulldog revolver that used to belong to her father, and a small Ruger she sometimes ran with.

Perry tried Sophia's number, but her hands were shaking so hard she called Troy's favorite carry-out delicatessen instead. She tried again. She kept the phone to her ear as she made her way to the safe. Sophia picked up after three rings.

"Sophia," Perry said before Sophia greeted her. "I was followed on my run. Silver truck, C-ring lights, black trim around the wheel wells, black camper. Tinted windows. I don't know how many people were inside. They tried to run me down."

"Damn, Perry. Are you okay?"

She kneeled in front of the gun safe, her knees feeling as if she'd doused the open wounds in alcohol, and tucked the phone between her shoulder and ear as she worked the dial. "Yeah, but I'm banged up with hella road rash on my knees and face. Had to bushwhack and I lost my phone—but I think I know where I dropped it, and I have the Find Me thing on my iPad."

She got the safe open and quickly grabbed the Glock, then checked it.

"I need you to get over here. Troy and Olyve are safe. Nico is with a friend. He's two houses down. The house number is nineteen-oh-six and I want someone to pick him up or to stay at that house until this is finished. I have the lights off. Call this in, will you?"

"Yes. And I'm coming."

Perry stayed low as she hurried out the door, flipping the light off behind her. "Troy?" she yelled.

"We're in the bathroom," he said from just a few feet down the hall.

"Stay there." The bathroom window was high and small. Anyone on the outside who wanted to spy would need to stand on something.

"What are you doing, Perry?" Troy asked. "I can help you."

"No!" Troy had accompanied her many times to the shooting range and he was competent with a variety of firearms. Regardless of his competence, though, he knew that his wife was tactically trained. He would stand ready as backup, but until then he knew he would just get in her way.

She crouched as she moved down the hall to the den. Troy had turned off the television and lamp next to his chair, but the light in the bathroom next to the kitchen was on, illuminating the room. As she slowly moved to the window, Ripley began barking.

Don't kill my dog, she thought as a crack sounded.

Then another sounded as a bullet passed through the window above her head and hit her and Troy's framed wedding picture on the wooden shelf next to the fireplace. The glass above her and on the shelf shattered and shards hit the floor. Perry dropped and lay flat below the windows.

"Perry!" Troy yelled. "You okay?"

"Fine! Stay in there!"

She moved backward on her hands and knees to the front door, Glock in her right hand, her skinned knees burning from rubbing the carpet. Then she felt the broken window glass stick into her palms and knees.

She heard the truck engine rev.

On either side of the heavy wooden front door were five twelve-by-six-inch windows set vertically. When Olyve was seven, they had used watercolors to paint different colorful patterns on each pane. She could see through the paint that the truck had backed into their driveway, the red glow from the taillights coming through the colored glass. Then the tires squealed. She waited three seconds, then stood and turned on the front porch light.

The motion detector light had not come on. The first shot had taken it out.

She heard tires squeal, then the growl of the engine fading away. She limped through the mudroom to the back door, exited, then hurried outside and around the house as fast as she could. The truck's taillights were visible at the end of the street. It turned right, where the driver could access any number of paved or dirt roads.

She used Troy's phone to call dispatch to tell them which way the truck had turned. Then she went back into the house the way she'd exited.

10

"They're gone," she yelled to Troy and Olyve. "But stay put until others get here."

Perry wondered about the truck's occupants. They were not just drunk joyriders and they were not local rednecks. This was purposeful behavior. They knew where she lived.

She had only told Troy that she would be running. The truckers had been watching her. Or maybe there was a tracking device on her car and they knew when she got home. That seemed unlikely. Her fatigue and pain prevented her from thinking clearly.

Sirens blared in the distance. In another minute, red and blue flashing lights illuminated the den. She put down her weapon, then turned on the inside lights and opened the front door. She held up her arms so they could see her empty hands.

Two patrol cars stopped catty-corner in the street. The drivers got out and stayed on their side while the others opened their doors and remained behind them. All held AR-15s.

"Detective Antelope," Perry yelled. "The perp is gone."

"Perry?" yelled one driver.

Perry had known Officer Miguel Martinez for six years. He lowered his weapon and started for the house.

Two more vehicles sped up her street, the one in front driven by Sophia, the red, white, and blue lights on the top bar and between the headlights flashing. An ambulance followed.

Sophia pulled into the driveway, jumped out, and ran around to the passenger side to assist Nico. She picked him up and beat Martinez to the door. She wore a white V-necked T-shirt, pajama shorts, and flip-flops, and her hair was mussed like she'd just gotten out of bed. For a moment, Perry nearly cracked a smile—of course Sophia had fantastic bedhead, all thick and curly. Then she sobered. Sophia had tried to sleep while Perry went for an indulgent run.

Nico escaped from Sophia and ran to his mother.

"Mom!" he yelled. "You're all bloody."

"I'm okay. Dad is in the bathroom with your sister. Go. Run like a bunny."

"Perry," Sophia panted. "You're okay."

"I am."

"But you look like shit." Sophia hugged her.

"Ouch," Perry hissed. Sophia's ear had pressed into the puncture in her cheek.

"Troy and Olyve are inside," she repeated.

Sophia nodded and hurried through the door. Perry heard her shoes crunch on the broken glass.

Perry relayed what had happened to Officer Martinez and the seven other responders. Martinez sent out her description of the truck, although everyone knew how easy it was to meander the back roads. It would be a challenge to find the offending vehicle.

Two paramedics hurried up the driveway.

"Come inside and sit down, ma'am," one paramedic said.

Her nametag read LETA. She took ahold of Perry's arm, guided her inside, and pointed to the beige sofa.

Leta scrutinized Perry's body, starting with her face. Her gloved hands gently held Perry's jaw as she turned her face from left to right. Then she lifted each arm and studied them from fingertips to shoulder, then her legs and feet.

"I'm not telling you anything you don't already know, Detective. You have some serious road rash. Last time I saw this was when I worked the Tour de Tucson. You know how many bikers wiped out and destroyed their skin? Very few lacerations, just a lot of missing skin after they fell and skidded." Leta rummaged in her bag. "Did you hit your head?" she asked.

"No," Perry replied immediately.

"You sure?" Sophia asked from the hall. "Your head's pretty hard."

"Yes, and I'm proud of it."

"All right," Leta said as she dabbed Perry's face with a gauze pad. "You have no perforations from metal. I don't see too many wood splinters, although your cheek has an impressive puncture."

Leta took out her tweezers and began extracting bits of cedar and grit.

"Mom?" came a high voice from the hallway. Perry saw her wide-eyed son, Nico, standing next to one of the officers, Troy and Olyve behind him. Nico paused for a few seconds, then ran to her, arms outstretched. He hugged her around the neck. She winced but was not about to let go.

"Okay, son," Troy said, pulling their bloodied son away. "Stand here by me. The paramedic will be done in a minute."

"I'm not gonna lie," Leta said as she resumed pulling out particles. "Recovery won't be smooth. You need to scrub these cuts and scrapes—it'll hurt. But if you don't, then you might see infections. Really, you should come in and have this done properly. Scrubbing wounds is crucial."

"We can do that," Troy said.

Leta turned and gave Troy a once-over. "Well now," she said. "Nice to have a man like that take care of you."

Perry started to smile but gasped when the movement pulled on her cuts.

"Look at me," Leta said as she shone a light into Perry's eyes.

Perry sat still.

"You said you didn't hit your head. You sure about that?"

"No concussion."

"You seem coherent."

"I'm always coherent." She shot a glance at Troy, expecting a sarcastic comment.

He said nothing.

Leta put away her light. "You can go to the hospital and they can clean you up. Or . . ."

"No," Perry said.

"That's what I thought."

The other paramedic, a newbie by the look of him, fidgeted and inhaled as if he was about to declare something. "She needs to be checked out by a doc—"

Leta held up her hand. He quieted.

"Detective, I know your case is important. But I am telling you as a paramedic with many years of experience that you need to see a physician. At the first sign of infection, you will need antibiotics. Actually, you should just go ahead and start them now. And even though you say that you didn't hit your head—"

"I didn't." Perry stood.

Leta held up her hands, palms out. The two left.

Several officers walked around the house with spotlights, searching for evidence that the perps had exited the truck and maybe tried to enter the home. None of the flowerbeds were disturbed and there were no scratches on the doors or locks.

Sophia stood in front of Perry with her arms folded across her chest. "You had a heck of a nap."

Officer Martinez chuckled.

Perry shrugged. "I tend to thrash around."

Perry's weed-whacking neighbor appeared in the doorway, clad in his usual Oklahoma State T-shirt.

"Hey, Patrick," Perry said.

"Everything okay over here?" Patrick had his hands on his hips as if he were planning to take charge if things were not okay.

"Banged up, but yes."

"I've seen that truck before."

"What?" Troy blurted.

"You have?" Sophia asked. "Where?"

Olyve moved in to listen, and Perry couldn't help her attention drifting to her daughter. The tall, thin teenager wore her long hair in a bun atop her head. The scent of the chlorine removal shampoo and bodywash she'd recently used wafted through the room. Her skin had tanned almost to the color of a coconut from long hours in the intense sun; it was a shade darker than the week before. Even though Olyve sat under the lifeguard umbrella while on the guard stand, she still had to pick up towels, scoop out frogs and insects, and teach swimming lessons. At least she minded her mother and wore sunscreen.

Officer Martinez and two others stepped closer.

"Well, it's like that one." Patrick turned and pointed out the door to Sophia's truck. "Plus black trim and a black camper. It was parked in front of the Wylers' house." He motioned to a two-story redbrick house with white shutters two houses down from his one-story gray-brick structure with stark landscaping. "I saw it when I went to the store this morning and wondered why it was there. It was gone when I got back, but it showed up again when I was mowing this evening."

"You're sure it was the same truck?" Sophia asked.

"Yup. My son has those same front lights."

Perry looked to Sophia, who glanced at her, then back to Patrick.

Sophia asked, "This morning?"

"Yeah. Silver F-250. I took a picture but there wasn't a plate on the front."

"I'll inform Raquel," Sophia said.

Troy sat beside his wife. She was covered in dirt and dried blood and he was not sure where to touch her so he put a gentle hand on her shoulder.

"Perr, we need to take care of those cuts. Let me look." He pulled her around so he could see the large bloody gash on her left thigh, the road rash on her knees and left cheek, and the puncture and laceration from a tree branch across her right cheek. He let out a long sigh.

"Mom," Olyve said quietly. The sixteen-year-old stood two inches taller than her five-seven mother, and at the rate she was growing Perry thought Olyve might approach the height of her six-foot-two father.

She opened her arms for a hug. "Honey." Olyve leaned in. "Easy," Perry whispered.

"I can help," Olyve said.

Olyve had completed advanced first aid as part of her lifeguard certification and thought she had the skills of a paramedic. Perry kept a fishing tackle box filled with first aid supplies and Olyve knew how to deal with basic injuries after countless times falling off a bicycle, tripping over tree roots, and cutting her finger while filleting fish.

"Hey, Perry," Officer Martinez said. "We got the APB out. We also scouted around the house again. Like you said, no tracks under the windows and since there's grass everywhere we can't tell if anyone else came around."

"Thanks."

"You need to deal with all that," he said as he motioned with his hand from her face to her ankle. Then he leaned in and said quietly, "And you might want to take a shot or two of tequila. That road rash is gonna hurt like hell."

"Yes, sir." Despite herself, Perry grinned.

"I'll have an officer outside tonight," Sophia said.

"Good idea," Troy said. "Perry. To the bathroom. Now."

Perry took a step forward and gasped. Her ankle and knee had already started to stiffen and her thigh throbbed. The road rash would be the absolute worst. Troy saw her limp and put one hand under her left armpit while Olyve moved to her right side. Nico walked closely behind her.

The other officers were discussing who would spend the night watching the Antelope house as they exited through the front door and walked to their vehicles.

Olyve ran ahead to gather supplies while Troy got Perry to the guest bathroom, Nico trailing behind.

"We've been here before, Perry," Troy said. He guided Perry to the edge of the tub. He sat on the toilet.

"I wasn't hit," she said.

"You could have been."

They heard Olyve's footsteps.

In an attempt to distract her while Troy washed her thigh with a washcloth, Olyve timidly spoke up. "I heard that a woman was taken and a kid was killed."

Perry looked at Nico, who was sitting on the bathroom floor, back against the wall. His young face remained impassive. She wondered if they would need to consult a child psychologist. If she had seen her mother bloody and surrounded by lights, sirens, and police when she was his age, she would have had nightly terrors.

"Nico," she called to him. "I'm fine. I beat the bad guys. I'll be fine." Was that enough to say? She was never quite sure.

"Tell us why this happened," Nico said.

Perry decided that being upfront might allay his fears.

"I'm putting my trust in you and your sister—you two know you can't mention this to anyone."

Perry gritted her teeth when Troy doused her thigh with hydrogen peroxide.

"Two Indian horse relay riders were assaulted at that rest stop off I-40. A woman was taken and a man was hurt. We don't know by whom." She did not discuss the oil and sugar in the tanks or the flat tires. She would talk to Troy about that later.

"Were they Indians?" Olyve asked.

"Yes, both of them. Choctaws. And they were part of the Chahta Riders team. You should see their horses—incredible. Ow!" she yelped.

"Sorry," Troy said. "You have grit embedded in here. I have to get it out or else the skin will grow over the little pieces. And it won't feel good when they work their way out. And if they don't it'll look like a weird tattoo."

"Ugh," she moaned. She stared at the tiles and took a deep breath. She was so exhausted she thought maybe tiredness would dull the pain, but her fatigue only seemed to magnify the stings. The scrubbing, objections, and cursing continued for ten minutes.

A hand placed a tumbler in front of her. She took it. Deep Eddy Lemon Vodka. This was a generous pour. Perry was grateful.

She turned her head and saw Olyve. She smiled.

"Thanks, daughter." She took a sip of the sweet and deceptively strong drink.

Perry saw movement in the doorway. Zeus and Odin crept in to sit by Nico where he sat cross-legged on the floor, staring at the rest of them.

"Why did they take her?" Olyve asked.

Perry had a few ideas but now was not the time to express them in detail. "I don't know, sweetie. It's not an uncommon thing. Bad things can happen when a woman is alone in a broken-down vehicle."

"She wasn't alone," Olyve said. "There was a guy with her."

"True. But some people are opportunistic. And these perps decided to take a chance."

"You should have taken your gun on your run," said Troy.

She did have a small Ruger she sometimes wore in a waistband, but she usually just ran around the neighborhood and to the lake with a small cannister of mace. There were always plenty of people on her route and the extra weight of a gun would bother her. The last thing she'd wanted today was a tight waistband that would make her even sweatier. She also had a taser, but that would be ineffective unless the perp confronted her.

"I don't think that my small gun would have done much to the truck," Perry said. "The driver didn't get out."

"You could have fired at the truck so he'd back down," Olyve said.

Perry took a drink and felt the warm liquor surge through her. She knew she should drink water, but damn this tasted good. "Maybe."

Olyve handed her father the gauze and tape.

"You're gonna hurt tonight, Perr," Troy said.

"I'll probably stick to the sheets."

Olyve didn't say anything. She had been in a similar situation after a mountain bike wreck. A stick went through her front spokes, causing her to fly headfirst onto the trail and slide six feet on her front. Her helmet saved her from a skull fracture, but she lost skin on her knees and the palms of her hands. The healing process was grim.

"Vaseline helps, Mom," Nico said. "Remember when I fell off the wood pile and my knees got all bloody?"

"Good idea," Olyve said to her little brother.

"Don't do any more wrapping," Perry said. "I have to shower and get this blood and dirt off me." She downed the rest of the vodka and turned on the cool stream.

Olyve took Nico by the hand as they left.

"Let me help," Troy said. He helped her undress and lifted her leg into the tub. He handed her the handheld sprayer.

"Thank you," she said.

Troy asked, "Why would you thank me? I'm always here for you, Perr."

Perry's eyes burned. They had been together for more than twenty years and Troy still had the power to take her breath away.

"I'll get your pajama pants and a long-sleeved T-shirt," he said.

Perry thought about how ungratefully she behaved. Troy infuriated her on a weekly basis, yet she depended on him. Not just that, she loved him deeply. She needed to work on expressing that feeling.

She gritted her teeth and washed her face with the bland Cetaphil, even though she normally used the almond scrub. After a painful rinse, she patted herself dry and Troy dabbed the wounds with Vaseline before covering the raw skin with gauze. "This'll keep the blood from sticking to your clothes."

She brushed her teeth, then limped to the kitchen, where Olyve waited to ladle a bowl of tortilla soup. Perry dropped like a rock into her chair. "I smelled chicken earlier."

"I just tore it apart and put it into the soup Dad already made."

Perry stared at it.

"Mom. Just eat half a bowl. Then you gotta lie down. You have some Tylenol 3s for your headaches, right?"

"Yeah, and another prescription I can have filled." She ate without tasting her soup.

"Nico's reading," Olyve said.

"Good."

"What's her name, Mom?" Olyve asked.

Perry put her spoon in the bowl and wiped her mouth. Her cheeks burned and her legs throbbed. She thought about how to answer.

"Dels Billy. She lives outside of McAlester. The young man's name is Lee."

"I saw the team on YouTube." Olyve twirled the bottle of Cholula hot sauce. "Where would they take her?"

"We don't know that yet, honey. Lee is still unconscious. He handles the horses."

"So, she's like one of those missing and murdered people."

"Missing." *Hopefully not murdered.*

"How're you gonna find her?"

Perry stirred her soup. The chicken, onions, and carrots swirled like thick detritus in a whirlpool.

"We now have a description of the truck from this evening."

"And you think that person had something to do with it?"

She thought for a few seconds. *Probably.* "It's a start," she said.

"Where do they take women?" Olyve asked again.

Troy stood at the sink, rinsing dishes and silverware. He turned off the water.

Perry sighed and reached out to place her sore palms over her daughter's hands. "Sweetie, that's not easy to answer. Sometimes the women—and boys and even men—are found alive. Some are runaways. Unfortunately, many victims are assaulted and murdered and they are found, uh, like that."

She realized that was not a graceful way to explain this issue. Troy turned around to listen.

"Like what happened to those girls at school."

"Yes."

Three years prior, two Kickapoo girls who were a year ahead of Olyve in school were abducted one summer afternoon as they walked home from the local Dairy Queen. Despite there being witnesses who claimed to have seen the girls speaking to a passenger in a white van, the perpetrators of the girls' rapes and murders were never found. Olyve and Nico had also overheard their parents discussing the disappearances of other girls and boys. Olyve had grown used to hearing about the dead people whose murders her mother had to investigate. It filled Perry with pain to think about all the realities Olyve knew that her classmates did not, because of her mother's line of work. She didn't want her kids exposed to such things. But maybe, in the end, it would help Olyve face the real world someday.

"Some are not found. Their disappearances remain mysteries. You know, honey, human trafficking occurs all over the world. Some people are kidnapped and sent to other countries to work in houses, drug factories, and as, uh, sex workers."

She wondered if she should have said that. Olyve had a quick wit that Perry envied, but she had never discussed human trafficking with her. She trusted that her beautiful, smart daughter could handle what she told her.

She expected Troy to say something, but he did not.

"We don't know what happened to this young woman, but every bit of evidence gets us closer to finding out. The problem is that with every hour she could be farther away."

Olyve stared at her mother for a few seconds, then surprised her and Troy by saying, "You won't be able to find her if you don't sleep, Mom."

Tears burned Perry's eyes. She let go of Olyve and dropped her hands to her lap.

She barely registered it when Troy picked her up and carried her to bed.

11

The next morning Perry again sat at the table in her regular chair, a bowl of oatmeal covered with pecans, cranberries, and blueberries in front of her. She looked at her husband, who sat next to her.

"You should have woken me, Troy. I haven't slept until nine o'clock since I was in high school with a hangover."

"That's not true. We slept until ten o'clock the day after Thanksgiving last year."

"We had Covid."

"So we did." He reached into his shorts pocket and pulled out her phone. He placed it on the table. "I used the Find My app on your tablet."

Perry breathed a sigh of relief. "Thank you. Where was it?"

"In the cedars. Close to where we found those antlers last year."

Those antlers being a huge eight-point set dropped from the buck that had frequented the grassy area behind their house for the last five years. They had always wondered where he left his shed.

"It's fully charged."

"Of course it is."

Troy put his hands on top of hers. He gently squeezed her fingers.

"How're your knees?"

"Feels like they're in a cast. And my cheeks are swollen. It's hard to eat this."

He removed his left hand to push a tall glass of some kind of purple milkshake toward her. "Smoothie. Yogurt, berries, whey, and half a banana."

She picked it up and tried to drink it. It spilled onto her chin. Troy held up a spoon.

"Why aren't you in class?" she asked.

"I texted the students I'll be an hour late and that they need to use that time to work on their poems."

"Olyve?"

"Another twelve-hour day at the pool. She left an hour ago."

"You're kidding."

"At least she's able to save some money."

"That's not what I meant."

"Don't worry. Sophia let me know that a patrol car will be there. Just in case.

"And Nico's at the pool, too, with Sean. He's got money for lunch and I'll get him after class. Now drink the rest of that," Troy said. "You'll need it."

"A pool lunch of a brand-X hot dog and Cheetos?"

"I meant, money to supplement his turkey sandwich and applesauce. Same with Olyve."

Perry stared at him.

"Seriously."

"All right. I gotta hurry. Sophia will be here soon."

She looked at her phone. Dickinson had called three times.

"Oh boy."

"What?"

"Dickinson."

"You need to call her," Troy said as he took the plates to the sink.

"I will."

He gave her a look that meant he was aware that she would not check in. At least not right this second.

"There were enough officers here last night who'll tell her how I am."

"Sophia called at seven to ask how you're feeling."

"How'd she get your number?"

"She asked before she left."

Perry could not recall seeing Sophia talking to Troy. But her cuts hurt so bad she did not pay much attention to anyone.

"Well, gotta motor." The detectives had planned to meet Sealy at his home in McAlester at nine o'clock, but because Perry had slept through her alarm, Troy and Sophia thought it best if she slept another two hours. Troy even suggested postponing for the day. Sophia rescheduled for eleven o'clock.

Perry preferred to drive, but her left knee had stiffened, her right knee was scabbed, and her left ulna throbbed. She was afraid her wounds might hamper any quick driving moves. Sophia was happy to take her truck.

Perry managed to wind her hair into a bun and brush her teeth. Troy stood at the door, watching her get dressed, to make certain she put on her vest under her white shirt. She strapped her backup weapon above her right ankle. Troy did not see that she had already strapped her knife to her left leg. It threatened to rub the abrasion on her ankle, but she had wrapped gauze around the wound and hoped that it would guard against the sheath.

"You look good," he said.

"My face looks like a pin cushion."

"I don't see any pins."

"Troy. I . . ."

Troy gave her a small, pained smile. "Just let me know how you're doing."

"Always do."

They stared at each other for a few seconds, then Troy stepped in and gave his wife a gentle hug. "My phone is charged, the volume is up, and I'll have it with me."

"Troy. We have to find her." She refused to cry. "I'm with Sophia and Raquel, so don't worry."

"Go find that girl." He handed her a travel mug filled with sweetened iced coffee.

She kissed his cheek, then picked up her daypack and headed out the door.

Sophia sat in the driveway in her own silver F-250. She left the motor running while she got out to open the passenger door. She watched as Perry carefully made her way down the four porch steps.

"A truck like this almost killed me."

"Lots of F-250s out there. The most popular truck, right behind their puny siblings the F-150s. And silver and white are common colors for hot climates." She waited a beat, then said, "Hey, it wasn't me."

Perry reached into her pocket and pulled out a horehound candy. She threw it at Sophia.

"Missed me," Sophia laughed. "You going to be all right today?"

Perry handed Sophia her pack, which she put in the back seat. "I'm coated in Vaseline and I have extra rolls of gauze and tape, wet wipes, and most importantly, my little white helpers. I'll be fine."

Sophia knew "little helpers" meant Tylenol with codeine. Perry often developed headaches and Sophia had seen the amber vial with the white top plenty of times.

Perry slowly got into the seat. Her cheeks were shiny with Vaseline, which covered the vividly red cuts and punctures. Sophia thought if a person was going to die from a thousand cuts, they would look like this.

"You sleep enough?" Sophia asked after she'd gotten back in the truck and shut the door.

"No. It'll take a week to get up to speed."

Sophia laughed. "That's for sure. I've never gone that long without at least taking a nap. By the way, I talked to Raquel. She's still looking at the allotment information. I told her we're headed to McAlester. She's making headway, so I told her to stay put and call us."

"Good. I want to see what's going on with that family."

"Sealy doesn't seem like he'd be part of anything worse than toilet papering a house."

"Hopefully."

With lights flashing, occasional sirens, driving ten miles above the speed limit, plus one stop to pee, they arrived at the Line Billy residence in an hour and twenty minutes.

Sophia stopped in front of the house on West Stonewall Avenue, several blocks from where Line Billy worked at the Oklahoma State Penitentiary. A red 2000 Toyota Camry sat under the carport. The one-car garage door was open and the detectives saw tools and extension cords hanging on the walls over boxes stacked two high. A bike hung from the rafters and fishing poles lay across the beams.

Perry thought it an impressively clean garage given how much stuff was crammed into it. This reminded her of the crowded garage where Nathaniel McGee had been shot. There was room for one more vehicle on the gravel area next to the metal carport. A padlocked shed stood at the end of the carport, which made it easy to unload items from a truck backed into the structure.

The brown front-yard grass contrasted with the thick and colorful moss roses in the half whiskey barrel next to the sidewalk. Perry appreciated the flowers. Her grandparents put moss roses in their large cement porch planters. She loved the orange, pink, red, and yellow blossoms that flourished when other plants wilted in the dog days of summer.

Three high-backed Adirondack chairs sat under the covered porch. The front of the house faced west so the rolled-up awning made sense.

Perry yawned. "We gotta get going on this," she said to Sophia as they walked to the door. "The more pooped I get, the crankier I become."

Sophia yawned in response to Perry. "Maybe we can get a nap in today. Not that you'd need it, since you slept in. I mean, sleeping until nine o'clock. How decadent can one be?"

Perry ignored the good-natured jab. "Don't count on naps. Let's just do this and see where it leads."

The women climbed the porch steps and Perry pressed the doorbell. They heard the ding-dong and the vibrations of footsteps. Sealy opened the inner door. His lush dark curls looked tangled, as if he'd thrashed around trying to sleep. She envied his tousled hair and his dark eyelashes, which looked like they were coated with mascara.

"Oh hey," he said from behind the screen door.

Sophia pocketed her sunglasses. "Mr. Billy, again, sorry to have been a bit late. We ran into an issue."

Sealy looked at Perry and his eyes widened. "Wow," he exclaimed. "What happened to you?"

"Just a little fender bender."

"Geez."

"Mr. Billy," Sophia continued. "We have a few more questions for you."

"Like what?"

"Is your father here?" Perry asked.

"No."

"Can we come in?"

"Did you find out anything?" He unlocked the screen door and pushed it open.

"We're still collecting evidence," Perry said, stepping into the house behind Sophia. She grimaced. The cut on her thigh burned.

The detectives entered the sparsely furnished living room.

"Y'all can sit here if you want." He removed a pillow and blanket from the sofa. A large-screen television perched on its stand in the corner. A cable snaked from the back of the screen to the antenna attached to the wall. A worn oriental rug lay over the vinyl floor. Perry thought that the brown lounge chair was probably where Line Billy sat. A box fan blew toward the sofa, where Sealy had apparently been napping.

"How're you doing?" Sophia asked.

Sealy pushed hair from his eyes. "Not so great," he said. "I have a headache. But I mean, who cares, right? Dels is out there someplace."

Perry and Sophia sat on the sofa. Sealy sat in the lounge chair.

"I'm sure this is difficult for you. Dels is your cousin." Perry paused a moment. "We just have a few questions."

Sealy nodded.

"Tell us about your allotment."

Sealy's lethargy disappeared. "What?" He looked from one detective to the other. "What does that have to do with anything?"

"We're just looking at all angles," Sophia said. "Your allotment is owned by your father and Dels."

Sealy fidgeted. "That's right."

"They inherited it from Line's father. Who is also Dels's grandfather?"

"Yes. Dels got her father's portion after he died."

And you won't inherit any of it until your father dies, she thought but did not say.

"My family allotment is outside of Red Oak. It's surrounded by land that was bought by whites in the 1940s. Are there allotments around your land that are still owned by Choctaws?" asked Perry.

"Not anymore."

"Has your father thought about selling it?" Sophia asked.

Sealy's eyes shifted to the ficus tree in front of the window, then to the rug at his feet. Clearly, he was trying to figure out how they knew that. The detectives continued to watch him.

"He's mentioned it."

Sophia cocked her head. "Who wants to purchase it?"

"Uh, there are a few people who've asked."

"Why would you sell it?"

Sealy shrugged. "I don't know—the money, I guess."

Perry knew that oil companies, ranchers, and farmers greatly desired the resource-rich allotments. Perry asked, "What about Dels?"

Sealy's eyes widened. "Hey. Are you thinking I did something to Dels?"

Perry held out her hands, scraped palms up. "We're just gathering information. Time is very important."

"Well, I sure as hell didn't do anything or plan anything." Sealy stood, his hands fisted at his sides. His voice increased in pitch as he said, "Dels is my cousin."

Perry was unfazed. "Did Dels want to sell?" she repeated.

Sealy huffed. "No."

"Do the allotments around yours have pump jacks?"

"Yeah."

"Have any hit oil?"

"I think so."

Perry now knew that Sealy was aware there was a chance

their allotment would strike oil. Therefore, this young man also knew that he stood to inherit some of that black oil profit if his father died.

Perry continued. “Finding oil is hit-and-miss. One allotment might hit a gusher and the one next door is dry as a bone.”

Sealy shifted on his feet.

“Please sit down, Mr. Billy,” Perry said.

He did, then crossed his left leg over his right.

“Is there water on the land?” Perry asked.

“Yeah. A well. A creek that floods after a rain.”

“Trees?”

“Yes. All kinds. Especially by the creek.”

Perry nodded. Resources made the land more valuable. Farmers and ranchers who wished to lease the land would pay to have water for crops and shade for cattle. The allotment was even more valuable if there were minerals underground. She could not get comfortable and adjusted her sitting position.

“I know there must be pressure to sell. My family has always had to deal with it. My husband is Comanche and he gets offers every week.”

Sealy looked out the window.

Perry shifted on the sofa again. Her ankle throbbed and she felt a bead of blood or sweat sliding down her cheek. She put her hand to her face and then looked at it. Just Vaseline.

She decided to switch gears. “Tell us about Rhonda.”

Sealy’s eyebrows jumped up his forehead. “Rhonda Paul? What about her?”

“Are you two dating?”

Sealy seemed rattled by the question. Or embarrassed.

Perry prompted him. “She came to see you at the race.”

“Yeah. We’ve been out. And we talk.”

Perry knew that “talking” was the new term for dating. Or sort-of dating. Olyve had said that she was “talking” to one of the boys on the swim team even though their only "date" had been to get a slushy at Sonic.

Sophia leaned forward and put her strong forearms on her knees. "She's interested in the relays?"

"Yeah. She's just learning about them."

"Did Rhonda come to the race by herself?"

"Well, yeah. I mean, I think so."

An engine sounded in the driveway.

"That must be Dad," Sealy said.

"I assume he worked the night shift?" Perry said.

"No. He went to the store. He starts a late shift tonight."

Perry and Sophia stood. They watched as Line Billy walked in front of the large bay window. He walked through the door with two full plastic grocery bags.

Line stood an inch taller than Perry and four inches shorter than Sophia. He parted his straight black hair on the side and it fell to his earlobes, a 1970s style. Perry thought he looked like Tom Nardini, the actor in the 1965 western movie *Cat Ballou*. One of her favorites. Line sported a slight paunch, but his shoulders were wide and he looked strong. Like a former football or baseball player.

He set the bags down and grinned. His teeth were crooked but white and he appeared to be wearing lip balm. Perry took note that his eyes did not smile.

"Who do we have here, son?" He wiped his hands on his jeans. He wore a large turquoise-and-silver ring on the index finger of his right hand. Perry could not imagine writing with such a huge ornament on her finger.

Sealy shuffled his feet. "The detectives I told you about. Um, Detective, um—" Perry let him struggle for a few seconds before interjecting.

"Detective Perry Antelope, and this is Detective Sophia Burns," she said. She felt a coolness coming off Line. He held out his hand. She did not want to shake it, but did. His ring scraped her abraded palm.

Line's gaze moved from one injured cheek to the other but he did not comment.

Instead, he said, "Oh yeah. Halito, Ohoyo Choctaw."

Perry thought it odd he would call her "Choctaw woman." He read her face and then quickly said, "Issuba Vmbinili Tvshka," which meant "Lighthorseman." That was technically incorrect because she did not work for the tribe, but she did not say so.

The two maintained eye contact long enough for Sophia to clear her throat.

Perry could not put her finger on why, but she did not trust Line Billy.

"Mr. Billy," Perry said in a low voice. She made herself go still. She did that when she thought she might act impulsively.

"Sir," Sophia interjected. "Good to meet you."

Perry relaxed. She felt simultaneously angry and relieved at Sophia interrupting what she'd wanted to say to Line Billy.

"We don't want to take up your time," Sophia said.

Perry waited for his response. Her ankle pulsed and her knees burned.

Line reached into a bag, took out a black-and-green Monster energy drink, and popped the tab.

"You have any word about my niece?" he asked before draining half the can, then looking at Perry again.

She noted that his gaze landed on her left cheek, not her eyes.

"Not yet. When was the last time you saw her?"

"Hmm. Last week. She came by to pick up a bag of feed."

"Dad helps manage the team," Sealy said. "He orders the horse feed, supplements, and equipment. He's our accountant."

"Well, I'm not really an accountant," Line corrected. "But I keep track of everything. Deliveries come here and then the racers pick them up."

"You store the items in that shed?"

Line looked at Perry with an expression that read, *Where else would I put it?* He said, "Yes, ma'am. Everyone on the team has a key."

Sophia pulled her phone from her pocket and looked at it. "Oh, excuse me. I have to take this," she said and hurried out the door.

"Were you at the races this weekend?" Perry asked.

"No," Line said before he swallowed the last of his drink. "I had to work."

"What day did Dels come by?"

Line tapped the empty can with his left index finger as if it were a drumstick. "Hmm. I think that would have been last Wednesday. Like I said, she came to get feed. Oh, and a new bridle for Worf. That's one of her horses."

Perry nodded. She knew that. "I figured. And was anything out of the ordinary?"

Line stopped tapping and looked back at Perry. "What do you mean?"

"Did it seem as if anything was bothering her?"

"Not at all."

Sophia walked back in. "Sorry about that. Unavoidable call."

"Did you two talk about selling the allotment?" asked Perry.

Line glared at Perry the same way his son had. "What do you mean by that?"

Sealy cleared his throat. "They asked me that too, Dad."

"Are you trying to say that our allotment discussions have something to do with my niece going missing?"

"Not at all," Perry said calmly. "As we made clear to your son, we're just collecting as much information as we can."

Line pursed his lips, then said, "Well, you have your information. I just came home to change clothes. I have to get to work."

"The Pen or as a gaming commissioner?"

"We have a gaming meeting."

"All right." Perry did not have anything else to ask and was happy to say, "I think we're done here for the moment." Her head pounded and she longed for a Tylenol 3 and another sugary, alcoholic drink. Still, she added, "Unless you have another question, Sophia?"

"No." Sophia turned to father and son. "Please stay in town in case we need you again."

"I really appreciate you looking for my niece," Line said without expression. He did not look at Perry.

Perry couldn't tell if he meant it.

12

"He drives a tan 2000 Chevy S10," Perry said as Sophia started to pull out of the driveway. "I knew you went outside to look. Your phone sounds like chimes when it rings, but I didn't hear that or the vibration before you pulled it out of your pocket."

"Where is that silver F-250?" Sophia muttered.

"We'll find it."

"Now where?" Sophia asked.

"I'm starving. Let's go see Rhonda."

Fifteen minutes later, Sophia pulled into the parking lot of the Choctaw Casino off Highway 69.

"I need something sweet," Perry said as they sat in the parking lot surveying the vehicles. "And with caffeine."

"I could eat," Sophia said. "I already had too much caffeine. How are your many wounds?"

"I think they're pulling apart."

"I know what it feels like to have road rash. It takes a long time to heal because you keep moving. And yours are deep."

While Perry regarded the front of the casino, Sophia got a good look at the abrasion on her left cheek. She knew Perry would try to power through fatigue and minor wounds, although facial wounds could be especially distracting.

"Did you take a pill?"

"I'm about to." She pulled out the prescription vial and tapped out a fat white tablet. She popped it into her mouth and took a few swallows from her now warm coffee.

Sophia knew it would do no good to try to get Perry to slow down, so she took the only tack she knew.

"Let's hit it." Then she climbed out and waited on her.

The pair made their way across the circular drive and under the large portico that shaded the entry. Sophia walked with her regular stride, and Perry kept pace a few steps behind her. Sophia didn't want Perry to think that she believed her weak; she had quickly learned that if Perry was having difficulty, it was best to allow her to admit it.

The smell of cigarette smoke assaulted them as they walked through the large front doors.

"Damn," Sophia muttered. "I forgot about the smoke."

"At least it's cool in here. Let's find food."

"Trophy's Bar and Grill right over there." Sophia pointed.

"Thank God. My stomach's roaring."

There was no server in view so the two detectives sat at a table next to the wall, facing the television. It was almost 12:20 and the place was only about ten percent full.

"The parking lot is packed," Sophia said. "I guess feeding the machines takes precedence over eating."

Perry put her sunglasses on the table. She closed her eyes for a few seconds, willing her headache to dissipate.

"For people who are addicted, well, you are absolutely correct," she said. "They play slots until they drop or run out of money. It's easy and you don't have to interact with anyone."

A brunette server with multiple braids extending to her

waist and wearing a short pink skirt, purple top with puffy short sleeves, and red ankle boots with six-inch heels clicked to their table. Her approach sounded like a flamenco dancer pouring her heart and soul into her stomping. Her small white apron looked comically useless.

"Hi, y'all," she greeted. "What can I getcha to drink?" She chewed a large wad of gum. "Specials today are Old Fashioneds. All day long." Her nametag read CHERRY.

"Sounds great," Perry said. "I'll have coffee and a lemonade. And water. No ice."

Cherry laughed, causing her necklace with a dozen strands of tiny Disney characters to shake. "That's different."

Perry took a closer look at the woman: Cherry looked to be around thirty years old. Her purple eyeliner extended a quarter of the way to her temples and her false eyelashes looked so heavy Perry wondered how she managed to blink. Perry had never seen purple eyeliner. This server's eyebrows were blond and did not match her brown hair. At second glance, Perry realized she wore multiple braid extensions.

Perry pushed stray hairs from her face. They had stuck to the Vaseline covering her wounds. "Well, I need caffeine and sugar."

"Oh. If that's what you need, we have a Mountain Dew, Redline Xtreme, and vodka energizer. Oh, and there's a shot of orange juice in there."

Perry stared at the happy server for a few seconds. Cherry's suggestion triggered her and she felt a pang of queasiness. A few years prior, her family had traveled to Glacier National Park. After a hike, they stopped at an East Glacier store and she tried a Diet Red Bull. She took two large gulps and her stomach immediately churned like an out-of-balance washing machine. She had leaned out the door and puked onto the parking lot.

Troy's response had been, "I told you to drink water."

Many of the newer energy drinks were more potent than what Cherry offered. Perry knew of several young drinkers who had launched into cardiac arrest after mixing Mountain Dew with alcohol and any number of other overly caffeinated beverages. This casino drink was no doubt a strategy to get people to stay awake so they could spend more money.

She was not in the mood to upset Cherry by mentioning that.

"Just coffee, lemonade, water, and the catfish platter." Perry ordered fried catfish when they ate out, which was not often. She and Troy either pan-seared or baked it. "And okra, if you have it." Perry looked at Sophia.

"Uh, lemonade. Also the 'shrooms and meatloaf."

Perry knew there was no way Sophia would have said "'shrooms" unless she saw it on the menu.

"Perfect," Cherry cooed. The waitress turned to go.

"Oh, wait," Perry said. "When does Rhonda come in?"

Cherry twirled on the ball of her left foot. Her heel did not even touch the ground. "Rhonda's a bit late today. She said she'll be here by one." Then she clicked off to the kitchen.

"Cherry," Sophia said.

"I suspect that's a nickname."

"Cherry," Sophia repeated.

"Sometimes we have no control over what others call us."

"But most of the time we do," Sophia countered.

Perry laughed. "She has a tip name. The real one is probably Linda Marie or Melinda Louise."

"How'd your parents come up with your name?"

"My grandfather on Mom's side was named Perry. He and my grandmother were both Choctaw. I want to say that my parents were romantic and knew that Perry means 'adventurer,' but as it turns out they just liked the sound of it."

Sophia laughed. "Well, my father had a crush on Sophia Loren."

Perry snickered along with her—her partner did not look a thing like the Italian actress. Sophia Burns resembled a forty-year-old athletic Vanessa Redgrave, who, depending on her mood, could wither you with a stare or throw you through a wall.

"My father liked Ali MacGraw and Katharine Ross. I wanted to name our cats Daryl and Dixon but my husband won that round so they're Zeus and Odin. But I got to name our dog Rip after Ellen Ripley."

"You have cool cats," Sophia said. "Laid-back and huge. And Rip is a sweet thing."

Perry sat back in her chair. "Anyway, we might have to slam this down so we can talk to Rhonda."

"I can do that," Sophia said. "But you eat slower than cold molasses."

"I can always wrap it up and save it for later."

"Fish?"

"Heck yes. I mean, not fish that sits out overnight. But I'll eat it as long as it doesn't smell bad."

"Gross."

Cherry appeared with a carafe of coffee and two tall glasses of iced lemonade and a glass of water. "Enjoy," she chirped.

Perry picked up the glass of water and downed half of it. She looked out of breath.

"You feeling better?"

Perry shrugged. "I'm in the process of healing." She took a swig of the lemonade. "Wow. That is tart. It tastes like Deep Eddy."

"Who?"

Perry laughed, then grimaced as she touched her right cheek. "Fuck. That hurt." She took a few breaths and said, "Not who. What. A vodka that tastes like lemonade." She wished she had a glass of that right now.

"Ah yes. I know those lemonade drinks that are not lemonade."

"Have you ever had a Long Island iced tea?"

"I don't think so."

"Troy and I went to New Orleans for Mardi Gras a few years ago and had those at . . . I forget. Maybe Pat O'Brien's. That's an old bar in the French Quarter. Anyway, that drink tastes like iced tea, but it's really a mix of rum, vodka, tequila, gin, and other stuff. Lordy we got drunk." She drained the rest of the lemonade and laughed, although their hangovers had not been funny.

Sophia refrained from telling her story about chugging a bottle of Boone's Farm Strawberry Hill in high school and then vomiting for the next twenty-four hours. "So, Sealy and his dad seem to be indignant that we asked about the allotment."

Perry nodded, then picked up the coffee and took a sip. "They did. You never know what you might discover when we're just gathering data."

"We have to ask him if he has his own land," Sophia said. "The only way I can see Bake being a part of this is if Sealy and his father want the land and Bake is a part of a scheme with them. But, there is no way they would give him anything." She sighed. "Hell. I don't know. We need to ask him."

Perry chuckled. "Don't overheat. We need more information."

Cherry appeared with a tray full of food, then stood up straight like a student at West Point.

"Do you want catsup?"

"I would love catchup, and lemon slices," said Perry.

"Would you like Tabasco?"

"Ah. No. That's okay."

Cherry hustled away and quickly returned with a bottle of Heinz and the lemon. "Anything else?" she asked.

"Not a thing," Perry answered.

"Why do you say 'catchup'?" Sophia asked once Cherry had walked away.

"My mom said it like that."

"Cherry said 'catsup.'"

"'Catchup' is easier to say. But I hear 'catsup' a lot."

"All right. You put *catchup* and hot sauce on everything."

"Almost." Perry reached into her daypack and pulled out a small yellow bottle, the same type of soft bottle that people use to put shampoo in when they travel. It held three ounces. She squeezed red liquid all over the fish.

Sophia dug into her meatloaf. "How often do you change that out?" She was now used to Perry and her traveling Cholula hot sauce.

"I'll use up maybe a third of this today and maybe another third tomorrow. When I remember, I clean it, refill it, and put it in the fridge. Don't worry. I won't get sick."

After a pause, Perry said, "My grandparents are buried here in McAlester. My mother's parents. At the Oak Hill Cemetery."

"Where are your other grandparents?" Sophia asked. "And your parents?"

"My father's parents are buried in Antlers," she answered. "My parents are in Red Oak."

They ate while listening to random eighties rock music. Duran Duran's "Rio." Michael Jackson's "Beat It." Perry stopped her assault on the catfish fillets to sneeze from the smoke that wafted in from the casino.

As Whitesnake's "Here I Go Again" began, Sophia took a bite of fried mushrooms, then said, "Look to the bar. That might be Rhonda."

Perry had not quite decided why she wanted to talk to Rhonda. Maybe it was Raquel's comment that a woman could have sabotaged the tires. Or maybe because Rhonda might have some insight or maybe saw something suspicious.

Perry turned her head to see a blond woman with her hair tied back in a severe high ponytail. She wore a tight white blouse, and her large silver hoop earrings reflected the light. Perry stared at her for a few seconds and smiled. Now that she knew who she was dealing with, her thinking shifted. The older woman Rhonda was hanging around a young Indian man. She had seen too many Native men with blond females, and in many cases, the Native men latched on to these women because they were desperate for social status in the white man's world. To Natives, however, the pairing looked comical. Perhaps she was being cynical, but now that she had seen Rhonda, she was even more intrigued.

"Ready?" Sophia asked.

"Piece of cake," Perry said as she held on to the table for support to stand. "Holy shit."

"The day after an injury is when you feel it the most," Sophia said.

After a moment of hesitation, Perry sat down again. "Go get her, Sophia."

She hesitated. "Are you okay? Should I call Troy?"

Perry kept her eyes on her uneaten fries. "If you would like to be dunked headfirst into a creek with snapping turtles, go right ahead and call him."

Sophia pondered that.

"I'm not going to chase her, Sophia. Go get her."

Perry watched as Sophia approached the bar. Rhonda hurried to the tall detective with a smile. Cherry spoke to her, probably asking what she wanted to order. Then Sophia responded, held up her badge, and Perry could see Rhonda's face change from helpful bartender to worried target of a homicide detective. Sophia motioned to their table. Rhonda moved from behind the bar to follow Sophia to where Perry sat. Her cowboy boot heels clicked as loudly on the hard floor as Cherry's did. Perry thought she looked at least thirty-five.

Rhonda stuck out her hand to Perry, who shook it. "Please sit, Ms. Paul," Perry said.

Rhonda smiled, then sat down and looked from Sophia to Perry. "So, how can I help you?" Her eyes went to Perry's left cheek, then to her right.

"Well," Sophia began, "as you probably know, one of the racers you met on Sunday is missing." She did not mention Lee.

"I know. Sealy told me. How awful." Rhonda sat straight, her tight white blouse slightly gaping in between the buttons. Her eyes glistened as if she were about to cry.

Perry could not comprehend the connection between this cougar and the wet-behind-the-ears Sealy.

"How well do you know Sealy Billy?" Sophia asked.

"We've been out a few times. Saw a movie. Why does that matter?"

Sophia ignored the question and asked her own. "Do you know Dels Billy?"

"No. I only met her at the last race. I mean, after the races were over. She won and I went over to where the team was with the horses."

"What did you talk about?"

"Nothing of consequence—I just said congratulations. Dels had a funny-looking dog and I petted it. Let's see. I met the other racers and that was it. I left after less than ten minutes."

"And you didn't see the racers again that day?"

"No. I came home. I knew that Sealy had to stay and deal with the horses and do other team things."

"Were you going to see Sealy again this week?"

"Yes. We had planned to meet after my shift last night, but I ended up having to stay longer than expected. It was really busy."

Perry watched the exchange. She felt convinced that this woman had played a role in the disappearance of Dels Billy and the attempted murder of a teenager. She thought that maybe it was because of a combination of her fatigue and distracting pain.

"Do you know Line Billy?" Perry asked.

"Sealy's father? I met him once. I don't know him." She glanced at the bar where several people were milling around, looking for the bartender.

Perry was aware of Rhonda's anxiety. "Did you see anything unusual at the races?"

"Like what?"

"Did you sit in the stands?"

"I did. In the middle section, about the third row up."

Sophia leaned forward. "Did you notice anyone who took an interest in Dels?" Perry thought that was a bad question.

Rhonda laughed. "That would be everyone in the stands. The races are crazy." She shook her head. "Really crazy. Everyone on the bleachers watches. I mean, a food truck could blow up during a race and people wouldn't even notice."

"When you were speaking with the team, did you notice if any of the truck or trailer tires were flat?"

"What? No. Tires were flat?" Rhonda seemed genuinely perplexed. She looked to the bar again, where Cherry was waving her over. Rhonda put her hand up in a "stop" gesture.

"Just a few more questions," Sophia said. "Can you think of anyone who seemed overly interested in the team, or anything odd?"

Rhonda shook her head again. "Sorry. Not a thing."

"Thank you for your time," Sophia said. She took out her card and wrote Perry's number on the back. "Call us if you think of anything."

“I sure will. And I hope you find Sealy’s cousin soon. He’s really upset.”

“I’m sure he is,” Sophia said.

Rhonda stood and hurried back to the bar, where half a dozen patrons waited for service.

Perry watched her. “That is a cougar.”

“No shit. You gonna eat that okra?” Sophia asked.

“Nah. Go ahead.”

She reached over, took four little square pieces, and dipped them in the Heinz.

“Catchup,” she said.

13

Perry reclined the passenger seat back as far as it would go and sat with her legs stretched out in front of her. Sophia slouched, looking through the file of recent reports of missing women she'd brought with her.

Perry had guided Sophia to where her grandparents lay buried in the Oak Hill Cemetery. She had limped out of the truck and considered the mossy headstones. Perry had not visited these graves in ten years. She thought that relatives should have scrubbed them and left plastic flowers, at least, then realized that she could have done it. She thought about everything she had accomplished in the past decade while her ancestors had not done anything. Perry knew she was hardly the only person to consider life and death, but cemeteries made her think about her mortality and she did not like it.

She said a few words to her grandparents, then got back in the cool truck.

"Too many cold cases," Sophia said when she returned. "Shootings, stranglings, rapes. Too many recent cases with no leads. And too many still missing. Not just women. Girls, boys, and men too. It might sound funny," Sophia said as she looked out the window at the expanse of headstones, "but I had always wondered what it would feel like to be shot. I figured it would be intense. Painful. It is. I've wondered what it would be like to be overpowered to the point that you can't fight back or get away. I mean, I'm big and it wouldn't be easy for a regular-sized guy to wrestle me to the ground, but there are plenty of men a lot bigger than me. I've never had to deal with that."

Sophia quieted and Perry looked at her. She had wondered the same things.

"You were shot," Perry said.

"Three times. Twice my vest caught it. That still hurt like hell. My left boob got it both times. It was black and blue for a month and I had to wear an XXL jog bra so it wouldn't rub. The other shot was the real deal. Went through my left deltoid." She exhaled. "That could have been a heck of a lot worse."

Perry knew about the shoulder wound, but not the other two that hit the vest.

Sophia continued: "Luckily, I had been through knee and rotator cuff surgeries from throwing and I knew how to manage the pain. And how to work out when one arm or leg is down."

Perry shifted in her seat. Her thigh ached and she felt a headache emerging.

"So many women assaulted and killed," Sophia said quietly. "I've been doing this for a while and we've both seen a lot of things."

"We have," Perry agreed. "But you've seen more than me, being a patrol cop in Las Vegas. I cannot imagine what you've encountered."

Sophia closed the top file. Instead of responding to Perry's statement, she said, "I study psychology and read books about killers. I know that some of them, and some rapists, are mentally unstable and others are so greedy that they're willing to hurt others to get what they want. I don't understand how they can do it. Any of it."

Perry took some Vaseline from her bag and applied a thin layer to her cheeks. "That's why many of us are in this business, Sophia. I don't understand a lot of what we have to deal with either. Just remember we're here to catch the bad guys. Let the psychologists and God deal with them afterward. We can't solve every problem."

Sophia continued to watch the blue jays perched on top of a large marble headstone adorned with a vase and plastic flowers on each side. She could hear the birds' shrill calls.

"I wonder where Dels Billy is," she said.

Perry started to reply when her iPhone rang. She looked down. "It's Raquel." She clicked on the speaker. "Yes?"

"How you doing?"

"I'm hanging in there, thanks."

"Sophia told me."

Perry did not respond and Raquel did not ask more questions. "I found out about Dels's allotment and the tribal records through Ancestry.com. It's all there, if you know how to look."

Perry reached back into her pack and got her notebook and pen. "Go ahead."

"I traced the original allottees. Those are the original enrollees on the Dawes Roll. Long story short, Dels's grandfather passed what he inherited to his sons—Dels's father and her uncle Line Billy. After Dels's father died, his portion went to her. Dels's mother died four years ago and her father died two years later. Her mother had no part of the house or the land that Dels now lives on. She's Chickasaw."

"So it's all on her dad's side."

"Yes. Mom had her own allotment, however, and Dels inherited that parcel too. Mom had no siblings."

"Where is that parcel?"

"Chickasaw land. Outside of Davis by the Washita River."

"What's on it?"

"I don't know yet."

"Okay. So that land is Dels's and her Billy relatives have no stake in it."

"Correct."

Perry considered the issue of the Billy property. She knew that the inheritance of allotments could be tricky. She scribbled a family tree on her pad with arrows indicating how the Billy allotment land was connected. The 1887 Dawes Severalty Act dictated that Cherokees, Choctaws, Chickasaws, Muskogee-Creeks, and Seminoles by blood were to be enrolled on the Dawes Rolls, also known as the Final Rolls. The United States government argued that the intention was to "civilize" Native peoples by giving them land so they could farm and ranch.

The real goal of allotment, of course, was to appropriate tribal lands that had been guaranteed to the tribes by treaty. After the head of each family received 180 acres, every unmarried person over eighteen years old received sixty acres, and every orphan under eighteen got thirty acres, the leftover acres that once were promised to the Five Tribes were auctioned off to white settlers.

Native people lost their allotted lands at extraordinarily high rates. Some sold their 180 acres for a pittance because they needed money. Once the land was gone, it was out of tribal hands—unless they could afford to buy it back, that is, which did not happen often. Others, such as the orphans and those deemed unstable, were assigned "guardians." It was not surprising that opportunistic guardians of the Five Tribes inherited the land after their charges suddenly died.

Many Natives, like Vera Spring and, apparently, Dels Billy would never sell their lands out of principle. In the early years, some profited from the oil that was discovered, although their white spouses then often took their oil revenues. Some Native women were murdered by their white husbands, such as what happened among the Osages.

As time passed, selling an allotment could be a nightmare. When an original allottee died, the land passed to their heirs. If there were five children, they all owned it equally. If one person desired to sell, they had to have permission from the other four. The bigger the family, the bigger the challenge. On the other hand, Perry liked that no one could unilaterally sell what might be valuable land—that is, land that might have undiscovered riches under the ground.

"Where is the Billy allotment?"

"Outside of McAlester. As we already know, Dels lives on it. She lives in her family home. It was her great-grandmother's, then her grandfather's, then it went to her father, and that's where she was raised."

"And Line Billy agreed that this was okay? That Dels could live in the house?"

"Apparently."

Perry thought that interesting. Many Native families kept their allotments, but they often did not live on them. After the elders passed, the younger generations did not want to live away from town. Many of this generation did not even want to live in their Nations.

Sophia tapped her pen. She got to the point. "So, if Dels dies, her share of the allotment that came from her father's side goes to Line Billy, then later to Sealy."

"Right. Blood relations."

"Where is Sealy's mother?"

"She divorced Line years ago and moved away. She's white."

That meant she was out of the picture.

Perry thought back to when she first met Sealy. She said, "Sealy seemed upset by Dels's disappearance."

"He did," Raquel said. She'd been there and had heard Sealy speak.

"So tell me about the land."

"Old rock house. Two stories. Built in the 1920s. Most of the land is pasture. A barn and several outbuildings. It's fenced."

Perry's great-grandparents never sold the allotments they received in 1906, and now that everyone was dead the land was in her name. Her family sometimes fished in the small pond that sat in the middle of the allotment and Troy hunted for deer and turkeys there. The land was almost three hours away so they did not go often, but she knew she had to make the drive to patrol her property to reinforce the barbed wire, remove illegal deer stands, and replace destroyed NO TRESPASSING signs.

The parcel had a creek running through it. As a child, Perry used to sit at the edge of the creek while her father hunted for white-tailed deer. He knew where she was, and she knew to stay put. Her personality was in large part shaped by her experiences in that place. She watched the crawdads swim past. Dirt daubers made their holes in the rise of the bank opposite her. Once she observed a snapping turtle make its way downstream, the huge reptile stopping to inspect a rock, but then she realized the awesome creature had nosed the stone over to get at the mugwumps underneath. Tiny fish darted in perfect synchronicity through the clear stream.

Now Perry leased the 180 acres to a farmer who rotated winter wheat, sorghum, soybeans, and corn crops. She didn't charge him much—three thousand a year—mainly because he didn't ask to cut the trees along the Little Turkey Creek where the deer and turkeys lived. Many Choctaw allottees, however, paid little attention to what their farming and ranching lessees did to their lands. If you neglected to check on your property, opportunistic lessees might cut all the timber and expand the crops to the fence line. And before you knew it, their cattle had polluted your waterways. Poachers would swarm in and take the white-tailed deer and turkeys. The same old post–Civil War Indian Territory all over again.

"I want to know if there are any oil and gas people asking to lease. Also, what about water, timber, fertile soil? And find out if it has been explored for underground goodies. If any well-bores have been dug."

"All right," Raquel agreed. "But you should see if Dels has any papers in the house."

Perry looked at Sophia. "Right."

"What's the address?"

Raquel told them and Sophia looked it up. "Less than two miles away," she said.

14

Sophia stopped in front of the gate that crossed the lane leading to Dels Billy's house.

"I'll do it," Perry said as she started to open her door.

"No, you won't. Save your legs."

Sophia got out and removed the padlock. It was not fastened—it just hung between two links to make it appear secure. She opened the gate, then came back to the truck to drive through. She left the gate open.

Dels's home sat almost a quarter mile from the gate under tall oaks and cottonwoods, next to a stream that ran by the side of the rock house. Sophia stopped in front of the structure. It had no cement driveway, and the narrow path that led to the front door was made of flagstone. As Perry opened her door, she heard a dog bark, which only got louder as she stepped out and onto the dirt. She felt a pushing on her pant leg. It was Gomer sniffing her, no doubt smelling the blood beneath the gauze.

Perry reached down to pet the dog and grimaced when she

felt a pull in her lower back. *Sophia is right. We always feel worse the day after the injury*. She scratched Gomer behind his ears.

"Hey, boy." The strange dog with huge butterfly ears panted as he looked up at her. He seemed to be smiling.

"That is one odd dog," Sophia said.

"He's cool."

"Detectives," a voice said at the corner of the house.

They looked up to see Bake Folsom holding a chicken. Two small goats stood at his side.

"You don't see that every day," Sophia observed.

"You might if you were around horses. Goats are great companions for them."

Bake came closer. His long hair was tied into a bun and a mask hung around his neck. He wore plastic gloves. "Are you here to tell me something I don't want to know?"

Perry answered quickly. "No. We're here to see if there is anything of use in her filing cabinets."

"As in, a reason why someone took her?"

"Yes."

"All she has is what you see here." He motioned with his arms to the land around them.

"Can we come in?"

"Yeah. I was cleaning the chicken coop. Come around this way."

They followed him around the house to the back entrance topped by a wisteria-covered portico. He put the chicken down. The orange hen with muttonchop feathers looked up at him for a few seconds, then flapped her wings and ran toward the barn with the goats at her side. A chain-link fence surrounded a red-painted coop. A dozen hens scratched in the dirt.

"That one keeps getting out," Bake said. "There's fencing on top to keep out the coons, but she scoots out when I open the door. Now look at her. She wants in."

A tall cottonwood shaded the back of the house. Ten feet from the porch sat a picnic table with benches big enough for four people on each side. The propane grill looked like the one Troy and Perry owned. Chairs of various types encircled a fire ring. There were numerous hot dog roasting sticks with char residue on them lying on the bricks. *The team probably ate here before the races,* she thought.

The modest garden looked thirsty. The three tomato plants were laden with bright red fruits, but the leaves appeared wilted, as did the climbing beans crowding the fence that protected the garden from deer. Perry grimaced at the sight of the eight-inch-long okra spears that looked like daggers. Perry and Troy grew more okra and peppers than anything else so they could freeze the harvest. If she didn't clip the okra before it grew more than two inches long she ran the risk of a fibrous mouthful.

"What happened to you?" Bake asked. He narrowed his eyes as he focused on her face.

"Got a bit of road rash and cuts from a hit-and-run."

"Hit-and-run? You were hit in your car?"

"No. I was on foot."

Bake just stared at her. "Someone hit you," he repeated.

"Well, I should say the truck didn't hit me. I was running by my home and a truck tried to run me down. The driver caused me to fall off the road and slide down an embankment."

"That looks painful. And you're limping."

"Road rash takes a while to heal."

"Who did it?"

"I don't know. But it looks just like my partner's truck. Silver Ford F-250."

He stood for a few seconds, not sure what else to say about that.

"The horses miss her," he finally said.

On cue, a horse whinnied.

"Is that Issi?" Perry asked.

"No. Worf. Issi's out in the pasture. She won't come in." Bake looked to the east.

"Can horses get depressed?" Sophia asked.

"I think most animals can," Perry answered.

"And it's not just Worf and Issi," Bake added. "Animals know when something's off." His gaze went to Gomer, who lay in the dirt outside of the barn. He was curled with his head facing the humans. He watched them but did not move. "Gomer never does that."

Perry chastised herself for thinking about overgrown okra and wilted garden leaves instead of this man's grief, in addition to what the animals were thinking in what her father referred to as their "pea brains."

"Do you ride?" Bake asked the detectives.

"Not me," Sophia said.

"I used to all the time growing up," Perry said. "My best friend had horses."

"So you know they can be sensitive."

"Indeed. Mr. Folsom, do you live here?" She wanted to know if he would tell them that he and Dels were married.

"I have a place of my own. Fully paid for. I prefer to stay with Dels, so I put money in her account every month. I'm not a man-whore, if that's what you're thinking."

Perry wasn't thinking that, but his statement was interesting. She thought back to when she and Troy took the plunge during his last year as a PhD student and she decided to move from Stillwater. She had her apartment with a view of the Oklahoma City skyline and was perfectly happy to be by herself. Troy was living with four men in an old house in Norman. One, Red Walker, was in the pre-med program at the University of Oklahoma and insisted that his roommates be quiet so he could study—not just a few nights a week, but every night.

In contrast, Luther Walkingstick attended every powwow in the Oklahoma City area and three nights a week he slammed the door behind him when he came home between midnight and four A.M. Stan Lawrence, the quiet diesel mechanic, had the habit of filling his water bottle with ice multiple times a night and the echo sounded throughout the old house. Troy was the last guy to move in and had to take the smallest room on the third floor. It was too small, and the closest bathroom was on the floor below him. Perry did not like staying overnight with him in that house, so he began spending more time at her place than at his.

She wondered if Bake had a similar situation.

"Do you have property like this?" she asked.

"No. I just have a small apartment." Then he added, "But it's nice. There's a pool and weight room."

"How long have you known Ms. Billy?"

He cocked his head. "You already asked me that. Six years and we've been together almost three." He took off his gloves. "You said you wanted to look at her files."

"Please."

He put his arm out toward the door and said, "This way."

The door led to a spacious mudroom with a huge, deep sink and a chest freezer. Running shoes and sandals lay in piles under the window. Several pairs of winter boots were lined up on shelves next to the sink. It appeared that Dels and Bake did the same as Perry's family and kept shoes out of the house. Bake pulled off his tall rubber boots and put them by the door.

Normally, Perry would have asked if she should remove her shoes, but not while investigating a kidnapping, assault, and now a possibly related murder.

Bake led them through the kitchen. It had an old linoleum floor, and a small wooden table covered with a sunflower tablecloth sat in the middle. The Formica countertops were clean and adorned with a block of knives, a Mr. Coffee, paper towels, a toaster, and various spice shaker bottles. Perry noted the empty flower vases on the oak table and the pepper-filled bottles in liquid on the windowsill. Her grandfather filled bottles with little hot peppers and vinegar and set them on his sill to marinate. The walls were gray and in need of paint. The sink was deep, like the one in the mudroom. The yellow Frigidaire looked like it was decades old, but she also knew those things could run a very long time. The kitchen reminded Perry of her grandparents' home.

They followed Bake through the doorway into a larger dining room. An evaporative cooler that took up an entire window space shot moist, cool air into the room. An enormous oak table surrounded by wooden chairs with embroidered needlepoint seats took up most of the space. A chandelier with at least one hundred elongated crystals hung from the low ceiling. The carpet—like the table, chairs, and the wood molding around the doorframe—was dark. It looked as if the house had not been updated since Dels's great-grandparents lived here.

They followed as Bake led them up five steps, across a landing with stairs leading up into darkness, then down five steps.

"Here we are," he said. He went to the doorway and flipped a switch. A ceiling fan pushed cool air onto the detectives.

The room was clearly an office, possibly converted from a bedroom. Bookshelves lined two walls. Windows with heavy wooden moldings lined the third. Perry and Sophia looked out to the drive, which was covered by a shingled roof. Pecan trees shaded the entire west side of the home. Breeze from the ceiling fan and window cooler circulated in the small space and felt soothing. Perry could take a nap in here.

An old secretary desk with many cubbies took up the other wall. Next to it was an out-of-place metal filing cabinet.

Perry noted the low ceilings and worn carpet. *Just like my grandparents' home*. Their home had many closets, but all were tiny. People in that time had no need for multiple outfits. The closet in her grandparents' small office was always filled with puzzles and games such as pick-up sticks, Chinese checkers, marbles, and Mouse Trap.

"Dels keeps all her stuff in those drawers," he said. "She gets a lot of advertisements in the mail and she just dumps those. She keeps all the letters from companies and people who want to buy her property."

He opened the top drawer. Perry and Sophia stepped forward to look.

Perry stifled a gasp. She received many offers for her allotment, but nothing like this. She usually just threw her mail into the recycle bin. Dels was clearly overwhelmed. The metal drawer was filled from front to back with neatly labeled file folders. The first one in the top drawer was clearly marked JULY of this year. The one behind it was JUNE.

"May I?" she asked.

Bake shrugged.

She took out the file and laid it on the desktop. There were four pieces of paper inside, each one an unfolded letter. Colorful paper clips attached the envelopes to the letters. Her eyes went to the back of the desktop. A letter opener lay on a small plate.

She looked at Sophia. She kept her eyes on the top letter. If Dels had this many offers, that meant the land looked promising to many people. She had to dive in but needed a break.

"Mr. Folsom, where is your restroom?"

"There's one right there." He pointed to the dark hall. "On the left."

"Thanks. We need some time to look at these."

"I hope you find something that will lead to Dels." He took

a deep breath. "I need to tend to the animals. There's Gatorade and beer in the fridge." He turned around and left the room.

Perry waited a beat until Bake was out of earshot. "Sophia, get started. I gotta pee."

Perry made her way to the dim opening framed by the same heavy wooden molding as every other doorway. She pushed open the heavy white door and found herself standing in the same bathroom as her grandparents'. The floor was the same honeycomb mosaic design. The tall toilet had what looked like an Adam's apple base. The bathtub had a chain attached to the plug and under the medicine cabinet mirror was a slot for used razor blades. There was a bathtub but no showerhead.

I'm having childhood flashbacks in a real setting, she thought.

The push-out window over the toilet was the same. A sweet-gum tree stood right outside, its branches touching the house. The crazy seed balls they dropped had sharp points that Perry had stepped on more times than she wanted to recall. Still, she remembered them fondly. One time, she got back at her sister, Asp, by putting the seed balls on the floor next to her bed. She remembered laughing at Asp's screech when she got up in the middle of the night.

She quickly did her business and went back to the files.

"You all right?" Sophia asked.

"I am." She realized she had been crying.

She wiped her eyes with her sleeve, then took out the second file. The first letter was from the oil company First Flight and was addressed to Dels Billy.

She opened the second drawer and randomly pulled a file. Inside was a letter from a man named Walter Wilbur, who politely inquired about Dels's possible interest in selling her land: "It would be my honor to care for your lands that the Choctaws have so reverently cared for for so many generations."

"This person offers one hundred dollars per acre," Perry said. "Big whoop."

"I wonder if that First Flight company knows something," Sophia added. "Why is it addressed to only Dels if her uncle owns part of it?"

"Companies often do that. They send out individual letters and don't mention the other property owners. I know that in instances that don't involve allotments, companies will offer to buy a person's parcel of a tenancy in common property."

She went back to the first drawer and to the third file. She pulled a letter. "This is from the Central Oklahoma Cattlemen's Association, asking in a businesslike manner what their price is for leasing the land. This is pretty common. Ranchers or farmers lease the land from the owner. I do that with our land. And Troy's family has two allotments. One of those has a few test wells but they haven't found anything yet."

Perry pulled file after file, each filled with letters ranging from formal, polite, and businesslike to rather rude, demanding to purchase the property. Dels had received several unsolicited contracts that required only her signature to sell. The brazenness shocked her.

She looked at the earlier letters addressed to Dels's father. There were no copies of letters or notes indicating that he or Dels had responded to any of them, but that didn't mean that no one had answered the queries. She wondered if Line Billy kept similar file drawers.

Perry felt her eyes burn. She wiped them and sniffed.

"What's wrong?" Sophia asked.

She leaned back in her chair, her knee aching, straightened her leg out in front of her, and sighed. She knew that time was short and they had to hurry.

"Look at these files." She motioned to the rifled-through filing cabinet. "Her grandparents kept every letter. And so did her father. These go back to the 1920s. People have been asking this family about their land for over a hundred years. This particular allotment. I get these kinds of letters every week and it becomes annoying, and some letters are aggressive. I just ignore them, but they keep coming. And some of these people have discovered my phone number and call, asking for me to sell."

She looked at the low ceiling. It was dull gray, unlike the walls of the office, which appeared to have been recently painted blue. Perry thought Dels may have picked out the cheerful color in an attempt to brighten the darkness in the filing cabinet.

Sophia pulled out the next three files. "Look at this. This company is offering fifteen thousand dollars an acre." She opened the calculator on her phone. "Times one hundred and eighty acres, so this offer is for two point seven million dollars. That's a far cry from the offers ten years prior that offered just one to two thousand per acre." Sophia took out the file marked 2021. "Two letters. One offers ten grand per acre and the other eight grand."

"Who are those from?"

"Oil and gas companies."

"They know something," Perry said. "No one is going to offer that amount regardless of how great the hunting is. This house is sturdy, but it's old. I would think that anyone who could afford to pay that amount would just tear this place down and start over."

"Oil and gas companies aren't going to build a new house," Sophia said.

"No, they won't. They want to drill."

"So they figured out that this is a prime spot to put in the pump jacks. Or to frack."

"Right," Perry agreed. "And that would be a problem since it makes the ground unstable. You may not know since you weren't in the area then, but in 2016 a five point six quake hit Pawnee Nation and damaged stone buildings. They felt it in Kansas City."

"And here I thought we only had dirt devils."

"The tornadoes here are bad. The earthquakes are usually minor, but they happen."

"All right. What do we do with this?" Sophia asked.

"These letters show how desirable this land is. And they tell us why one family member might get pissed off and decide to off the one relative who blocks their path to making some big bucks."

Perry stood, then bent over and reached for her pack. Feeling dizzy, she sat back down and unzipped the outer pocket. She took out the tube of Vaseline and pushed out a small glob, which she gently massaged onto her cheeks. Sophia thought she glowed like an ice rink.

"You okay?"

"My cheeks burn."

"I can get some ice from the freezer."

Perry sighed. "No. We don't have time for that. Someone had it out for Dels, maybe more than one person. This land is worth a lot. We see that Dels was concerned. No one keeps records like this if they're not concerned. She's only twenty-four years old, Sophia. I was an idiot until I was thirty."

She huffed. "I doubt that."

"It's true. When Troy and I got married my hands shook so hard the petals fell off my bouquet. I had Olyve when I was twenty-four. I was scared shitless. I was too young to have a kid."

Sophia knew of people who had kids at age fifteen. Her sister had twins when she was twenty-one. That seemed normal to her, but Perry was not her sister.

Perry took the water bottle from her pack. "Dels kept records after her parents died," she continued. "I bet her parents warned her. They knew something was imminent and Dels paid attention."

"They couldn't have predicted what happened to her the other night," Sophia said.

Perry leaned forward to touch her ankle but got only as far as her knee. "Don't be too sure, partner." She huffed and sat back in her chair. "I don't think Bake was part of this."

"No?" Sophia continued to look at the letters.

Perry sighed and clasped her hand across her belly. "Look at how he manages this place. He appears as if he just hiked the Appalachian Trail—dark circles under his eyes and he seems dehydrated. He's trying to be attentive, but stress is getting the best of him. I don't know why I thought of him as a suspect."

"Yes you do," Sophia countered. "You always look at the partner or spouse."

Perry thought she might slide out of her chair. "I'll show you why I changed my mind. Go get Bake."

After Sophia left, Perry sat in silence and stared at the filing cabinet. Most of the people who'd asked to purchase Dels's land were likely dead, no longer interested, or had moved on. The exceptions were the first five files in the top drawer. One company had asked repeatedly if Dels Billy would sell. The company first sent a map and an estimate of the value of the land. Another sent a ten-page document that had stickies for Dels to sign. All packaged and ready to go. Perry had received a few of those and she thought she might pay those people a visit, but tempered her anger instead and filed their gross offers away. The next letters added more extraneous verbiage. If one did not understand the ins and outs of property purchasing, one might be inclined to say yes. Dels would not budge, but it appeared that her uncle wanted her to. Or, if she were out of the picture, it would be up to him alone.

Bake and Sophia appeared. Gomer followed them in, then lay down.

Perry stood. "Mr. Folsom," she said.

Bake looked at the floor, then moved his eyes to a window.

"You and Dels are married."

Bake did not respond. He stood with his hands at his sides. Perry thought his pose looked awkward.

"Okay," Perry said. "Why did you marry?"

Bake shuffled his feet. "I love her."

Perry, Sophia, and Gomer watched him.

"Plus, I have good healthcare and she can be on my plan now," he blurted. "We can also use Indian Health Service, but that might be cut." After he spoke his shoulders slumped.

Perry looked at Sophia, who gave a quick smile.

"All right. Congratulations. Do you have a key to this filing cabinet?"

Bake took the opening. "Right here." He opened the small top right drawer of the old secretary and pulled out a lanyard with a key attached.

"Good. Keep this locked. Do you have video surveillance of this property?"

"We got Blink cameras. I put them in last year after the Black Friday deals."

"Engage the cameras. You told us the other night that you have a weapon?"

"Yes. When we travel I carry a SIG Sauer P365."

"Anything else around here?"

"I have a shotgun."

"Do you know how to use it?"

"Yes, I do. My father gave it to me. I learned when I was ten years old."

"That it?"

"A .357 Magnum."

Perry was not an advocate of homeowners keeping guns unless they lived in a high-crime area, but in this case she believed owning a weapon was warranted. Regardless of how much time one spent at the shooting range, most people had no idea how to react to shocking and sudden situations such as a home invasion. If you had a gun in your hands, all sorts of things could go wrong. You might kill a relative who came into your home late at night because you forgot that you gave them a key. Or you might shoot an inebriated person who tried to open the front door but was simply at the wrong address. The worst case would be a child who found your weapon and shot a sibling. Or you. To wield a deadly weapon, a person should be a thoughtful personality who could stay calm and assess a stressful situation before firing a potentially killing shot. Once you pulled the trigger, you could not take the bullet back.

"Does Dels own any guns?"

"A Smith & Wesson revolver. And a Colt Diamondback. They were her father's."

Vera had mentioned that Dels knew how to shoot but did not carry a weapon with her. Perry wondered how the kidnapping would have turned out if Dels had had one of those with her. Someone had quickly overpowered the strong and athletic young woman. Maybe a weapon would have prevented that. But as Troy said about carrying a knife, she probably wouldn't have escaped without injury.

Bake didn't blink when he said, "Look, Dels is alone here. Except for me and the team. She knows how to shoot. She's smart and she won't allow any weenie asshat to take her down. Whoever did this is bigger and stronger than her. But if she can, she will get away."

He got louder as he spoke. His face reddened and his eyes glistened. Perry liked to think that Troy would speak of her in such a manner.

"Is there anyone who can come stay with you?"

"Benny." He shrugged. "Vera said she'd come too. There's room for all the animals."

Perry grasped the armrests, pushed herself up, and took a step toward him. "I will not allow anyone to take advantage of Dels Billy," she said. Her tone was even and calm. Sophia knew what that meant. "Lock this up. Lock the gate and this house. Make sure the cameras are on. Call your friends." She smiled. "It might be good if they were here."

Bake nodded. She squeezed his arm. "We will find her."

They walked outside to Sophia's truck.

Issi whinnied loudly. They all turned to see the filly pacing the fence line. Perry wanted to believe that the horse heard her.

"We're heading back to Oklahoma City. Mr. Folsom, once again, let us know if you think of anything. Call either of us anytime."

Bake held her stare for a few seconds. "I will."

15

Back in Oklahoma City, Perry and Sophia sat in Sophia's truck under the shade of tall oaks in a neighborhood park eating sandwiches from Schlotzsky's. Perry ordered a turkey and avocado with extra mustard and jalapeño chips. Sophia ate a pastrami Reuben with barbecue chips and loaded baked potato soup. Perry kept eyeing the Reuben.

"That looks good," she said.

"Want a bite?"

Actually she did, but she declined. "No thanks."

"My soup's too hot," Sophia said. "I should have thought of that."

"When we get out just leave the soup in the truck. It's almost one hundred degrees outside and it'll get up to one-twenty in here. It'll stay good." She sipped her iced tea. "Probably."

They watched a thin Black man in running shorts take off his tank top and wet it in the water fountain. He walked to the picnic table and took off his shoes and socks, then lay on top of the shaded table with the folded wet shirt over his forehead.

"Why would anyone run in the heat of the day?" Perry asked. "And it's humid as hell."

Sophia put down her sandwich and looked at her. "You ran last night."

She shrugged. "The sun was behind clouds when I started."

"Maybe he has a race coming up and knows it'll be hot."

"Any race around here would be a five or ten K, and it would be in the early morning."

The man on the table did not move.

"I recall wrestlers in my high school would do stuff like this," Sophia said. "They'd put on plastic tops and pants and run in the heat of the day."

Perry snorted. "Wrestlers can be extreme. You heard of Dan Gable?"

"I think so."

"Long time ago I read about his workouts. I used the one where he'd get a deck of cards and whatever card he turned over was how many push-ups he'd do. And he'd go through the pack several times."

"I don't know if I could do that once."

"You're stronger than anyone I know. How in the hell did you launch that shot put as far as you did? You were the NCAA champion."

Sophia sighed. "Long days of painful training."

Perry understood that statement. She had run cross-country through high school and for two years at Eastern Oklahoma. She often wondered what she would have done instead of running fifty to eighty miles a week. For sure, if she didn't expend energy running she would weigh five hundred pounds. Throwers like Sophia normally did not run, but they spent endless hours in the weight room, plus jumping, sprinting, and working on their form like dancers.

Perry wrapped the remainder of her sandwich and put it back in the bag along with the half-empty bag of chips.

Sophia gaped openly. “I’ve never seen you not finish a meal.”

“Too hot to eat.”

Sophia narrowed her eyes at Perry. “That’s never bothered you before.”

Perry kept her eyes on the shirtless man lying on the picnic table, his wet T-shirt still over his forehead.

“Watching that guy makes my entire body hurt. And I have a headache.”

Sophia poured the remnants of her chips into her mouth and balled up the bag.

Perry watched a crow land on the branch above the man. It hopped around, trying to figure out if there was something useful it could take.

“We’re missing something,” she said. “We know Delș’s family wants to sell and she does not. Her uncle Line must have copies of the letters we saw.” She took several swallows of her drink.

“Seems to me that Line has a clear motive to get rid of his niece,” Sophia said. “And so does Sealy, provided that he’s in on it with his father.”

Perry’s phone chirped. She saw that it was Raquel.

“Raq—”

“There’s another uncle,” Raquel interrupted.

Perry’s eyebrows shot up. “What do you mean?”

“Line has another brother. In California.”

“What’s his name?”

“Poinsettia Sean Billy.”

Perry looked at Sophia, then at her iPhone. “Say again?”

Sophia stifled a laugh.

Raquel repeated his name.

“Yikes,” Perry said.

“Yes, it is different,” Raquel agreed. “Sealy’s middle name is Ceviche.”

Sophia put a hand over her eyes and shook her head.

“No way,” Perry said.

"And there's more. Line is actually Lyon Maize Billy."

"Ha!" Perry blurted.

"Dels and Sealy's deceased grandfather was Henry Amaranth Billy. Dels's deceased father was Salen Absinthe Billy, so there is a precedent."

Sophia blurted out, "Oh my God."

"So Sealy's father, Lyon, had a strong hand in naming his kid," Sophia said. "I wonder if his mother argued about that."

Perry could not imagine saddling her children with food names except maybe Sage, Ginger, or Coco, and nicknames like Pepper, Chip, Tootsie, and Cookie. At least Lyon's and Sealy's food names were their middle ones.

"Hey, if I named my kids after my favorite foods, they'd get Relleno, Egg, Grapefruit, Okra, Tomato, and Deep Eddy, while Troy would argue for Pasta, Oreo, and Bloody Mary."

Sophia laughed. "I'd use Brisket, Enchilada, and Whopper. And don't forget the waitress Cherry."

"You two okay?" Raquel finally asked. That Raquel had not laughed made the names even funnier to Perry.

"What's your middle name? Don't tell me it's Cardamom."

"Chula."

Perry thought that a brilliant name. "Fox?"

"A fox family came through our yard the morning I was born."

"Raquel Chula. Nice. We have a fox family in our neighborhood. All right. Why has no one mentioned this Poinsettia Billy?"

"I can't answer that, but I can tell you that he's a half brother. But he also inherited that parcel because he's a legitimate son of Henry Amaranth Billy."

Perry thought a moment. "Vera only said that Dels and Sealy argued about selling the allotment."

Sophia tapped her finger on the wheel. "Either she didn't know about the other uncle or the uncle is not in the picture at all."

"How old is he?" Perry asked.

"He'd be forty-four. Apparently Henry remarried a few years after his wife died. The new wife was not enrolled in any tribe, according to what I've seen so far. Poinsettia is six years younger than Dels's father and five younger than Line Billy."

"Well, now," Perry said. "This alters the landscape. Raquel, look a bit longer and see if you can find out anything more."

"I'm hogging my cousin's laptop as we speak." She clicked off.

Perry took her vial of Tylenol from her pack as she huffed a laugh. "So now there are three people who own that allotment. And Bake and Sealy have stakes in it."

"What do you want to do?"

"For the moment, we need to think about it. I took pictures of the letters."

"Of course you did."

They watched a white SUV park in the lot across from them. A man got out from the driver's side and a woman from the passenger's side. Three kids who looked to be between the ages of eight and eleven piled out and ran to the swings. Mom and Dad took coolers from the back of the vehicle and carried them to the picnic table across the park from the runner.

"It's too damn hot for a picnic," Perry said.

"No shit." Sophia set the potato soup on the floorboard between her feet. "Something will come up. It always does." Perry's phone chirped again.

Sophia grinned. "Like I said."

Perry tapped the speaker icon. "Antelope," she greeted.

"Detective Antelope?" asked a young woman. Perry didn't recognize the voice.

"It is. Who is this?"

"My name's Yarda Red Plume."

"I watched you race. On a tape. How can I help you, Ms. Red Plume?" Perry asked.

Yarda said, “Well, I heard about Dels being missing.”

“Do you have information about her?” Perry asked, hoping she would get to the point.

“Well, not her exactly. I parked in front of Dels’s truck at the race.”

“You were in the same race, correct?”

“Yes.”

“Where are you, Ms. Red Plume?”

“East Glacier.”

“Montana?”

“Yes. My team was on the racing circuit and we decided to go to Oklahoma. I know Dels pretty well. I have a dash cam in my truck.”

Perry stifled a gasp. Could the dash cam answer how Dels’s truck got its flat? “Did you speak with her on Sunday?”

“Well, yeah. Before and after our race. We’ve raced against each other several times. Dels is cool. We always speak after we finish a race. She hurt her knee jumping off one of the horses and was going to ice it.”

“Go on.”

Yarda continued. “Like I said, I live in East Glacier Park, so we left right after the women’s relay. It’s a long way to drive. A teammate told me about the text Mr. Ryder sent out. I don’t really look at my phone a lot. I don’t have Facebook or any other social media.”

Perry continued to gaze at her phone.

“I planned to call Dels yesterday to ask about her knee. And to tell her that we’re going to race at Fort Hall later this month.”

“Fort Hall?”

“Idaho.”

“Okay.”

Perry and Sophia heard a horse whinny in the background.

“Sorry,” Yarda said. “I’m in the barn.”

"No problem."

Yarda was quiet for a few seconds. "I was really shocked. I called Mr. Ryder and he only told me a little bit, but he gave me Vera Spring's number. She told me what little she knew about what happened."

"Dels Billy has been missing since eight-thirty P.M. Sunday night," Perry said.

"I know."

Perry felt Sophia tap her arm. She looked at her. Sophia held up her hand, signaling Perry to let Yarda talk.

"I left after the ladies' race. I mean, I said goodbye to Dels, then my team packed up the rest of our things. We had a long drive, you know?"

"I imagine so. How long did it take you to get home?"

"Over twenty-six hours. It takes a while when you have horses. We drive slowly and we have to stop a lot. The horses need to walk around and eat. It's a real haul. And we stop at hotels that have a field nearby. We have to take turns with watching. Even with the cameras, it's hard to sleep because we're always afraid someone will steal them. You know?"

"I can imagine." Perry thought that sounded like a trip from hell, but she would never say that. She and Troy had traveled plenty of times and worried about their truck packed with camping gear. She never could sleep well in a hotel. Right now, she wished that Yarda would speak faster.

"I thought about the races last night. There wasn't anything strange on Sunday. But then I remembered my dash cam. At the relay I had the camera set to the front of the truck, so it was recording out the front windshield. So today I thought I should look at the video. I recorded when just a few people were around during the ladies' relay and then turned it off when we started driving. I recorded again when we stopped for the night outside of Wichita, Kansas. It was late when we left the races and we were tired. Normally we drive about five or six hours at a time, then let the horses out. It was so hot that we stopped more than normal. We stopped at Limon, someplace north of Denver, Cheyenne, Casper, you know. Anyway, it took a while to get here."

Perry felt the sweat running down her back even though the air was on.

A horse whinnied. "Shush," Yarda scolded it. "Sorry, the horses are glad to be home and have a lot of energy. Anyway, I watched the recordings for the first day of the races and nothing happened. Then I got to the recording during our ladies' race. No one was with the vehicles or the horses. The next recording is before we left the rodeo grounds for Glacier. It recorded the entire area of Dels's team. A blondie with a lot of turquoise stuff came over to Dels. Dels had her leg up with a pack on her knee. I also saw the other team members, you know? Vera Spring—she's the only one whose last name I remember. Benny—he does the chief's race. Lee. He's a cute young kid who wants to race. Sealy, he's the one with the great hair and I think he's related to Dels. And Bake. He's really . . . uh." She hesitated. "He's Dels's guy."

Perry realized that Yarda did not want to say that Bake was hot.

"And then what?" Yarda had Rhonda on video. She waited for more.

"Well, in the foreground, you can see someone come up to Dels's team and crouch by the tires. They're in a hoodie so I don't know if they were male or female, you know? I thought maybe it was a team member checking to make sure the tires were inflated. We all do that. You know?"

"Yes. Yes, I do."

"But this person moved really fast and went from tire to tire. And it was super-hot so I don't know why they would have on a hoodie."

A horse nickered so loudly Perry thought its nose was touching Yarda's phone.

"Stop it, Shakira."

Perry almost laughed.

Sophia tapped Perry's arm. "Tell her to send," she mouthed.

Perry nodded.

"Ms. Red Plume, can you send that recording to me?"

"Sure. It lasts about ninety seconds or less."

"Send it by text and to my email to make sure I receive it. Let me give that email address to you."

"Just a sec. Okay. Go ahead."

Perry gave it to her. "Oh, and let me give you two more. Another Choctaw officer and a Seminole." She gave her Raquel's and Osceola Tiger's contacts.

"Do you think this will help?" Yarda asked.

"Miss Red Plume, it absolutely will."

Yarda sniffed. "Do you have any information? Do you know where Dels is?"

"We're working on it," Perry said as she looked at her phone, waiting for the video to come through.

"Dels is a good person. I can't believe this happened to her. It keeps happening to *us*." Perry and Sophia heard the sobs begin. "I lost my cousin and an auntie. They just disappeared. This is the norm for Ind'ins."

Perry did know. "I'm so sorry, Miss Red Plume," she said. She knew she was not the best at comforting victims' friends and relatives, but she was not indifferent; she just knew it did no good for her to cry as well. "What you told us is important. We will look at this right now." Then she said, "Thank you so much. Please keep your phone nearby and check your messages throughout the day. I might need to contact you."

Yarda took a big breath. "I will. I'm home this week and will have my phone with me."

"Again, I'm sorry that you have to deal with this. I'll call you as soon as I learn something."

Perry clicked off her phone, then sat back in her seat with an *oof.*

"Drink some Gatorade."

She heard the sound of crickets, indicating that the video had come in. "Let's look."

As Yarda had told them, the frame extended from where Dels sat in a chair at the front of her truck, which was next to Benny's Hummer. Yarda had parked to the west of the vehicles and trailers, with a clear view of where Dels would sit. A figure in a gray hoodie slowly approached the left side of Dels's truck from behind Benny's Hummer.

"Whoa," Sophia muttered.

Dels was a distance away, but they could see that she sat on a lounge chair with her injured leg supported on something.

"Dels Billy," Sophia said.

"Yes."

A man moved into the frame. He came to Dels and placed the ice pack on her knee, then leaned down to kiss her. Dels put her hand on his.

"That's Bake," Perry whispered.

Bake squatted and put his hands on her foot. He said something and Dels laughed. He stood and moved out of the frame.

Vera Spring moved into the frame to the right and spoke to Dels. She carried a large water container in her right hand. It seemed to be empty because Vera lifted her right arm to wipe her brow.

"Vera's about to fill those containers for the horses," Sophia said.

"Mm-hmm," Perry agreed.

Vera disappeared and for four seconds nothing happened except for Dels dropping her head back onto the headrest of her chair.

"Look," Sophia said.

They watched as a thin woman in tight jeans, a long white ponytail, and a visor entered from the left of the screen and walked around the front of Dels's truck to face her. Perry sat up and leaned in. "Rhonda," she whispered.

They made out high-heeled boots, a long-sleeved white blouse rolled up to her elbows, and a lot of jewelry. Perry identified a squash blossom, a silver Concho belt, multiple rings, and long earrings almost to her shoulders. Perry snickered. "Rhonda's got an Indian fetish. Ostrich-skin boots too." The glittery purple visor with a silver howling coyote brooch pinned to the band could not protect her face from the intense western sun. She appeared to be a white woman, but Perry knew there were plenty of tribally enrolled thin bloods in Oklahoma who looked Swedish. This one obviously had bleached her hair to an almost snow-white shade. It did not match her black eyebrows and tanned skin.

Rhonda's animated hands gestured as she spoke with Dels. Then she turned and stuck out her right hand to Benny, Sealy, and Bake. Vera entered the picture, hands on hips, and ignored the woman's proffered hand. The three men turned and walked back toward the barn.

Perry held her breath. The figure in a hoodie took something from the small cross-body bag at their right side, and then moved to the back left tire. They watched as the person squatted and did something using their right hand.

"Puncturing the tire," Sophia said.

Then the figure quickly moved from behind Dels's truck to the back of Benny's Hummer and squatted by the back right tire. Then he or she stood just as fast but stayed hunched over as they pulled out a larger item as they went to Dels's gas tank.

"That's a push opener," she said.

"It is."

They watched as the person inserted what appeared to be a bottle at the opening, held it for a few seconds, then dropped it back into the bag.

"Holy shit," Sophia said. "And I think that's a woman."

"Why do you think that?"

"Walks like one."

"We'll look closer on a big screen. Let's keep going."

The person moved to Vera's trailer, walked toward the back, then disappeared out of the frame.

Rhonda spoke again to Dels, then looked to her left. A slight movement, but one that Perry registered.

"Did you see that?" she yelped as she backed up the tape.

"What?"

"Watch."

Rhonda did it again.

Sophia said, "She looked back toward the camera."

"Agreed. But she can't see it. Why is she looking?"

A second later, Rhonda waved goodbye and hurried to the north in front of Benny's Hummer.

The film stopped.

"We need to look at this on a larger screen," Perry said. "Maybe Raquel and Osceola can make out more than we can before we get to a monitor."

"Okay," Sophia said. "But let me look at it again."

Perry handed Sophia the phone. Sophia replayed the last few seconds, then she replayed them again. "She's not just randomly looking around."

"What do you think she's looking at?"

"She's looking to see if the tires are flat."

Perry stared at the last image without blinking. "Why did Sealy turn off his recorder right as Rhonda arrived?"

"Because he wanted to talk to her without the camera?" Sophia posited.

Perry shut off the laptop. "Or he didn't want to film the person messing with the vehicles."

16

"What do a shampe, a woman in a hoodie, and a horse relay have in common?" Perry asked Sophia and Raquel, who had joined the conversation twenty minutes prior and had been brought up to speed on the case.

"Is that a joke?" Raquel asked through the speaker.

"It sure has the makings of one," Sophia agreed. "You still think a shampe is out there?"

"What?" Raquel asked. "What are you two talking about?"

Perry sighed. "Lee Robinson told the doctor that a shampe attacked him."

Raquel stayed silent so long that Perry finally asked, "Raquel?"

"Well," Raquel began, "shampes are seen quite a bit in Choctaw land. But not along I-40. He's deluded."

Perry laughed. "No shit."

"So what's the punchline?" Raquel asked.

"I haven't figured it out yet."

"I don't know what's going on with this strange case, but I

did call Osceola Tiger to ask if he's learned anything. Nothing. Still no witnesses from the highway. And I watched that video," Raquel said. "Rhonda was absolutely looking at the tires."

"She didn't do all this by herself," Perry said.

"Sealy?" Sophia asked. "He's a smitten teenager. Rhonda's a manipulative older woman."

"I found out she's thirty-five," Raquel said.

"I knew it!" Perry yelped.

Raquel asked, "Why did he turn off his camera?"

"If he's interested in Rhonda, maybe he felt awkward with a camera on his hat," Sophia suggested. "He was standing in a perfect spot to film whoever left those nails and screws."

"This is truth," Raquel said.

"But," Perry countered, "who also lives close to the casino and is there a lot for gaming commission meetings?"

Sophia tapped her fingers on the steering wheel. "Line Billy."

"Line Billy. Why not? Sealy seems like he could be easily fooled. He's cute, but he's a kid. Rhonda is a clever woman."

"Wouldn't be the first time it happened," Raquel said.

Perry thought about that. Rhonda was thirty-five and Sealy was twenty. Line Billy was forty-nine. Perry was not against age differences in relationships, but it did give her pause when one partner was that much younger.

"Line works down the road at the penitentiary," Sophia said.

"Just a few miles," Raquel agreed.

"Yes," said Perry. "Rhonda plays Sealy to get access to the racers."

"She could be in it with Line," Sophia said.

Perry touched her cheek and looked at her fingertips. They looked moist and pink. Her wounds were still oozing. "Maybe."

"Line did seem a bit smarmy," Sophia admitted.

Perry did not respond to that.

"And they would know each other from the casino," Sophia continued.

"They sure would," Perry agreed. "Rhonda's a bartender and Line's a gaming commissioner. She'd get to see Line a lot. Sealy is young and naïve. She could easily wiggle her way into his world."

Raquel agreed. "I'd like to know how she juggles the two of them but will leave that investigation up to you two."

Sophia said, "Rhonda gets to know Line and Sealy and somehow finds out about the allotment issue. Maybe she thought she could seduce Sealy and his father. I don't know. But the idea would be to get rid of Dels."

"But Sealy is not a co-owner of the land," Raquel interjected. "Line is. I think she used Sealy to get to Line."

Everyone was quiet for a few seconds.

"What about the possibility of her connecting with Bake?" Sophia asked.

"I feel sure that's not the case," Perry answered.

Perry took her pill vial out and considered the Line connection. "Seems to me she could just go straight to the father and not deal with Sealy."

"But she is 'talking' "—Sophia made quotes with her fingers—"to Sealy."

Perry pulled out lip balm and slowly uncapped it.

"Regardless," Sophia said impatiently, "the goal is to sell the land."

"If Rhonda went for Line, then what would they do with Sealy if they got the allotment and could sell it?" Raquel asked.

"Hmm." Raquel's voice sounded like the beginning of a song. "That would be awkward and I doubt if the son would like what the father is doing with his girl."

Perry sighed. "You're right."

The three mulled over the situation.

"I don't know for sure what the deal is," Perry said, "but I do believe there is something up with Rhonda and the Billy family."

Raquel did not respond to that. Instead, she said, "Let's proceed. What do you want to do?"

"Where are you?"

"My cousin's house in Norman. I'm going to look more at the Billy family. I only got as far as the allotment."

Perry looked at her left elbow. Blood had seeped through the gauze and her white shirt. She felt that the same was happening on her knees and ankle, but she didn't know for sure because her pants were black. She opened her mouth as if she were yawning and felt the cuts on her cheeks pull with the effort. Twenty-one years as a law enforcement officer, fourteen of those as a homicide detective, and she had never faced this challenge. She could always depend on her body. Now she wondered if she could trust her thighs enough to squat on a toilet.

Perry's phone chirped. "Raquel, call if you find something."

"Okey dokey" was the response.

"Troy," Perry greeted.

"Hi, hon," Troy said in his deep baritone. Perry slumped. She wanted to be next to him when he said those words to her. He had said them many times before and she had taken them for granted. Now she understood everything he had been telling her for the last two decades. *Family is everything. You work too hard.*

"How're you doing? Do you hurt? And don't lie."

"Sore. My knees and thigh feel tight. Ankle is stiff." She stopped there. She didn't need to continue with her litany of aches and pains.

"Keep putting Vaseline on the scabs."

"I will. It helps."

"What about your cheeks?"

"I try not to look. I can feel it."

"Put Vaseline on your face too."

"I will."

"I made chicken and okra enchiladas."

She didn't respond. No matter what she got herself into and no matter her outbursts, Troy always supported her. Even when she was wrong and then realized it, Troy gave her space and let her bring up the issue. He never faulted her.

Perry smiled. She was a perfectly good cook, but Troy was better. He had not known much about cooking when they first met, but after watching her, he decided that he could be a fine chef and began looking at cookbooks. Besides, Troy was never satisfied with restaurant meals and always said that he could do better. He took cooking as a challenge.

"There's wine too."

"Sounds perfect."

"Love you," he said.

"Love you more," she responded. "Tell the kids." She clicked off and turned to Sophia. "I think we need to go talk to Line Billy. He'll be at work."

"You think he and Rhonda took Dels and are keeping her someplace?" Sophia asked.

"Better than her being dead," Perry answered.

"It's almost eight o'clock," Sophia said. "I don't think either of us are up to driving back to McAlester. You're shrinking."

"What?"

"You're slumping. Your color is different. And you're slow to respond."

Perry started to argue, but she sighed instead. "You're right. How about we call it a night and go back that way early in the morning?"

"Good idea."

After a few seconds, Perry sat up straight and said, "No. We need to find Dels. If we stop for the day then we lose twelve hours. She may not have that kind of time."

She called Raquel to tell her their plan.

"McAlester, huh?" Raquel asked.

"How you feeling?" Perry asked. "You rested?"

"Well, I—"

"We have to go," Perry interrupted.

"Ten-four," came the response.

17

Sophia turned on the lights and sirens and began the trek back to McAlester.

"Do you want more people involved?" Sophia asked as they sped down I-40 past Del City.

"Not now. We need to find Line first," Perry said.

"Why don't we just call the warden and have him detained?"

"I don't know if he can do that. And if the warden says something, then Line will know we're onto him. I'd rather surprise him."

"Are we going to check in with Dickinson?"

"In a bit."

Sophia chewed her lower lip and did not respond.

She called Raquel. "Where are you?"

"Express Travel Center off of Martin Luther King."

"All right. You're not far behind. We decided not to tell the warden ahead of time. Surprising Line might be the best course of action. If he runs, we might lose Dels."

"If you think that's the way to go."

"I do."

An hour and ten minutes later Sophia pulled into the lot of the penitentiary. She had turned off the lights before they were in view of the prison so they would not alert the guards.

Perry scanned the lot but did not see Line Billy's vehicle. Nor did she see another silver truck. There were, however, plenty of other trucks painted black, red, and white, and another looked faded blue with rust around the wheel wells.

Raquel pulled up next to them ten minutes later.

She and Sophia rolled down their windows. "Ready?" Sophia asked.

"I'll follow."

Sophia pulled up to the guardhouse that sat under the curved metal Oklahoma State Penitentiary sign. She showed her badge to the older Black guard, as did Perry.

"There is a Choctaw Lighthorse officer in the truck behind us," Sophia said. She saw a Pringles tube and two Pepsi bottles on his small desk. "Is this where the guards park?"

"Guards come through here and park in that lot," the guard said. "What is your business here?"

"Confidential."

The guard looked at Sophia and Perry. "Let me see your IDs, again please."

They handed them over and the guard wrote down their information. "All right. Go on through and park over there."

Sophia pulled into the smaller lot. Perry looked back and saw the guard speaking to Raquel. Less than a minute later, she joined them.

Raquel asked, "How're you doin', lady? I mean, you look like shit and you're moving like you just crawled out of a car that flipped a dozen times."

"Well, I feel better than I look."

"Bullshit. Come on."

Perry smiled, but it hurt. She needed another pill. She said, "Line's truck isn't here."

"Maybe he got a ride to work," Sophia suggested.

Perry didn't believe that, so she didn't respond.

They went through building security, and on their way to the warden's office a man appeared in the hallway. Their escort, a tawny-skinned blond man with a nametag reading RICARDO, held out his hand. They all introduced themselves.

"The warden is—oh. There he is. Warden Zinski, these officers want to speak with you."

The imposing man with a blond crew cut and a neck as thick as a linebacker's said, "I was on my way home. I had to stay late today. How can I help you?"

Perry said, "We're here to see Lyon Billy."

"Line? Why?"

"It's rather crucial and time-sensitive."

The guard, Ricardo, said, "He's not here."

"Not here?" Sophia repeated. "We saw him earlier today and were told that he had to work the late shift."

"He called in sick."

"Flu, cold, Covid?"

"I dunno. I wasn't the one who talked to him. Another guard told me. Lucas was pissed because he wanted to go home after Line showed up to relieve him. Now he has to stay."

Warden Zinski said, "I hadn't heard about that." He turned to his visitors. "Why do you need him?"

Perry looked at Ricardo, then back at the warden.

Warden Zinski said, "Thanks, Paddy. You can go."

Perry glanced again at Paddy Ricardo. Irish Mexican. She thought of the Mexican restaurant that she and Troy had visited in Lawrence, Kansas, called Carlos O'Kelly's.

"What's this about?" the warden asked.

Perry nodded to Sophia, who answered. "It's in regard to

the woman who was abducted at the abandoned rest stop on I-40 Sunday night. Her companion was seriously injured. They're Indian horse relay riders."

The warden's eyebrows shot up. "Ah, yes. I did read about that." He thought for a few seconds. "You think Line had something to do with it?"

"We do."

"Did he do that to you?" He pointed to Perry's face.

"Honestly, I don't know," Perry said. "Look, if you see him, we need to know about it. We were hoping to surprise him here. If he comes back to work and goes about his usual business, do not mention that we were here. If he could be detained that would certainly be helpful."

Warden Zinski stood straight. "I understand."

Perry took out her card, as did Sophia and Raquel. "Please call the moment you see him."

The warden nodded. "I'll do that. Good luck."

Raquel's phone dinged. She looked down, then said, "Excuse me." She walked about ten feet away and listened. After another minute, she put her phone back in her pocket. When she returned to the others, Sophia and Perry were shaking hands with the warden.

"Thank you for your time," Raquel told him. She turned and walked quickly toward the exit, the detectives on her heels.

"How's the ankle?" Sophia asked Perry. "You're limping."

"It's hardening like cement."

"You need to keep moving it."

When they were outside, Raquel looked around. As Sophia started to ask if they should go to the Billy home, Raquel interrupted. She turned to them and glared like a hawk zeroed in on a rabbit. "That was a colleague who called me. A dead male was found about twenty minutes ago. ID in his pocket says Lyon Billy."

18

Sophia did not turn on her siren during the three-mile drive to where Raquel said Line was found in Oak Hill Cemetery. Perry leaned her head against the window and allowed the cold air from the vent to blast her face.

"Got any other ideas?" Sophia asked.

"A glass or bottle of wine sounds good. Or lemony vodka."

"We'll have those later, believe me."

Sophia pulled into the cemetery off East Washington Drive and stopped behind a Choctaw Nation cruiser with its lights flashing. Raquel parked behind her.

"Choctaw jurisdiction," Sophia said.

"It is."

"Isn't this where we were parked earlier?" Sophia asked. "Your grandparents are right about there." She started to point, then realized where everyone was looking.

Perry did not move.

"Holy shit," Sophia said, steeling herself for what was to come. "Let's go." She glanced at her partner. "Perry?"

Perry sighed. "I can do it." She opened the truck door and unbuckled her belt. She felt like time had slowed.

Sophia hurried to Raquel's truck and told her that it appeared that the deceased had been deposited on top of Perry's grandparents.

Raquel listened without expression. Then she turned to Sophia and asked, "Are you shitting me?"

"I am not. We were here earlier today."

She didn't look at Sophia when she replied, "And so were the people who were watching you."

Sophia waited for Perry to unfurl herself from the truck. She looked like a spider stretching her legs.

A few seconds later the three women approached where the dead man lay. Raquel greeted two of the Choctaw Lighthorse officers. As Perry stared down at the dead man, Sophia assessed her. Granted, they were mainly surrounded by darkness while the bright beams of the flashlights shone downward, but Sophia still thought that her partner looked smaller than she had ever seen her. Perry's shoulders were slumped and she opened and closed her left hand as if trying to loosen a knot in her forearm. Sophia resisted the urge to put her arm around her. She knew that Perry would rebuff her. Instead, she followed Perry's gaze to the graves.

A man lay on his side, legs crossed as if he had been tossed and rolled. His right arm was behind him and his left out to the side as if he were pointing at the headstone next to him. His clothes were torn and blood saturated the gray short-sleeved prison guard shirt. Line Billy wore his black nametag over his right breast and his laminated guard ID was attached to the left pocket. A bloody tarp lay half underneath him.

"It looks like he was thrown from a vehicle," Perry said.

"Yeah," Sophia agreed. "His clothes are a jumble and so are his limbs."

"Line Billy," she heard Raquel say to one of the Choctaw officers who squatted next to the body. He had a baggie in his hand. Inside was a wallet and a loose driver's license.

"Yup," the Lighthorseman replied. "One Lyon Billy. Says so right on his chest. Also has his tribal CDIB and Oklahoma Penitentiary ID cards in the wallet. A MasterCard and some small bills."

Perry had been so sure of her theory about Line's role in Dels's disappearance that she hadn't even considered it a theory at all. Rhonda and Line Billy had orchestrated this horrendous event so that Dels would disappear. They would then sell the allotment and split it with Sealy.

Perry was wrong.

"Who found him?" Perry asked.

A third Choctaw officer answered. He stood about five-six and looked like a power lifter. Although the force was called the Choctaw Lighthorse, some of the officers were white and Black. This one looked Scandinavian. His nametag read ERIKSSON.

"A lady who came to put flowers on her son's grave," he said. "She's over there." He pointed to a silver Mazda. A noticeably shaken large lady with a messy gray bun and dressed in a long floral housecoat and flip-flops sat sideways in the driver's seat with the door open. "She didn't see anyone here when she arrived around eight forty-five."

Raquel conferred with the Choctaw officers and motioned to Perry and Sophia. She introduced them.

"What happened to you, Detective?" asked a thin Choctaw Lighthorseman who looked like the Cherokee Wes Studi when he was thirty. His nametag said WRIGHT.

"Hazards of this case," Perry replied.

He continued to appraise her. Then his eyes widened. "That silver F-250?"

She nodded.

"We heard about that."

"Hey, Peter," Raquel said. "Detectives Antelope and Burns have been investigating the disappearance of that man's niece and they spoke with him today. Let's allow them to continue, okay?"

Peter Wright held up his hands. "Go ahead." He took out his iPhone and began to take pictures of the corpse.

Perry pulled on gloves, then squatted next to Line's body. She almost squealed when the scab on her knee pulled open. Sophia watched her and knew Perry was in pain but did not assist her. If Sophia did help her and the others saw, Perry would never forgive her. So she watched as Perry took out her penlight. She shone the light on one side of Line's face, then the other.

She looked to the others. "Hickey on his neck," she said. "I don't recall seeing that earlier."

"Me neither," agreed Sophia.

"It looks like some of his hair was torn out," Raquel observed. "Above his right temple."

"Yeah," Sophia agreed. "A good chunk. You can see where it bled some."

"And his left cheek looks like it's been hit pretty hard," Peter added.

She shone the light on his mouth. "Split lip and at least two missing teeth. Those teeth were crooked, but very white. I recall thinking that."

"Someone knocked the crap out of him," another white Lighthorseman said. His nametag said CRENSHAW.

"Are there cameras around here?" Perry asked.

"None," Crenshaw answered.

Perry put her left hand on the ground and pushed up. Normally she could do a one-legged squat, but not today.

"Tracks?"

"None that we could see," Peter said. "But it's all grass."

"The area needs to be combed," Sophia said.

"We'll do it."

A white SUV stopped twenty feet away and a man in jeans and a light green shirt with the sleeves rolled up got out. He pulled a bag from the back seat and strode to the scene.

"Coroner," Raquel told them.

The man hurried over, then nodded to the group. "Jim Scott," he said.

Sophia introduced herself and Perry.

They watched as he pulled on his gloves, then bent to look at the dead man. He leaned in closer. "Shot in the base of the skull," he said. "I'll look for more after the techs finish the scene and he gets to the morgue, but at least you know you're dealing with a homicide. Theoretically."

Perry asked, "Can you tell the type of bullet?"

Scott craned his neck to look at Line's head without moving it. "It looks like a near-contact shot. The hair is singed. The skin might be burned, but there's too much blood to tell. It's a penetrating wound. That is, the bullet did not exit his head. It's still in there. Possibly a hollow-point."

He stood and turned off his light. Dozens of other beams lit the scene.

"We're working the case of the woman who was taken on I-40 Sunday night," Perry said. "A young man was severely injured." She turned to Line Billy on the ground. "We spoke to this man earlier today. He called in sick to work and, well, here he is. As soon as you have any information, please call me." She gave him her card.

"Of course."

Jim Scott looked again at the dead man. He cocked his head, squatted, and pointed to Line's left hand. "Abrasion on the knuckles of this hand." Then he lifted Line's T-shirt. The right side of his rib cage was pushed in and discolored. "He was hit here. Ribs are broken."

No one needed to repeat that this was a brutal assault.

"We need to find Rhonda and Sealy," Perry said. She pulled off her gloves and wadded them into a ball and stuffed them into her pocket. "Call me, Dr. Scott." She walked toward Sophia's truck.

"I'm right behind you," Raquel said. She looked to her Lighthorse colleagues.

"We'll deal with this," Officer Crenshaw said. "I know how to get ahold of you."

Raquel followed Sophia's truck as they approached the Billy property. Sophia stopped at the curb in front of the house. Raquel parked two houses back.

Sealy's car was not under the carport, and the garage door was closed.

"Maybe his car is in there," Sophia said. "I'll ring." She pulled her Glock and approached the door. Perry stood back twenty feet on the sidewalk while Raquel moved to the side of the garage, staying out of view of the front window.

Sophia rang twice. Raquel motioned to Perry that she would move around to the back of the garage.

No one answered the front door. A moment later, Raquel returned.

"No cars in the garage. I could see through the side window. The door is locked. I didn't see a camera."

"We should see if Rhonda is at work," Sophia said.

A few moments later, they parked in front of the Choctaw Casino. Raquel waited outside while Sophia and Perry went to Trophy's Bar and Grill.

Perry sneezed from the smoke. "God, that hurt my face."

They entered the restaurant and saw Cherry carrying a tray

laden with drinks. Perry's eyes went to the bar. A handsome young man stood behind it holding a cocktail shaker, vigorously mixing something. Perry thought a daiquiri would hit the spot. It would certainly dull her aches for at least a few minutes.

Cherry saw the detectives and smiled. After she served drinks to six inebriated men, she hurried over. Tonight she wore her hair in two braids with red bows at the ends. She had on red eyeshadow and thick false eyelashes. Her black-and-red-checked miniskirt went well with her puff-sleeved white blouse and black fishnets. Her footwear looked and sounded like tap shoes.

"Hellooo," she drawled. "If you're looking for Rhonda, she's not here. In fact, she was supposed to relieve me three hours ago."

"Did she call in?" Sophia asked.

"Nope. And she's not answering her phone."

Three laughing women entered. "Look, I gotta go." They watched Cherry hurry to grab three menus from the counter, then escort the giggling women to their table.

"Damn," Sophia muttered.

"Hang on a sec." Perry walked over to where Cherry stood taking the women's drink orders. "Cherry," she said. Perry was not going to wait for her to finish getting the orders.

Cherry whirled. "Yes?"

"What kind of car does Rhonda drive?"

"Oh. Well, she just got a new silver Audi. She used to have a small Hyundai Kona."

Perry's jaw dropped. "An Audi?"

"Yeah. Cool, huh?"

"Does Rhonda have another job besides this one?"

"No."

"Do people tip well here?"

Cherry kept her smile but her eyes revealed that she was not amused. "Sometimes. But not *that* well."

"All right. Thanks."

Perry met Sophia outside the bar, then said, "We'll talk outside."

The two officers returned to Raquel in the parking lot. She rolled down her window. "Not there?"

"Nope. She didn't show for work. And Cherry, the waitress, said that Rhonda just got a new Audi to replace her Kona."

Raquel whistled. "Damn. I knew I was in the wrong profession."

"Yeah."

"Y'all still think Sealy is part of this?" Sophia asked.

"He sure didn't gift her with vehicles out of his weekly allowance," Perry answered.

Raquel laughed. "Someone did."

Perry looked around the parking lot. "And I hardly think that kid could have beat his father to death. No. We're looking for the owner of the silver truck. I think we should get some food and regroup. But not here."

19

The three drove to Wendy's by the freeway intersection. Perry preferred the Braum's Ice Cream and Dairy Store, which was located across from the cemetery, but it had closed fifteen minutes prior. Perry had gone to Braum's numerous times after she and her parents made the drive to put flowers on her grandparents' graves. Visit the cemetery, then have ice cream. At least she had a good memory of each trip.

They drove past the graveyard and saw that the crime scene had diminished. The coroner's vehicle, the ambulance, and half the patrol cars had left. They could see yellow tape and the Lighthorsemen walking around the area, looking down. Perry thought it ironic that the area was cordoned off because there was a dead person in the cemetery.

Sophia parked in the Wendy's lot, then turned in her seat to look at Perry. "Be honest. How're you doing?"

"My head is throbbing. Ice cream sounds good."

"Headaches are not unusual for you."

"This is true."

"I think you get them because of stress and tension."

"What makes you think I'm stressed and tense?"

"Because you always are. And you have good reason for it now."

Perry looked out the window. Raquel sat in her truck, waiting for them to get out.

Sophia put her hand on the door handle. "If that's how you're feeling right now, then we're good to go. Your headaches are nothing out of the ordinary."

Perry jerked the door open and got out. Before she closed the door she said, "Don't psychoanalyze me, Sophia. I get enough of that from my husband."

"It's not a criticism. Just an honest observation."

Perry slammed the door.

The three weary officers sat in a booth. They got their orders quickly. Raquel dug into a Jr. cheeseburger. Perry ordered a chicken wrap and a Diet Coke, and they each got a vanilla Frosty. Sophia got spicy chicken nuggets and a handful of ketchup packets. Before dousing the nuggets she held up the little packet and pointed to it. Perry raised an eyebrow and Raquel looked confused.

"Catchup," Sophia said.

"And so?" Raquel asked.

"How do you say it?" Sophia asked.

"Catsup."

"It says ketchup on the packet. Ketch-up."

Raquel shook her head as she chewed. "It does, but I say cats-up."

Perry tuned them out. She just stared at her food.

Sophia popped a nugget into her mouth, then put her elbows on the table. "Another long day," she mumbled as she rubbed her eyes with the back of her hand.

Raquel dragged fries through the ketchup and pushed them into her mouth.

Perry clicked her teeth.

"Stop it," Sophia said.

"What?"

"You told me recently that you cracked a tooth doing that. And one bite into one of those dang horehound candies is gonna split a molar in half. Are you wearing your mouth guard when you sleep?"

"Don't worry about me, Mom."

Sophia ground her teeth. "I'm not your mommy, Perry."

Raquel watched the exchange. After she swallowed a third of her vanilla shake, she interjected, "Someone wanted to destroy Line Billy."

Perry huffed. "Any time you take aim and pull the trigger your goal is to destroy."

"I mean that Line Billy was destroyed before that trigger was pulled. His injuries were cruel."

Perry picked up her shake. "Someone wanted him to hurt."

"And they left him on your family graves," Sophia added.

"They're making it personal," Raquel said.

Perry set down her cup and twirled her straw. "Whoever did this knew about my family."

"No big mystery. Just like we knew about the Billy family. Ancestry.com. Anyone with an account and knowledge of your name and your parents' names can trace your lineage and find their graves. Hell, just use Find a Grave. Your ancestry is not a secret. And if the person or persons knew you were here looking around, it would make sense they might taunt you."

"Same reason they tried to run you down," Sophia replied.

"Assholery," Perry finally said. "They want a delay in the investigation. They could have done it to either of you. They dumped him here because it was more convenient than taking him back to Oklahoma City and throwing him on my lawn."

Raquel picked up her shake and licked the thick ice cream from the end of the straw. "Maybe they see you as the biggest threat."

Perry shrugged. "Sometimes people do things just to be mean."

"True," Sophia said. "But you are a bulldog when it comes to solving cases and the perps probably sense that."

Perry huffed.

"It's true. You don't like to fail."

Raquel stirred her shake. "You remind me of my older sister."

"Is she in law enforcement?" Sophia asked.

"No. Academia. She's a historian. A truth teller who gets her butt kicked every time she tells a fact about our past. She spends so much time in archives figuring out demographics that she's wrecking her eyes worse than a welder working without eye protection. Truth telling is a liability these days and she's a target. James doesn't give a shit."

"James?" Perry asked.

Raquel smiled. "Yeah. My mother loves that name. James. So she gave it to my sister." She sat back, put her arms over her head, and stretched. "My father was a Raquel Welch fan, so he named me."

A worker behind the counter dropped something heavy and the sound reverberated through the building.

"Sorry!" the woman yelled. Everyone behind the counter laughed.

"What about your mother?" Sophia had a feeling that the daughters got their moxie from her.

"Our mother was, uh, unique. She's Black and Choctaw. And she's blind."

"Blind?"

"Yeah. She made us read to her even though we were just learning. She and my father would sit on the sofa holding hands while we struggled to read to them. I mean, we were first and second graders. We learned fast." She laughed. "Mom scared the hell out of us. She was like Dr. Clair Huxtable on *The Cosby Show*. You know. Phylicia Rashad. You either come up with the goods or you crawl under the sheets and stay there. I read more books when I was in junior high school than most adults do in their lifetime."

Perry turned to look at Raquel. She thought her a singular woman who perfectly fit the axiom "still waters run deep." Perry wondered again what her partner might be like. Maybe when this was over, she could meet him. The thought of an evening with Troy, Sophia, Mike, Raquel, and her man made her smile.

"Well," Sophia said as she wadded up her napkin and laid it on the tray. "Good fortune found me. After my shoulder surgery, I thought my law enforcement career was over, but I healed quickly. Now I have a strong and experienced partner."

Perry guffawed but also thought she might cry. Either from the compliments or the pain of her wounds.

"Now what?" Sophia asked.

Perry sat back and looked at the white ceiling. Her legs stung from road rash and her thigh felt like she had pulled a muscle. "I'll be back." She stood, picked up her pack, and made her way to the restroom.

She heard Raquel quietly ask Sophia, "Is she okay?"

Before the door shut behind Perry, Sophia responded, "Not really. But she'd rather lose fingernails than admit that she can't solve a case."

Sitting on the toilet with her pants around her ankles, Perry took off her left knee dressing and assessed her wound. Nothing looked infected, though the scab had split in two places. She added a bit more petroleum jelly, then applied a new bandage. Her thigh felt angry, but she saw only a broken scab. A strip of gauze and white tape covered it. After she stood and fastened her pants, she pulled up her pant leg and removed the knife sheath to look at her ankle. It seemed about the same as her knee. The real pain from her ankle came from what must be a pull or sprain. She thought about wrapping it, but that would have to go over the torn flesh.

"Shit," she said.

Perry exited the stall and washed her hands, realizing she should have washed her hands before touching her injuries. "Oh well," she said aloud.

The vials in her pocket called to her so she took two pills from the bottle in her jacket, even though she was aware that she might throw up in a few minutes if she didn't eat more than a milkshake. The cold water from the faucet tasted good and after five swallows, she looked in the mirror. Dirt stuck to the Vaseline on her face.

"You look like a drowned rat that had leprosy," she said to her reflection. "If you had a beard, people wouldn't be able to see all of this mess." She picked out some offending dirt from both cheeks.

Perry checked her phone and saw that Troy, Olyve, and Nico had texted to ask how she was doing. Troy asked her to *Tell me that you're okay!!!*

She kissed her phone and sent her family heart emojis with the note, *Feel good. Don't worry. Am with Sophia and Raquel.* As usual, she would deal with the fallout later.

This was not a new situation. Just a year into her job as a patrol officer, Perry and her partner, Jim Blackstone, responded to a domestic disturbance call. A man had beaten his wife almost to death and was threatening to shoot her. He opened fire when Perry and her partner arrived. The man shot Jim in the leg. Another bullet glanced off of Perry's zygomatic bone, leaving a gash from the corner of her left eye to the middle of the temporal region. A plastic surgeon sutured her wounded ear, but a thin white scar remained on the side of her face. The pain and blood loss had caused her to lose consciousness, and when she awoke she realized she had been out for almost eight hours. After the initial fuzziness cleared, she was able to recall what had happened to her with perfect clarity.

The acetaminophen surged through her and she felt a blast of warm relief to her wounds. She also felt a hit of euphoria. She pulled out her vanilla rose lip balm and smelled the sweet fragrance as she rubbed it across her lips.

In that instant, she knew who had taken Dels, assaulted Lee, and killed Line Billy.

20

Dels Billy awoke. Her right cheek throbbed but her left knee hurt more. *And it will be worse tomorrow,* she thought. Like other athletes, she knew from experience that injuries hurt more in the days to come.

She had a vague recollection of awakening in the night and speaking with someone who held a water bottle to her mouth. Dels smiled. It was her mother. Long black hair, which she wore partially pulled back with a tortoise-shell barrette. Her mother preferred vintage T-shirts. Last night she wore the red one with the *In the Court of the Crimson King* album cover on the front. That face creeped her out.

Dels's head ached with a light pounding that developed whenever she slept too long.

Her eyes flew open. That had not been her mother.

Why was her nightlight off? Why was her bed so hard? She lay on a mattress so thin she could feel the buttons digging into her thigh. As her eyes adjusted to the dark, she made out a chain-link fence, the poles of the sections, and a long-shackle padlock through the gate latch. Faint light reflected off the metal. The fencing stretched from one wall to the other, about eight or nine feet.

Dels sat up, supporting herself on her left elbow. The chain link behind her backed up to another wall. In front of her were two more elongated cages along a left wall. What appeared to be a small refrigerator stood against the right wall next to some boxes. A portable toilet stood in the corner of her enclosure.

In the moment she ascertained her surroundings, Dels realized where she was. *I'm in a truck. The cargo box.* A cool breeze blew some hairs off her face. *Air-conditioning.*

She tried to stand but felt too dizzy. She kneeled, her left hand on her knee and the other on the mattress. Her right eyelid felt heavy. Had she accidentally bumped herself? She touched her temple and realized that her skin was sticky. *Dried blood,* she thought. *I got hit in the head.* Then she sensed that her shoes were missing.

She recalled that she had been at the relays and was driving her truck home. With Lee. *Where's Lee?* She tried again to stand. She grabbed the chain link and a corroded spot stuck into her skin. She let go and shook her hand. The small movement caused her to sway. She grabbed another section of fencing and held on. She was not swaying by herself. The truck was moving.

"Just sit," a soft voice said from the cage to the left. "You can't get out."

"What? Who're you?"

"Colleen. I'm in a cage like yours. And the others. They got me two days ago in Jenks."

Dels sat down hard on the mattress. She felt the jolt in her coccyx, the ball of nerves she had hoped never to feel again. Xena threw her the year before and the hard landing had sent shock waves to the top of Dels's head. She took a few deep breaths and accepted the pain. "Took you?"

"Yeah. I work at the aquarium in Jenks. I just finished my environmental science degree and got a job as an apprentice. I normally go home around six, but that night there was a wedding reception and I had to work. I answer questions, keep the inebriated guests out of the EcoZone where we keep the stingrays, and make sure no one gets in the tanks with the otters or the bull sharks. They grabbed me when I stopped to pee at a QuikTrip. Less than two miles from home—I should have waited. They put a rag over my mouth out back because the inside toilet didn't work and I had to use the porta potty by the dumpsters. I woke up in here. Then they put you in here after that. I dunno when."

"Who's 'they'?"

"Two men. At least. One had on boots. I heard them click when they came up behind me."

"You sure they were men?"

"I guess. The one that grabbed me was strong."

Dels could not remember what had happened to her.

"Who are the others in here?"

"I dunno. They've been asleep since I got here."

"How many?"

"Three, I think."

The truck slowed, then made a left turn.

"Where are we?"

"In a truck. You were asleep, then kind of woke up. A woman came in and gave you more to drink and you conked out again."

"Drugs?"

"In the water. You drank it and then went back to sleep. We're always thirsty."

"What about you?"

"I pretended to be asleep."

Dels put her hands on the chain link and tried to stand again.

"There was someone else in here before me," Colleen said. She spoke only loud enough to be heard. "I could tell."

The truck ran over a pothole, the cab and trailer wheels dipping into the hole enough to make Dels stumble and drop back to the mattress.

"We're not on the highway anymore," Dels said. "We're going slow on a dirt road, I think." She put her hands back on the chain link. "Where are we going?"

"No idea." They sat in the darkness for a few moments before Colleen asked, "You Indian?"

"I am. Chahta. You?"

"Muscogee. Do you look like one?"

"What?"

"Do you look like a skin?"

Dels was about to ask, *What difference does that make?* when she realized that actually it wasn't a stupid question. "Why?" she said instead. But she knew the answer.

The truck slowed again, then made another left turn, this time much slower, as if the corner was sharp or there was not much room in front of the cab.

"You know men take Native women, right? And girls. And boys."

Dels already felt sure her situation was dire, but with the reminder of the vast numbers of missing and dead Natives who had been assaulted and trafficked, this unfamiliar fear hit her from a different direction. She put her hand to her head again. She had not been knocked out initially by chemicals or an injection. Someone had hit her. Hard. She sat up straight and pulled at the chain link.

"Have you tried to get out? Have you seen the lock? What else is in here?"

"I have. It's a basic padlock, but I can't reach mine even if I could pick it. I don't know anything about how to do that."

"Who are these people?"

"I don't know, but he brought me a Whopper earlier today."

The vehicle kept its slow pace. It slowed more and then stopped. Dels got to her feet and held on to the sharp chain link. She suddenly reached for her hip. She still had her shorts on. Good.

Dels was scared of many things: suffocation, burning, solitude, homelessness. Becoming a victim of sex trafficking was on the list, and if this was the situation she was in, she would fight.

The truck began backing up.

"You're right. I am thirsty." Dels needed liquid. Her throat hurt when she tried to swallow, like the time she had strep throat. Maybe she was sick. She felt around and found a bottle. The dim light allowed her to see the Aquafina label.

"You'll pass out if you drink that."

Dels considered the bottle. "How do you not drink?"

"I rinse my mouth but try not to swallow."

She opened the top and allowed a small amount of water into her mouth. She swished it around. Her throat hurt and needed liquid. She held the water in her mouth for a few seconds, then spit it out. That did not help her thirst. She tried again, but before she could stop herself she swallowed. She took a few deep breaths and felt drowsy.

"It only takes one swallow," she heard Colleen say before her eyes closed.

21

Perry appeared across the bright room. With a smile on her face, she walked over and sat with a plop.

"You good?" Raquel asked.

"I am."

Sophia raised an eyebrow.

In response, Perry said, "Yes, I did take some relief."

Instead of commenting, Sophia asked Raquel, "What did your father do?"

"Ran a pet store. Fish, lizards, birds, gerbils. He wouldn't sell cats and dogs because he knew those came from breeders. I remember we always had dogs and cats all over the house. All our pets were older animals when we got them. I never saw a puppy or a kitten."

"So then why the Marines? And why law enforcement?"

"I saw the Marines as a challenge. I can't abide misbehavior. And I will not tolerate people who take advantage of those who can't defend themselves."

Raquel looked down at her empty tray. Perry knew there

was much more to her story. She pulled the top off her milkshake and took a long drink, then a second, followed by a piece of chicken that fell out of the wrap.

"You want a burger with that?" Sophia asked.

"Sounds good now." She drank half her Diet Coke. "The shampe," she said.

Sophia looked to Raquel. "Perry, what did you take?"

"I know how to monitor my pain, Sophia."

"How many?" she persisted.

"It doesn't matter how many I took, Sophia. They wouldn't kick in this fast."

Actually, they had kicked in.

"Then what about the shampe?" Sophia asked.

"It's not a shampe."

"Good to know," Raquel responded.

"Delphine Adele Billy," Perry said. "Salen Absinthe Billy. Sealy Ceviche Billy. Lyon 'Line' Maize Billy."

Sophia and Raquel watched her.

"Poinsettia Sean Billy," she continued. "Henry Amaranth Billy."

Sophia looked around and saw that there was no one else in the place and the workers were busy behind the counter.

She and Raquel waited for Perry to continue.

Perry drained her drink, then slammed the cup onto the table. "Why is his plant name the first name?"

"You mean Poinsettia Sean?" Raquel asked.

"Yes." Perry grabbed Sophia's water and took a few swallows. "I want to know why it's not his middle name."

Raquel and Sophia waited as Perry reached up and adjusted her bun. She smiled.

"If his name was to fall in line with the rest of the family, it should be Sean Poinsettia."

"I guess," Sophia said. "So?"

Perry nibbled on a piece of chicken. "No kid in his right

mind would allow anyone to call him Poinsettia. He goes by Sean. Sean P., to be exact."

Raquel sat still. Sophia stared at her partner, then back at Raquel. In unspoken unison, Sophia and Raquel pulled out their iPhones. They spoke simultaneously.

"We need an APB on a Poinsettia Sean Billy. He drives a silver Ford F-250. Probably registered in California. Send that plate number ASAP."

They hung up almost at the same time.

"Sean P.," Sophia repeated. "Shampe." She shook her head and laughed. "Holy shit."

"That's bizarre," Raquel said. "Like that Facebook picture of upside-down plates. Among all the upside-down plates there's one that is right side up. And when you see that one, suddenly *all* the plates look right side up."

Sophia looked to her partner. She wanted to say that she knew perfectly well that Perry always solved every case they tackled together. What she did not say was that this might have been inspired by pain meds.

"Well, I'm sure as hell not going to call him Shampe or even Sean P.," Perry said. "He's plain old Poinsettia."

A minute later Perry's iPhone chirped. "Antelope," she answered.

"Detective," came the familiar voice of Sarita, the lead forensics investigator.

"What's up?" Sophia asked.

"We identified the woman at the bike trail."

"Who is she?" Perry asked.

"One Teresa Bennett. Her roommate reported her missing. Teresa was supposed to come home Sunday night after work, but she never arrived. The roomie says she had a dentist appointment at eight Monday morning. The roomie knew that because Teresa had been complaining about a toothache from a cracked tooth and had been trying to see a dentist. Roomie says there was no way Teresa would miss that appointment. She was using ice packs and went to the drugstore to get clove oil. It was bad. Anyway, she didn't take any overnight things with her and the roomie said Teresa hadn't planned to spend the night with anyone."

All three officers knew that Teresa Bennett still could have spent the night with someone or stayed alone at a hotel without an overnight bag.

Sarita said, "The roommate described the victim perfectly, right down to the tattoo and bracelet."

"Where did Teresa work?" Sophia asked.

"She moved to McAlester about six months ago, which was when she met her roommate, who works at the food distribution center. Then she worked at the Choctaw Casino in Wilburton. She was the casino teller."

Perry's eyebrows shot up. "The teller?"

"That's what the roomie said."

"How old is Teresa?" Perry asked.

"Thirty-two."

"Anything else?"

"Not at the moment."

"Sarita, let us know immediately when you learn something."

"Will do. Be safe."

Perry set her phone onto the table and watched it, as if expecting it to chirp again.

"So this Teresa Bennett worked at the casino," Raquel said. "Which meant she would have met Line Billy, the same way Rhonda did."

Perry nodded. "I would bet on it. A casino teller handles money, the paperwork, and the chips. The teller cashes out for the customers and that means they need good interpersonal skills. They interact with patrons, some of whom might be drunk and perhaps belligerent. That person safeguards the casino, which means tellers probably are not right out of high school. I assume she had a mature personality, was patient and intelligent."

"If Line Billy wanted to know about a casino, it seems a teller would be a good person to ask," Sophia added.

"Indeed."

Raquel's phone barked.

"Hit on a Poinsettia Sean Billy from Barstow, California," came the automaton voice. "Silver Ford F-250 plate number one one two George Frank three eight. Registered to that name. No outstanding warrants."

A few seconds later Sophia got the same call from a different voice.

"APB/Blue Alert it is," she said after clicking off and calling in the information.

"You think that Teresa Bennett was working with Rhonda?" Raquel asked. "The one wearing the hoodie in the video?"

"Not just Rhonda," Perry said. "Something went sideways."

"Where is Sealy in all of this?" Sophia asked.

Perry reached into her pack for eye drops. "I don't know, but at this point," she said as she looked to the ceiling and squeezed several drops into each eye, "I hope that kid is alive."

"Maybe Cherry has seen the dead woman before," Sophia suggested.

Perry tapped her fingers on the tabletop. "Yeah. Maybe."

"What do you want to do?" Raquel said. "The casino is just a few minutes away."

"I think we go see Cherry again."

Sophia sniffed. "I can smell the smoke already."

The three officers walked through the entry to the casino, along with a stream of laughing men and women who dispersed when they got into the lobby. Most made a beeline for the slot machines.

"I came here once to gamble," Raquel said. "I allowed myself to spend six quarters on the slots and I won fifty dollars. I can see how people get addicted."

"I've never gambled," Sophia said. "Except once I played strip poker in college."

"Did you win?"

"No."

Raquel laughed, but Perry limped ahead to Trophy's Bar and Grill. She stood at the entrance, scanning the room. When she spotted Cherry at the bar she made her way through laughing patrons to where the server waited for a drink order. Cherry leaned on the bar, clearly tired.

"Hello, Cherry," Perry said.

Cherry turned. "Oh. Detective," she greeted with a weary smile. "You're back." She saw Raquel and Sophia and did not look pleased.

"I am. And we need to talk."

"As you can see"—she motioned with a wave of her arm across the room—"this is a full house. And it's just me and the newblet Pixel."

Perry followed Cherry's gaze to a small, thin woman dressed in a black sleeveless turtleneck, black leggings, and boots with three-inch heels who was carrying a tray filled with food platters. She wore her red hair in a high ponytail that reached to her waist. *No way is her hair that long*, Perry thought.

"Now," Perry said. "Come with me." She took Cherry by the arm and led her out to the lobby. Cherry crossed her arms over her chest while eyeing Sophia and Raquel, who now wore a black zippered jacket and stood with her hands on her belt.

"What did I do?" Cherry asked. She looked nervous.

"You did nothing," Perry said. "But we want to know who has been to see Rhonda."

"To see her?"

"Yes. Men. Which men have been here to see her?"

"Lots of men come in here and ask for Rhonda. I mean, she's been here a long time. She's a good bartender and the regulars like her."

"Any one man come in a lot recently? Perhaps one she was receptive to?"

"Uh, yeah. A gaming commissioner, going by his nametag. An Indian guy with kinda long hair. Parted on the side. She left with him a coupla times. I never talked to him."

Perry knew that must be Line Billy.

"Any other men?"

"Hmm. No. Not that I saw. But she talked to men all the time at the bar."

"Did you see that man in the last few days?"

"I didn't see anyone like that. But it was the weekend and super busy. I don't have time to stop and notice people."

"Any women come to see Rhonda?"

Cherry did not blink. "Yes."

"One or more than one?"

"Just one."

"Tell me about her."

Cherry looked back into the bar. "I'm gonna get fired. Rhonda hasn't been back and it's just me and Pixel and she's new."

"Yes, I know. Talk fast."

"About my height. Long black hair. She's Indian. I dunno which kind. Not skinny. Not fat. In between. Braided string or something around her wrist."

"Right or left wrist?"

"Right," she said quickly. "Her hand was on the bar and she was looking at Rhonda. Anyway, before she left, Rhonda kissed her."

"Kissed her?"

"Yeah. I saw her do it as I came out of the back. She left right after that."

"When was this?'

"Umm. Last week sometime."

"Does Rhonda see both men and women?"

Cherry shrugged. "Well, uh, I dunno." She looked around nervously.

"It's okay, Cherry. Thank you. Go back to work."

Cherry turned to go.

"Wait." Perry reached into her inner pocket and took out her thin wallet. She pulled out two twenty-dollar bills and handed them to Cherry. The server took them without comment, then hurried back into the bar.

Perry turned to her companions. "Cameras," she said. She looked up and motioned with both hands. "They're everywhere."

"Rhonda was in on this," Sophia said. "What about Teresa?"

"Well, that is surely a possibility," Perry responded.

Perry called Sarita and told her what Cherry had said about the mystery woman.

Sarita did not hesitate. "We have prints. You took some from the Hummer, the truck, and the trailer. We took prints from the missing woman's truck and her trailer. We got partials from all of them. But as you know, it takes a while to get IDs."

"Call as soon as you know."

"Always do."

"Thanks, S."

As soon as she clicked off, her phone chirped again. "The rush has hit," she said before answering. She lifted it to her ear and heard the message from dispatch: "Detective. That silver Ford F-250 was just spotted at the Creek Nation Casino. Off 69 heading into Muskogee."

"Who called it in?"

"Off-duty officer."

"We're on it."

Raquel quickly typed in the site to her Google Maps. "Sixty-one miles," she said.

"You want to get another ride?" Sophia asked Raquel. "Get an unmarked vehicle from one of your stations?"

"No. It might be best if this guy doesn't see two unmarked vehicles. Yours is obvious to anyone who knows what to look for and the truck I'm driving now looks like a hundred others on the road."

"Do you want to ride with us?"

"No. I think we might need two vehicles."

They hurried to their trucks and within seconds were on Highway 69, heading north with sirens blaring and lights flashing.

22

Sophia sped north along Highway 69 with Raquel behind her.

Perry opened her phone and looked up Muskogee Lighthorse Police.

"Surely they know," Sophia said.

"I would think so," Perry said. "Still, we need to let them know we're coming."

Sophia picked up the radio. "This is Detective Sophia Burns with the Oklahoma City Police Department. I'm with Detective Perry Antelope and Choctaw Lighthorse Raquel Hunter. We're investigating the disappearance of a Choctaw woman, the assault of a Choctaw man, and the murders of two others. A person of interest is driving a silver Ford F-250, plate number one one two George Frank three eight. It was spotted a few minutes ago at the Creek Nation Casino in Muskogee."

"Copy. We have that information already and our Lighthorse were dispatched to the casino. The truck is gone."

Sophia figured it would be.

"Copy. I'm in my unmarked vehicle." She gave dispatch her

information. "We're ten minutes away. Are your Lighthorse looking?"

"Negative. We've got a busy night. Eleven-eighty. Multiple fatalities."

Just great, Perry thought.

"Copy. We'll check back in." She hung up.

"Damn," Sophia said.

Perry looked at the time on her phone. "Almost two-fifteen."

"How you feeling?" Sophia asked.

"Like shit. What about you?"

"Oh, I can keep going."

She called to tell Raquel they were on their own for the moment.

"Let's go to the casino," Raquel said. "Maybe someone saw which way he went."

Five minutes later, they pulled into the lot.

Perry looked out her window and saw the illumination of Raquel's iPhone.

Sophia opened the door and hot air enveloped the women. She looked back at Perry. "I'll ask if anyone saw the truck."

"I'll check out the routes," Perry said. Normally she would have jumped out first to take on that task. She looked down at the map and considered where the truck might be. If Sean went east, he would be on I-65 headed to the Cherokee Nation. If he went north, he would hit Kansas.

Perry closed her eyes. Her aches had eased a bit, but that was because she wasn't moving. She drank the last of the Diet Rite she'd left in the door cupholder, then opened the Diet Sprite. If she didn't keep drinking, she knew the pain of her headache would overshadow her injuries.

Raquel knocked on the window. Perry rolled it down. "You know that he's nowhere around here, right?" Raquel asked. "We're going to have to chase him."

"I do know. If he has Dels, where would he keep her? In his truck?"

"If he has a destination in mind for her. Or he already deposited her someplace, either dead or alive."

"If alive, where is she?"

"What if he's working with a trafficker?" Raquel asked.

Perry said, "Where would someone like that go?"

Raquel thought about it. "Likely a big city. Or a meeting place where the victims could be transported elsewhere."

Sophia returned and quickly got in. She had two Gatorades for Perry and Raquel and two Monster energy drinks for herself. She held up a small bag of pistachios and two kinds of chips. Raquel took the barbeque-flavored ones.

"One trucker thought he saw our silver Ford go north less than an hour ago," she said. "I asked if anyone saw the driver. A woman behind the counter sold a tall Indian with wavy hair to his shoulders and shaved on the sides an energy drink, a Pepsi, Hot Cheetos, a Diet Coke, powdered donuts, and a bag of Skinny Pop popcorn."

"Well, it appears that a woman is in the truck," Raquel said.

"Agreed," Perry said.

Raquel went back to her truck and they set off again.

A few miles north Perry called Raquel and put her on speaker.

"So we assume that Sean has Rhonda with him. If the now-deceased Teresa Bennett was at the races at the same time as Rhonda, and the tape shows Rhonda looking at the punctured tires, it makes sense that Rhonda played Teresa. She snuggled up to Sealy to get to Line. Regardless, the brother and uncle Sean P., aka the Shampe, entered the picture."

"It certainly seems to be the case," Raquel agreed.

"Maybe it's not trafficking. It's a kidnapping and a murder," Perry said. "Several murders."

"But what if they took Dels someplace where she would be trafficked?" Sophia asked. "It's hard to think of a woman being in on a plan as awful as that."

Raquel barked a "Ha!" through the speaker, then asked, "Ghislaine Maxwell ring a bell?"

"Since 2007 there have been more than two thousand cases of human trafficking in Oklahoma," Perry said.

"That we know of," Raquel corrected.

"True," Perry agreed. "And those victims were forced to work in private homes, massage parlors, and brothels. Some were shipped out of state and some out of the country."

"Dels Billy does not seem like the kind of woman who could be controlled in a massage parlor or brothel," Sophia said.

Perry squirmed in her seat. All of her scabs were drying or splitting. "I'm glad to hear you say that," she said.

"She's physically strong, has to manage horses, and takes care of herself. Literally. She has that property with no parents to help her. I think that if she can get away, she will. Just like you and Raquel would."

"If she's still alive," Perry said quietly.

"So how is this a trafficking issue?" Sophia asked. "I thought they wanted Dels's land."

"I guess not, really. But that might be what they wanted us to think."

They drove in silence for a few moments with the lights flashing. Luckily, there were few people on the road on this Tuesday night.

"Fuck, I'm tired," Perry said.

"I second that," Raquel's voice echoed.

"Thirds," Sophia said. "I don't function well without a shower at least every twenty-four hours and I need to brush my teeth. And I get mean. Like an overtired toddler who can't sleep and screams instead."

"That could be a good thing," Raquel said.

Perry realized they were chattering more than usual. They had to stay awake.

Sophia noticed. "Doesn't that pain med make you sleepy?"

"Sometimes. If I don't eat."

"I got a box of crunchy granola bars in my glove box. I took out the chewy ones because they melted."

"Crunchy it is," she said as she reached for the compartment latch.

"What if we don't see him soon?" Sophia asked.

Neither woman had an answer.

Sophia's radio squawked. "Ask and ye shall receive," Perry said.

The female voice came through as loud as a demolition car announcer. "Suspect was seen driving past the One Stop Food Mart at Big Cabin on 69."

"That's about forty miles," Raquel said.

Perry ripped open the granola bar and said, "Hit it."

23

Less than an hour later, Sophia pulled onto Main Street from Highway 69.

"Where do you want to go?" Raquel asked. "Clearly they're not here."

The radio crackled again. "The silver Ford F-250 was spotted on Highway 2 leaving Walmart in Vinita."

Perry picked up her pack and said, "Just ten miles away." She rummaged around and Sophia knew she was looking for her pills.

Sophia started to press the accelerator.

"Two highway patrol officers now headed northeast on I-44 on the lookout."

"Copy that," Sophia responded.

"Want to follow?" Sophia asked Raquel through the phone.

"Negative," Raquel said. "I say get on 69 going north, then 60 east and then hit Highway 2. If he knows he's being followed, Sean won't take the main route. I say he's going the back way. Still going through Vinita, though."

"Perry?" Sophia asked. She was not as familiar with Oklahoma roads.

"Let's do that. I don't know where Sean wants to be. Or if Dels is with him. Turn off the lights."

Sophia kept her speed ten miles above the limit. Raquel followed closely behind. They slowed as they made their way through Vinita then turned north onto Highway 2. Sophia accelerated and they drove seventeen miles until they arrived at the outskirts of Welch. She slowed down.

"Appropriate that we're going through Welch." Perry yawned. "A lovely little town except that considering what we're doing, its history seems to fit our travel plans."

"What happened here?"

"The torture and murder of two teenagers. Lauria Bible and Ashley Freeman in 1999. And the murder of Ashley's parents. After they shot the parents in the head, the perps burned down their house."

Sophia sighed.

"One theory is that the girls were dumped into mine shafts in Picher, which is a dead town to the north. You don't want to go there."

Sophia pulled the turn signal and washer fluid sprayed over the bug-splattered windshield. They watched the wipers ineffectively swipe over the dried innards of insect roadkill.

"Mine shafts?"

"Yes."

"Dang."

"Dark story, Perry," Raquel said.

"Hey." Sophia sat forward in her seat. "Is that him?"

Both detectives leaned forward in an attempt to identify the vehicle ahead.

"Definitely a truck," Sophia said. "I dunno if it's him, though."

"I can't tell," Perry said. "It might be. And it's turning onto Highway 10. Also called Highway 59."

"Should we call this in?" Raquel asked.

"I want to know where he's going. If we grab him right now he might not talk."

"The woman with him might," Sophia said.

"I say follow him," Raquel said.

Perry yawned again. The fatigue of this day had piled onto the exhaustion she'd felt even before Poinsettia Sean had tried to run her down.

"Drink some of that tea," Sophia said. "I forgot I have a Snickers in my pack. We'll split it if it's not gooey."

"Chocolate. Good idea."

"How's your fuel?" Sophia asked Raquel.

"Half a tank."

"Where is he going?" Sophia asked.

"Looks like Miamah."

"The sign says Miami."

"It's pronounced My-am-uh. Welcome to Oklahoma." She kept her eyes on the distant truck. "It's Shawnee land."

"You want to call their police?" Sophia asked.

"I do. First, I want to make sure this is our guy."

They drove for a few moments.

"He could be headed toward Joplin, Missouri," Raquel said.

The big silver Ford turned onto Northeast A Street.

"I guess he's not taking the direct route to Missouri," Raquel said.

Perry was puzzled. "Well, he can still get there from here."

They continued to follow at a discreet distance for five miles as the Ford rounded a gentle curve and went straight east.

Perry put her hands on the dashboard. "I'm thinking we need to call the Quapaw marshals so they can have some officers ready when he goes past. He might be headed to their land."

"If he stops in Quapaw, we'll do that," Raquel said.

They continued to follow the truck as it passed under the

arching metal GATEWAY TO MIAMI, OK sign that stretched over both lanes.

"Sophia and Raquel, slow down," Perry said.

"Copy that," Raquel said.

The vehicle looked light in color under the lights of Main Street. They passed a variety of businesses, all closed at this hour.

"Montana Mike's," Sophia said. "I could go for a steak."

"Right now?" Perry asked.

"As soon as we're done with this guy. Yeah."

"You're gonna have to wait about twelve hours before that steakhouse opens. Slow a little more."

"That's gotta be him," Sophia said.

A few minutes later they passed through Miami and entered the smaller town of Commerce. There were a surprising number of vehicles out, mainly big rigs. Perry hoped Sean had not noticed them following.

Perry consulted the map. "If he doesn't continue straight through, then he's headed for 69 and then probably Quapaw."

The truck took the turn and headed east. Instead of continuing, after a moment the truck's brake lights lit up and the vehicle turned north.

"No!" Perry barked.

"What's wrong?"

"Damn."

"What?" Sophia asked again.

"No. No, no, no."

"What?"

"Picher." Perry rubbed her forehead.

24

"Maybe they're just passing through," Raquel said. "They can stay on 69 and keep going north into Kansas."

"And perhaps not," Perry muttered.

"Picher's the place with the mine shaft?" Sophia asked.

Perry ground her teeth.

"Perry?"

"*Shafts,* plural. They're all over the place. This is the worst place they could go."

"Mining?" Sophia asked. "Here?"

"You don't need mountains to mine, partner."

"I've never heard of this place."

"This is a busy road," Perry said, "but I'm afraid he'll notice us now." She pulled up Picher on her phone.

"Not many lights," Sophia said.

"There isn't anyone here anymore."

"What do you mean no one is here?"

"It's a ghost town. A dead town. No buildings. As of a few years ago, when I last came through, there were only a couple of dilapidated structures about to fall down."

They reached the outskirts of the dead town.

"See all those mounds?"

The light-colored piles looked bright in the moonlight.

Sophia looked around. "Yeah. Mountains. Sorta whitish grayish."

"That's chat, a by-product of zinc and lead mining. And it's toxic."

"What do you mean?"

"Mining companies churned out lead for bullets during World War I. Then zinc became a big deal during World War II. They crushed the rocks to get out the zinc, and all that waste had to go someplace. You see the piles. It looks like sand. They call it chat." She motioned to the bare, light-colored hills. "Nothing can grow on them. Mining continued until it destroyed the town. They left holes in the ground too. And there are supposed to be three hundred miles of tunnels underneath this area."

"No way."

"Yes. The chat piles blew dust all over the place and particles got into everything. Behind the wallboards, inside cars, air conditioners, grocery stores, the water. Everything. The town started dying because people got sick. Really sick."

"Sounds like uranium."

"Poison like that, yeah. But the people here didn't know it was dangerous. So the kids played on the hills and parents filled up sandboxes with the stuff. It was too late to do anything about it after the mining stopped in the 1970s. Over half the children had lead poisoning. Teachers noticed that students were having learning problems. The pollution seeped into Tar Creek and then into Grand Lake. A lot of people use it for drinking water. Kids who swam in the water came out looking like they were burned. And they were. There was so much acid in the water that it burned their skin. Lead, zinc, arsenic, and manganese particles stayed in the air and people developed chronic lung disease."

Sophia made sure the air-conditioning was on inner circulation.

They rolled past Seventh through Fifth Streets. They saw only overgrown foliage that had steadily encroached into the lots where homes once stood. A few askew telephone poles remained, the broken lines torn and hanging to the ground. All around them were seven thousand acres of ridgelines, fourteen thousand abandoned mine shafts, and lots of acidic, chemical-laced water.

"I can't believe I've never heard of this Picher," Sophia said.

"You have now. Slow down. A tornado wiped out a good portion of the town in 2008. Destroyed something like at least one hundred houses—that's why you won't see any. Just streets and what look like broken or grassy foundations. Main Street got leveled too. Some people stayed until 2013, when the government bought them out."

Sophia's eyes went back and forth between the truck they followed and the desolation around them.

"This was a thriving town. Ten thousand people. Big high school. A gorilla mascot. Cheerleaders. I think they were even the football state champs at some point. The Quapaw Nation is doing its best to clean up the mess outsiders made. It's their land, you know."

"God, what a story."

"And we're going through it."

"Did you take any more pain meds?"

"No. Why?"

"You're talking a lot. And you're speaking fast."

"Where's the truck?" Raquel interjected.

"About half a mile ahead," Sophia estimated.

They watched the taillights in the distance. The brake lights briefly came on, then the truck turned left.

"Oh no."

"Where does that go?"

"Not to Joplin." She looked at her map. "That's Fourth Street. It just goes west into more of this." She gestured with her hand. "Into nothing."

"Maybe there's a building back in there you don't know about," Raquel offered.

"This whole place is a series of streets with only slabs or broken rock foundations." She sighed, then clicked her teeth. "There are all sorts of ways this can go. Maybe there's a trailer. Maybe there are more people in one of the hidden structures. Maybe . . . hell, I don't know."

Sophia leaned forward as if to see the truck better in the darkness. "We need to call the Quapaw marshals," she said.

"So you don't want to see where the truck goes first?" Raquel asked.

"I do. But this is their jurisdiction."

They reached the corner of Fourth Street and Highway 69.

"Pull over and park," Perry ordered.

Sophia and Raquel backed into the crumbled lot, the trucks facing west.

"I can't see anything," Sophia said.

Perry opened the door and put her right foot on the ground. She knew that if she gave in to the pain and moved slowly her mind would make sure everything else she did was slow. Despite the burning and pulling in her legs, she stood and found her balance. She took one step, then another. She walked as fast as she could to the intersection and saw the truck in the distance moving west. She knew there were side streets going to the north—Main and South Picher Street, according to her phone. Sean must have turned south on either South Treece Street or South Vantage Street. Those roads led straight into the chat piles.

Perry moved back to the truck and opened the door. Sweat ran down her back and face. The humid air felt like what one would breathe in a greenhouse.

"He turned south," she said. The vest she wore under her shirt felt like a vise squeezing her ribs and she wanted to take it off. "Let's head that way. Turn off the lights. There's enough moonlight. There aren't any street signs, so I have to use this map and count the roads as we go past them."

After Perry slowly got back into the truck, Sophia headed west onto East Fourth Street with Raquel behind her. They could see the road, but not anyone who might be standing off to the side in the trees. Perry counted what she thought were streets. Bushes had overtaken the intersections and the road signs. Those had been demolished by the tornado or pushed down by the machines that carried off the remains of the ruined homes. She estimated that they passed Main, South Picher, and Netta Streets.

"This place is big," Sophia said as they creeped down the road. They looked all around them, hunting for the silver Ford. "Not a single light."

"Trees and bushes are overgrown," Raquel said. "Great place to hide."

"Maybe," Perry answered. "There was a fear that the entire town might collapse into a sinkhole. Some parts of it did. And it still might. Which is why people aren't supposed to wander around."

"Or drive around," Sophia added.

"True," Perry agreed. "That's why Sean is here."

"This is a place of death," Raquel said.

"I know. But the Quapaws are doing what they can to revitalize it."

Raquel did not respond.

Perry consulted her phone. "I saw the truck go south. Right up here, Sophia."

Sophia slowed. "I can't tell for sure, but looks like it heads into that pile."

"That's what I see as well," Raquel said.

"I think most roads here lead to a pile," Perry countered.

"We need to park so Raquel can get in with us," Sophia said.

"I disagree," Raquel said. "Let's see what the deal is first. I don't like this place."

"Eggs in different baskets," Perry said. "We need both vehicles."

"I hear that," Raquel agreed.

"Let's call the Quapaws," Sophia said again. "They know this area better than we do."

Perry did not respond and neither did Raquel.

Sophia looked at Perry. Light from her iPhone emanated upward onto her wounded face. She thought Perry looked like something she once saw on the Shudder horror streaming service.

"This is like a forest with streets," Sophia said.

Perry nodded. "That's what it is now. Turn here."

"You sure?"

"No."

Sophia led the way down a dark road that looked like the one they had just traveled.

Perry looked at her map. "This has to be Treece Street."

"Do you want to turn here?"

She thought for a moment, then looked at her phone again. "No."

"No? You sure."

"Stop asking me that. I think if they're hiding they'll want to be back in the brush."

"If you say so."

Perry had nothing else to go on other than a gut feeling. But she knew that might be brought on by fatigue.

Sophia rolled slowly another one hundred feet to a dead end.

"This has to be South Vantage Street," Perry said. She looked to her right. "Go south."

The road looked like the others. Short brush and tall grasses stood where there might once have been sidewalks. Taller trees beyond that foliage used to shade the now-removed homes. Driveways were visible, but they were either broken cement or dirt now covered with grass and weeds. Occasionally, the moonlight revealed half a wall, chimney, or dilapidated outbuilding.

"Hang on," Sophia said. "I saw a light."

Perry's gaze lifted from her map. "Where?"

"Just a quick flash."

"How far?"

"Forty, maybe fifty yards. On the right."

"We need to hide these trucks," Raquel said. "How about we turn right and back into an old driveway?"

"Okay," Perry said. "Let's do it. Go slow. I don't want to fall to Pellucidar."

Sophia laughed. Raquel asked, "What?"

Perry sighed. *Yup. I am that old.* "Center of the Earth. Edgar Rice Burroughs."

"Yeah, okay," Raquel muttered. She found a spot thirty feet down the bumpy street.

"Lights need to be off when we get out. Raquel?"

"I heard you."

Perry checked her pockets and made certain that the holster on her right ankle and knife sheath on her left were attached.

Raquel exited her truck and gently closed the door. She took off her jacket, then adjusted her body armor. Perry and Sophia wore their bulletproof vests, which were never comfortable but now in ninety-degree heat were downright torturous.

"Got your light?" Perry asked Sophia. She had the same one as Perry, a Streamlight.

"I got it."

"Don't turn it on. Raquel?"

"Yep."

"Stay on the edge of the streets, but don't get into the yards. There could be holes or trash that might cut you."

She and Sophia moved silently down the west side of the street while Raquel moved down the east side. They hurried past the intersection and into darkness.

"*Pssst.*" It was Raquel. Perry and Sophia understood that she was pointing to the south. They heard an engine humming.

Perry put her hand on Sophia's arm. She pointed into the foliage. Through the brush, they saw glints of shiny paint. It looked silver in the moonlight. She moved quietly deeper into an overgrown yard.

"We better not be standing on thin ice covering a sinkhole," Sophia whispered.

Perry put her finger to her lips, then moved to her left a few feet and parted a bush. They saw Sean's truck backed into the foliage and heard the pops as the engine cooled—as much as it could in the nighttime heat.

"*Pssst,*" Raquel whispered again. Her companions followed her gaze. High clouds moved and the three officers saw another glint of reflection off a darker-colored object about thirty yards past Sean's truck. They moved across the street to join Raquel.

"It's a big rig and the engine is running," Raquel said. "Drivers sleep in the cab. It's too hot to turn it off."

The trio moved into the trees, mindful of where they stepped. Once they had retreated into the darkness, they moved parallel to the front of the silver truck.

"Be careful," Perry said to the others. "Remember that the ground might be unstable."

Then she stepped forward on her left foot and landed in a hole. "Shit," she hissed. The side of the depression rubbed against the gauze that covered the road rash on her ankle. The last thing that Perry expected was to be in the dead town of Picher creeping around in the dark after a probable murderer and human trafficker. She was exhausted, thirsty, and most of all, pissed off.

"Watch it," she said to the others. "Don't step there."

"Should we be wearing face masks?" Sophia asked. "Are we breathing poison?"

"Could be," Perry said. "We have no masks." Sweat ran down her forehead. She felt it trickle down between her breasts. The humidity made her clothes feel clammy. "Let's move through this lot, then cross the street so we end up on the other side of the big rig."

"Fuck a duck," Raquel said in a low voice.

"What?"

"I ran into something. It cut through my pants and got me."

Perry sighed and backtracked to Raquel's side.

"What is it?"

Raquel took Perry's hand and maneuvered it to what felt to Perry like a rusted piece of metal.

"An old barrel, maybe. You can't turn your light on. How deep?"

"I can't tell, but it hurts like shit."

Perry knew that Raquel had a high pain threshold so it must really be unpleasant, but she also knew that they couldn't do anything about the wound at the moment.

"Don't worry about me," Raquel said. "We gotta go."

"Copy that."

They made their way around a slab that had once supported a home, wary of a line of thorny blackberry canes. They'd almost reached the broken foundation that would have made up the front of the home when they heard male voices.

"What are they doing?" Sophia asked. "There's no building. Do you think they're talking in the back of that big truck?"

"Dunno," Raquel said.

The voices retreated, then went silent. After fifteen minutes of waiting in the darkness, the women heard a door slam.

"That could be the back of the trailer," Sophia said.

"It was," Raquel confirmed. "If they don't move in the next few minutes we'll call—"

The door to the semi-truck opened and they saw a man enter the dark cab.

"Move!" Perry exclaimed.

The three hurried through the brambles and clods of dirt to the south. The driver put the engine in gear and pulled forward, almost to the trees where the three women had been crouched. The trio dropped to the ground. In order for the rig to exit, the cab had to pull forward as far as possible, then make the left turn.

The rig kept moving forward onto the yard where they had been hiding a moment before. The driver turned left over the old driveway and ran over a few saplings. The trailer followed. Bright colors adorned the sides of the cargo container, the lettering reading HAPPYDALE FARMS WHOLESOME FRESH FOODS FOR YOUR FAMILY. Perry made out corn, tomatoes, chickens, and other painted farm foods scattered on the side.

"No lights," Raquel said. "They're trying to be clandestine."

A few minutes later, the silver Ford's engine revved, then the vehicle followed the larger truck.

Perry huffed, "We'll have to hustle to catch them." She limped to the middle of the road, then turned on her flashlight after the truck turned right. Perry's ankle ached, and her face hurt worse. "Let's go."

The trio hurried to the intersection and looked east. They could see the distant taillights. They jumped into the trucks and pulled onto Fourth Street sans lights.

They continued slowly. The vehicles ahead of them turned left.

Perry put Raquel back on the speaker phone. "They went north," Perry said. "We have to punch it. Turn on your lights."

Sophia accelerated, the tires spinning in the dirt until they gained traction. "Why did they stop here?" she asked.

"Good question," Perry answered. "This is a dangerous place and Quapaw law enforcement patrols these streets looking for drug dealers, kids, and curious tourists."

As they approached the intersection of Fourth and Highway 69, Perry said, "Turn off the lights." She looked both ways. "No one is coming from north or south."

Sophia turned north and Raquel followed.

"Still a bunch of nothing," Sophia observed.

She looked to her left, then did a double take. "Hey, it's a gorilla."

"That's the shrine to the high school. They won the state football championship."

"That's no small feat," Sophia said.

"I told you. This town used to be dynamic."

They passed East A Street and could see more slabs on both sides of the road.

Perry said, "Hundreds if not thousands of buildings all over the place in the old pictures."

"Damn," Sophia said. "These piles look scarier in the moonlight. Massive and deadly."

Raquel said, "It'll be daylight pretty soon."

"I think I broke my record for staying awake," Perry said.

"Hand me another one of those Monster drinks," Sophia said.

"Gross."

"I'll fall asleep without it."

"Where are we, y'all?" Raquel broke in.

Headlights shone in the distance. "Looks like a small car," Perry said. "Raquel, we're going to pull over on the right. It's a big area."

They parked on the broken cement and waited until the vehicle passed them.

Sophia looked at her. “Do you hurt?”

“Yes, Sophia, I do.”

Sophia waited a few beats, then said, “I can still see the taillights of the rig and that Ford.”

Perry hit the dashboard with her hand. “Go,” she said.

“They’re about to cross into Kansas,” Raquel said. “No more tribal jurisdiction.”

Perry sighed resolutely. “So what? We’re well out of ours.”

25

In another few seconds, Sean's brake lights shone.

The trucks turned left.

"Left?" Perry almost yelped. She looked at the map. "Shit. That road goes into the backroads of Picher. Right up to the base of some piles. They can take a right where the road stops but it goes north into Kansas and they end up taking back roads to, uh, nothing but pasture or grazing lands. And they might go past another dead town called Treece. It died the same death as Picher."

"Y'all . . ." came Raquel's voice. "Are we sure about where they turned?"

"Wait a sec." Perry consulted her map again. "I was wrong. They turned on the stateline road. East Tenth Road. That still goes past Treece but heads west."

They arrived at the turn, slowed, and continued to follow. The trucks in front of them stayed at twenty miles per hour. They passed a huge chat pile with a body of water at its base.

"That's Tar Creek," Perry said. "Where the residue flowed."

"And now it's all over my truck," Sophia said. "I'm afraid we inhaled poisonous dust."

The trucks in front of them suddenly braked and turned right.

"What the heck!" Perry exclaimed. She looked at her map. "There's no road here. Just a dirt road heading into the chat. And I don't see any structures on Google Earth."

"What do you want to do?"

"Stop." She consulted her map. "I don't see anything other than chat piles."

"Google Earth might not have been here in a while," Raquel chimed in. "There has to be a building in here."

"Just go slow so we can see where they went. Search to the right of this road."

Another fifty feet and Sophia said, "Look." A ten-foot concrete barrier spanned the width of the narrow dirt road.

Perry rolled down her window and looked down. "Tracks go around it. They ran over bushes and some small trees."

"All right. Do we follow in the trucks or walk?" Sophia asked.

"According to this map, they can't go too far before they hit a pile. I say pull up and park."

Sophia pulled forward until Perry said, "Stop. Right here. This is another road."

"You sure about that? Looks pretty overgrown."

"Just turn in here and park. We can go in on foot."

Sophia hesitated, then slowly turned onto the soft dirt and drove thirty feet. "I'm going to turn around so we face the main road."

"Go ahead," Raquel said. "I'm going to park closer to where we turned in."

Sophia backed up as far on the road as she dared, then turned the wheel and pulled forward.

Perry unbuckled her seatbelt. "Ugh." She rubbed her temples, then felt in her right pocket for her pill bottle. She pulled out two tablets and popped them into her mouth. Then she drained the Diet Sprite.

One of the tablets stuck in her throat. She gagged. It tasted bitter. Sophia handed her the energy drink. Perry took a swig and grimaced. As Sophia backed up again so she would miss a large dip on the side of the narrow road, the truck's back end suddenly dropped. The surprise fall caused the unbuckled Perry and the drink she held to fly upward. She landed hard, hitting her ass on the side of her seat. Liquid splattered over her face and onto the window. She banged her right elbow on the door armrest. The drink can in the cupholder flew out. Items in the back seat hit the doors.

"What the hell?" Sophia yelped.

The truck was still for three seconds. Then the back end began sliding slowly downward. Sophia started to open the door, then realized they were sinking so fast she might fall out and be crushed.

Sophia quickly gunned the engine. It was no use. The back wheels found no traction and the front ones could not pull the heavy truck forward. It continued to slide down.

"Oh shit," she said.

The front end was now at a sixty-degree angle to the lightening sky.

"Oh my God," Perry said quietly. She knew that some of the mining tunnels were more than thirty feet down. If this truck fell that far they could break their backs—or the truck could flip and the top could flatten. They couldn't stay in the truck long enough to find out.

Raquel jumped from her parked truck and ran over.

The truck settled another three feet.

Raquel stepped closer—as close as she could while maintaining a safe distance. The ground had caved in around the truck, allowing her to see into the darkness on the driver and passenger sides. She turned on her light.

"You're on support timbers," she said loudly. The light beam shot around the sides and front of the truck. "The truck broke at least one of them. Looks like the front wheels are on top of horizontal timbers—those aren't going to hold. Y'all gotta move."

An enormous crack sounded and reverberated into the truck. The big Ford F-250 plunged back another few feet. Perry yelped.

"Sophia, that was a post. We have to get out."

"How about we roll down the windows and climb out?"

"If this truck keeps moving we might slip and fall under it."

A light came through the windshield and blinded her. When the beam moved to Sophia, Perry could see Raquel's silhouette.

"Hey," Raquel said. "I can see the bottom. You might fall another ten feet."

Perry panted and looked at Sophia. She looked back at the light. Sophia grabbed her hand and squeezed. She squeezed back.

The truck slowly slid back atop the breaking support beams. As it moved, the angle became more pronounced. It went completely nose up, tilted to the right, and then began sliding backward again.

Sophia let go of her hand. "You better be buckled."

Perry quickly grabbed the shoulder strap and clicked her belt.

The truck shifted and the undercarriage scraped against something. From the pictures that Perry had seen of the Picher tunnels, it could have been a boulder or a heavy vertical support beam. She also knew that at some point many of the tunnels had become flooded with contaminated water. What if it continued to flow through the dark underground networks?

The vehicle continued to tip backward—then fell another two feet with a jolt, causing their heads to bounce off the headrests. Perry's pack flew upward along with her iPhone, used wads of Kleenex, food wrappers she had dropped onto the floorboards, and one of Sophia's half-eaten burritos.

"Oh God," Sophia said. "Are we done?"

"Roll down your window," Perry said. She pressed her window button, and instead of greenhouse heat she felt tolerable humidity. It was definitely cooler underground.

The engine continued to run.

"Y'all okay?" Raquel asked from above. Perry noticed that she was not shouting. Hopefully, the perps could not hear them.

"Just great," Sophia said. She leaned back into her seat, nostrils flaring.

"A fucking sinkhole," Perry hissed. She should not have taken the last two pills. She'd never felt like this before. The drug was altering her ability to speak coherently and she was nauseated.

"Move your asses." Raquel sounded like a Marine drill sergeant.

"How do we do that?" Sophia asked.

Perry unclipped her belt. She felt sluggish, but she knew what they had to do. "We have to exit through the windows. Get your stuff together." Perry reached behind her to find her pack, which now rested on the back window. She pulled out the penlight from her jacket pocket. "I got mine. We aren't getting back in this truck, Sophia. You got your weapons?"

"The ones on me, yeah. I need my pack—it's right behind me."

Perry pointed the light behind Sophia's seat. She reached for the pack and winced as the scab on her elbow split. She struggled to pull it forward between her seat and the shotgun locked vertically in the gun rack.

"You got another flashlight in there?" she asked as Sophia took her pack.

"I have two."

Perry looked at the shotgun between them. "We have to take that," she said. "And the AR. We can't leave those in here."

Sophia started to roll down her window and grunted.

"What's wrong?"

"I broke my finger."

"Which one?"

"Ring finger. Left hand."

"Let me see it."

"It's fine."

"All right," she exhaled. "Then get your shit together. Move."

Sophia grunted.

"Turn off the engine and lights," Perry said. "We gotta have the AR." She looked to the back seat. Sophia kept that weapon locked to the floorboard. "I'll give that to Raquel and you take this shotgun so we can get out of here."

"Electric lock." Sophia reached down to the lock on the floorboard.

When she glanced up, Raquel loomed fifteen feet above her. Perry shone her light outside her window and saw the wall of the tunnel at least twenty feet away. On Sophia's side, the wall was less than three feet from her window. Dark wood supports that looked like railroad ties were attached to the stone wall by long metal bolts. The beams had split lengthways, but there was room for a foot to stand on top.

There was no way out except to climb onto the windshield or exit through Sophia's window. "Sophia, never mind. We'll have to leave those. We won't be able to carry them. Just leave them locked."

Perry's pain dissipated and she felt a surge of energy, the same feeling she normally got after the initial drowsiness from the tablets wore off.

"Sophia, get on your knees in your seat and put on your pack. Then you have to go through the window and get ahold of that large beam."

Sophia hesitated.

"This is not one bit harder than you doing pull-ups," Perry said. Despite the pain meds flowing through her, she now felt impatient rather than mellow. "I've seen you do ten perfect pull-ups. You can do this."

With an inspired lurch, Sophia pushed off from the window-sill, as if rising from a Bulgarian split squat, and grabbed the taller beam with her right hand. Her right foot landed on the top of the lower beam. She looked up.

"Uh, Raquel," she said. "I got seven feet to go."

"Truth."

Perry put on her pack, then moved into the driver's seat and added her light to Raquel's.

"I see multiple handholds," Raquel said calmly. "You can use those handholds as footholds. Go."

Sophia did not respond.

"Sophia," Perry said calmly although she was feeling far from composed. "Sophia, we need to go. Move. You know what to do."

"Get your asses up here!" Raquel's voice was urgent this time.

The truck dropped again and this time the undercarriage protested. It sounded as if the oil pan had split. The next sharp snap told them that the back axle had broken. So they had not hit the bottom after all.

Perry looked up to see that Sophia had shimmied her way up the beams and stood with Raquel.

"Now, Perry," Sophia said.

Even without her many wounds, Perry knew that she did not have the same strength as the former Olympic thrower.

Perry followed the light that Raquel and Sophia shone on the beams. Neither of her colleagues said anything as Perry heaved herself up using the same beam that Sophia had grabbed. Instead of her hand grasping the back of the rotting wood, her fingernails slammed into the side.

The truck slipped once more, and then the window foothold slipped out from under her feet, leaving Perry hanging on to the wooden beam, biceps trembling with effort.

Perry's nails were tough—she kept them short and polished with Sally's Hard as Nails—but she felt them bending as she pulled herself forward. She had felt that pain once before, when she had clipped Ripley's leash and her dog took off like a sprinter before she had her wrist through the leash loop. Her lovely Ripley had bent her thumbnail backward in the process. The pain was intense and lasted the duration of her six-mile run. If she had stopped, Perry knew she would have cried and cursed. The run helped abate the shocking rip of her nail.

If all her nails pulled back as her thumbnail did that day, she would faint. She growled and quickly reached out with her left hand toward a rusted iron spike protruding from the wood. She pulled herself to it like the doomed Chrissy did with the buoy in the opening scene of *Jaws*.

"There's another handhold a foot above you to the right," Sophia yelled to her.

Perry reached for the timber that had rotted into several vertical pieces. Her hand grasped the splintered wood and she squealed. Despite the wood spikes in her palm, she pulled herself up and put her left foot on a horizontal slat. She reached up with her left hand and Sophia grabbed her wrist just as the wood underfoot snapped in half. Perry's partner yanked her up and over the lip of the pit with shocking strength.

Perry flipped over, the breath knocked out of her, and looked up at her colleagues.

"Let me see your hand," Raquel said. "Hold this light, Sophia." As Sophia kept the light on her partner's hand, Raquel pulled out two long splinters from the meaty part at the base of her thumb. "These came out clean, I think, but you also have a cut."

"Well, hell, what's another wound? I need a thousand more before I die, so I still have a ways to go."

"Now you, Sophia," Perry said as she stood. She took a few deep breaths to steady herself, then took stock of her condition. Everything burned. Raquel came into view and she looked in focus, although Perry knew that if she had to run she would not get very far. She took Sophia's light. "I don't think you have a broken finger, Sophia. It's dislocated."

"Don't set it," she panted. Perry understood her fear. What followed would hurt like hell.

She held Sophia's hand gently. "I won't." Then, before Sophia could blink, she did.

Sophia gasped, jerked her hand away, and bent over, her good hand on her right knee. To her credit, she did not yell.

"Wow," Raquel said.

"Oh God," Sophia moaned.

Perry pulled a roll of gauze from her pack. "Give me your hand."

Sophia regarded her. Perry thought she looked like a dog that was shocked her master had hit her.

Sophia panted but slowly held out her hand. Perry quickly bound the ring and pinky fingers together. "That's the best we can do for now."

"Let's go, y'all," Raquel said. "Same as before. They went down that other road."

After a few minutes of walking, Sophia muttered, "You call this a road?" She panted.

Perry took advantage of her partner's obvious distress. "Break time," she said, bending at the waist. She grasped a sapling tree with her left hand for support.

The other women stopped. Raquel kneeled and Sophia squatted as if she was pooping.

"What're you doing?" Perry asked her.

"Resting in maybe the oldest position known to man."

"Sleeping on your side or back is."

"I feel comfort in this pose."

"Congratulations."

Raquel ignored the banter. "What if the ground opens up again?" she asked.

"We climb back out," Perry answered.

The trio stood and followed the overgrown lane for several hundred feet. It was clear that several vehicles had passed this way recently.

After a few more minutes, Perry stopped. "Listen."

They heard a low hum. "The engine," Sophia whispered.

Raquel moved quickly ahead and then halted when she came upon what looked like a stream of white water.

"What the heck?" Sophia asked.

"It's chat water," she said. "It's coming off that pile." She pointed to the mound of deadly chat to their right. The watery stream of a light, powder-like substance had drifted across the road. And there were clear tire tracks running right through it.

"I don't want that stuff on me," Sophia said.

"Too late," Perry said. "We already inhaled it."

"Shhhhh," Raquel hissed.

They moved through the thigh-high brush until the path curved slightly to the left.

"Look," Raquel whispered.

At the base of the chat pile sat a metal structure measuring about fifty feet by twenty-five feet. It looked new. There was no rust streaking the sides and the white paint appeared unblemished.

"This might be a road maintenance building," Perry said.

The truck with food painted on the side sat on the south side of the building, while the silver Ford sat outside one of the garage doors. The only visible windows in the building were in the front door.

"We need to get some backup here," Sophia said. "There's at least two people in the building. We have to call—uh, who has jurisdiction here?"

"I'm not sure," Perry answered.

"We're in a different state," Raquel said. "I'll look it up in a sec.

"And then there's Rhonda," Raquel added. "She's gotta be in there."

"We think, but we aren't sure," Sophia said. "And there might be more people inside."

"True," Perry said. Her hand throbbed from the punctures and her ankle protested after the exertion of climbing. "We need to see what's going on inside that building.

"I'll look in the back," Perry said.

Raquel and Sophia stayed close to the wall while Perry moved to the back of the structure. There were no windows on the sides of the building, but the rear door that backed up to the chat pile had four small panes. Perry thought the placement of the door seemed useless. Who would walk out onto the contaminated leftovers of lead and zinc?

She wished she had a mask. *Too late now,* she thought. She slowly moved along the outer wall until she reached the door. The panes were filthy. A beam shone through a comparatively clean swipe across the middle of the left pane on the bottom. She peeked through.

A few seconds later, Perry was motioning for Raquel and Sophia to look.

"Two men," Raquel whispered.

Sophia squeezed in. “One is Poinsettia Sean,” she said. “Fits his description.” He stood about six feet tall and was dressed in a black T-shirt and slightly baggy jeans.

Raquel said, “And that must be Rhonda.”

Perry nudged her aside and peered in again. Rhonda wore jeans and the same tight blouse and high ponytail. “It is.”

“Look in the corner,” Raquel whispered.

Perry looked down and squinted. “Those wooden boxes?”

“Yes. Do you know what’s in there?”

“Flash-bangs.”

“You’re kidding?” Perry looked again. “How do you know?”

“I’m a Marine. And the lettering on the side reads ‘flash-bang grenades.’ ”

Perry snorted.

“I think the two bigger boxes might be grenades. And take a look by the wall.”

Perry did look. Then she glanced back at Raquel. The white sclera of her eyes shone bright in the moonlight.

“Long crates. Long guns?”

“At least. There’s a lot more. Look to the right.”

Perry saw a dozen stacked crates that were a bit smaller.

“Boxes of some kind of ammo,” Raquel said.

“Where did they get all that?” Sophia asked.

“Good question,” Raquel answered. “Central American cartels get all sorts of weapons, including grenades and flash-bangs, in Mexico. Probably surplus military items.”

“How do you get across the border with a truckload of weapons?” Sophia asked.

“There is always a way,” Raquel said.

“So they’re also running weapons,” Sophia said. “Damn.”

“Dels Billy first,” Perry interjected.

“What do you want to do?” Sophia asked.

“Besides grab all three of them?” She sighed. “Is this locked?”

She put her hand on the door handle and gently turned, then released her grip. "It's unlocked."

"Call the Quapaw marshals," Sophia said again. "They're the closest."

"It's not their jurisdiction," Perry countered. "We're in Kansas."

"They'll come," Raquel said. "I looked it up. So will Miami and Kaw Nation police as well as the Cherokee County, Kansas, police. We don't know who's in that rig. We might need ambulances. And the fire department."

Perry ground her teeth. Raquel was right, although she felt like the three of them could arrest Sean, Rhonda, and the mystery guy themselves. And more importantly, they needed to find Dels Billy.

"All right," she said. "Make the calls."

26

Raquel and Perry looked through the window again. The smaller man said something to Sean and Rhonda. Then the two men started toward the crates. Rhonda, on the other hand, quickly moved to the front door. She looked back at the two men and then appeared to take something from a pack by the door. As soon as she got it, she opened the door and ran out.

"What the . . ." Raquel exclaimed, then quickly moved to the corner of the building to peek at the front.

From where Perry and Sophia stood behind the building, they could easily hear Sean yell, "Rhonda! What the fuck? Where you going?"

The silver Ford F-250 rumbled to life. The detectives moved to the corner where Raquel was standing.

Rhonda gunned the engine. If she could have laid rubber, the truck would have left streaks twenty feet long. Instead, the wide back tires threw clods of dirt and rocks against the front of the metal building.

"Damn bitch!" Sean yelled after her, then he turned and slammed the door.

"I'll get her," Raquel said. "And I'll call the Quapaws when I get to my truck." Then she sprinted down the road.

"Now what?" Sophia asked.

"Front door," Perry said as she drew her Glock.

Both women rounded the building to the front, then Sophia moved to the metal door and put her hand on the knob. She positioned herself against the wall.

Perry started to tell her to stop, that they needed to know where the second man might be. In an instant, Sophia looked at Perry and mouthed, "One, two, three," then she opened the door and rushed in, her Glock pointed ahead of her. Sean stood in the middle of the room, his hands down. Perry followed, her eyes darting around the space, looking for the other man.

Two portable LED work lights sat on opposite sides of the building and shone on different spots. The illumination was not great, but she could see. Sean seemed to be a shadow. Dark clothes, dark eyes, and malevolent.

"Detective Sophia Burns," she started. "Oklahoma City homicide. Hands up, Poinsettia Sean Billy," she said.

Perry assessed his stance and the position of his hands, and then her eyes went back to his face.

Sean followed her gaze and smiled. Perry would not allow him to see her anger. She saw that he had at least three red streaks across his cheek. Someone had clawed him. Good. She hoped it had been Dels. She started to make a snarky comment and thought better of it.

"Where's the other one?" Sophia asked.

"Right behind y'all," came a nasally voice.

Perry closed her eyes, knowing what was coming. She turned her head and saw that the short, longhaired man held a Browning BDM semiautomatic pistol. He looked and sounded like the men on the *Swamp People* alligator hunting show, which Troy often watched. This one had a ghastly open wound on his cheek and nose, like a small gator had bit him.

She did not move.

The small man pointed the pistol at Sophia's temple.

"We got a camera outside, dumbasses," he said. "Throw your guns over there." He motioned with his chin to the open space on his right.

Neither woman moved.

"If you don't . . ." He took a few steps sideways so he had a clear shot at Perry's face.

Sophia sighed, then let her Glock 23 dangle by the trigger guard. The small man took it and flung it away, then stepped back.

Perry's eyebrows furrowed. She was not going to give up her weapon if she could help it.

"Toss yours over there too," he said to Perry.

She did not comply.

"Did you hear me?"

Perry did not respond.

He shook his pistol. "Toss the damn gun!" he yelled.

Perry nodded and looked at her pistol. She made a show of imitating Sophia and allowed it to hang from her finger. Sean still had not moved.

The small man cursed again, stepped forward, and took the pistol. He tossed it next to Sophia's weapon. *Thank God those didn't fire accidentally*, she thought.

"Legs too!" he barked.

Sophia sighed and slowly pulled up her left pant leg and using two fingers removed the Springfield Armory Hellcat pistol.

"Toss it!" the swamp man ordered.

She did. Perry did not move.

"You too, missy."

Perry stilled for a beat, then lifted her right knee and her pant leg. She did the same as Sophia. "Throw it over there," the twitchy gunman barked.

Perry's heart raced. If something bad was going to happen, it would within the minute. She flung the pistol, silently hoping it would not fire. When the small man looked to Sean for approval, Perry swiped at the end of the man's weapon with the palm of her left hand, hitting it hard enough to send it flying. She winced at the sharp pain of the metal against the laceration at the base of her thumb.

"What the fu—" the small man barked.

Sophia took two steps and tackled him. They both grunted as they slid several feet across the smooth concrete with Sophia on top, as if the smaller man were a sled.

Perry heard them gasp and hiss as she faced Sean, who continued to watch her, his hands at his sides. She still did not see a gun. Perry stood between him and the five weapons lying twenty feet out of reach.

Now what? Perry thought as she considered the man in front of her. He observed her with disquieting calm.

The blood rushing through her head sounded like the fast water in the log flume at Six Flags over Texas. Nico had insisted on sitting in front with Olyve right behind him. Perry thought she might escape getting wet, but the splash-down covered her and Troy, who sat at the end. Poinsettia Sean continued to stare at her, his head slightly cocked. She wondered if he was going to charge her or wait for her to make a move. Perry would wait him out.

Her sinuses were congested from the chat dust and she breathed with her mouth open. It occurred to her that the chat they'd driven through was already at work making the cells in her nasal cavity cancerous. Perry's thoughts swirled and Sean smirked as if he could read them.

Sean finally reached behind his back with his right hand. Perry's eyes widened, expecting him to pull forth a gun.

She wore her bulletproof vest and that would protect her chest, but it would not protect her neck, limbs, face, underarms, or any body part below her navel. These were the same thoughts she had every time she donned the vest. Two years ago, a colleague had been shot in the axillary artery under his armpit. A lucky shot—from the viewpoint of the assailant—but a deadly one for the officer.

If Sean had indeed assaulted Lee Robinson, kidnapped Dels Billy, and killed his own brother and Teresa Bennett, Perry knew that he had it in him to do anything. This man did not expect to be caught, but here they were. And his woman had just left him. Sean appeared to be a killer unconcerned about family. He certainly would not respect law enforcement.

Perry felt her strength waning. The pain meds were running through her system, but she also knew that was a deceptive feeling. Even if Sean had not tried to run her down almost thirty hours prior, her exhaustion would have weakened her.

In the few seconds that she mulled over her predicament, Sophia and the small man continued to roll on the floor. She could hear their grunts.

"You're under arrest, Poinsettia Sean Billy," she said.

He did not respond.

"Where is Dels Billy? In the back of that rig?"

"Dels?" Sean repeated in a baritone voice. "Why would Dels be in the truck?"

"You killed your brother. And Teresa Bennett."

"Why would I kill my brother? And who is Teresa Bennett?"

Perry digested that. For a few seconds she wondered if there was some other assailant involved.

A loud crash sounded behind her. A quick glance revealed that her partner and the smaller man had collided with the table. She swung her attention back to Sean.

He brought his hidden hand forward. It held a knife.

Oh shit, Perry thought.

Sean's weapon looked like a two-edged Gerber, but the

brand didn't matter. What registered for Perry was that in the scheme of knife fighting, her skills were minimal. Troy was right. She could dance around swiping at a tennis ball every day for years, but that was no comparison to a street fight. And if by chance Sean missed her neck and other extremity vessels, knives could cut through Kevlar. Her vest would not protect her vitals if his blade was sharp. She could only hope that he would not get close enough.

Perry quickly considered her opponent. If she weren't injured, she'd be thinking more clearly. She felt a wave of fear course through her because she also knew her body might not respond the way it should. He was at least four inches taller than she was and outweighed her by sixty or seventy pounds. They were built similarly. Rangy, long legs, and judging by his physique and the way he stood, Sean was a runner and lifted weights. Not heavy weights, just enough to maintain flexibility and agility. He moved more like a decathlete than a linebacker or a gym rat who just lifted for bulk and couldn't throw a punch. Perry sensed that this man could. She expected him to say "What ya got?" or something clichéd, but he was all business.

Sean the Murderer was agitated.

He stood in a corner, two feet from the north wall and four feet from the east wall, an angry killer with no place to go except forward. Such a man would be a determined person.

Perry visualized Sean kicking her, punching her solar plexus and thus disabling her, throwing her to the floor and strangling her. She bit down on her inner cheek. She had to put a clamp on her wandering imagination. It would do no good to create images of how she would die at the hands of a killer who knew how to wield a blade better than she did.

At least the pain meds took the edge off her anxiety. She tried to control her breathing and stay calm.

Sean slowly walked forward, moving his knife side to side in front of him as if he were hypnotizing a snake. Perry was no snake and he was not dazzling her. She acted like his movements scared her. They did, but not to the extent that he wanted.

The gasps and groans from the grapplers behind her sounded like something from inside an MMA ring.

Perry lifted her left foot up behind her so her pant leg fell back, then she slid the knife from its sheath. She lowered her leg and passed the knife to her right hand.

Sean stopped to consider this new development. While he scrutinized her, Perry flipped the knife so the tip of the blade pointed toward the ceiling. The hammer grip.

Sean opted for the ice pick grip, one often seen in movies when a person has no idea what they're doing—but Sean exuded confidence. Perry did not. Still, if Sean had expertise, he might try to stab her, but he would need to get closer than she would allow.

He raised his arm as if to stab downward. Quickly, Perry responded with a short horizontal slash, hoping to lacerate his forearm, but she only caught air. Instead of stabbing, he kicked out at her left leg. His foot connected with the oozing laceration on her thigh, and her left knee buckled. Unable to catch herself, she bent forward, stumbling. Taking advantage of her searing pain, he sliced diagonally across the back of her upper arm.

Her triceps stung, but she shook it off, immediately took three quick steps to her left, and twirled to face him.

Another crash sounded to her right and the lights dimmed. The two had knocked over one of the LED lights.

"Where is Dels?" Perry gasped. She felt warmth bloom on her arm where he had cut her. From the corner of her eye, she could see that the sleeve of her white shirt was now red.

Sean shrugged. "How would I know?"

"That's what this whole thing is about. You want her land."

Sean flipped his knife through his fingers casually, the same way Perry did with her Paper Mate pen when she was relaxed and thinking. She was so entranced by the smooth movement in his right hand that she nearly missed it when he threw the knife—straight at her. She dodged it, but just barely, the blade slicing her cheek and the top of her ear as it sailed past. Behind her, it skittered across the concrete floor.

Sean pulled a second knife from his waistband and with a hammer grip he lunged, the blade pointed at her face. Perry dodged, but this one cut along the length of her jawbone. She let out a cry. Sean was only inches from her.

Perry could not get her blade up to cut him, but, mustering her strength, she hit him with the handle on the side of his head.

Sean yelled and reached for his ear—she had hit him in the temporomandibular joint. Maybe even fractured it.

Sean roared and advanced, swinging the blade back and forth wildly. Perry danced backward with every step that he made toward her, until suddenly she found herself backed up to the boxes that contained arms and ammunition. Before she could sidestep, he growled and swiped the knife at her, slicing her left forearm. The pain spoke volumes: He had lacerated her from elbow to wrist.

She brought her knife up fast so that Sean took a step back, but not before she dragged her blade across his chest and arm. He grunted in pain and she scurried to her left, putting distance between them.

They glared at each other, then Sean looked down at his chest. A line of crimson expanded across his chest and upper arm where she had slit his shirt. Although her body ached as if she were tangled in an electric fence, she couldn't help feeling a bit of satisfaction.

But just as quickly as it came, it subsided. She knew that she was not going to get out of this alive if this fight continued. Despite his wounds, this angry man was stronger than her.

Sophia and the other man were still grappling, with no signs of one or the other winning, and there still were no sirens that she could hear. Where was Raquel?

27

Raquel watched the taillights of Sean's truck as she sprinted the four hundred feet back to hers. She arrived at her vehicle gasping and sweating, as if she had been doing burpees in a sauna.

Climbing in, she watched the taillights head east, back the way they had come. She assumed that Rhonda would take a right on Highway 69 and head toward Miami.

Raquel carefully steered onto the dirt road, mindful that a sinkhole might open its mouth and swallow her.

Once she hit the main road, she gunned the engine and held up her iPhone. She already had the Quapaw police contact info pulled up. She hit the call icon.

After two rings a female voice answered.

"Quapaw Police. If you . . ."

Raquel interjected. "This is Choctaw Lighthorse Officer Raquel Durant." She was still panting. After giving her badge number, she continued, "I am in pursuit of a person of interest in the murder of two people, the assault of another, and the abduction of another. I'm headed east on, no, wait, now south on Highway 69 into Picher. The person of interest is in a silver Ford F-250. Plate number one one two George Frank three eight. It belongs to one Poinsettia Sean Billy but is being driven by a Rhonda Paul."

Rhonda had punched the gas. Raquel continued: "Oklahoma City homicide detectives are outside a metal structure in Treece. Off Treece Road going west, approximately one point three miles in there's a road leading to the structure, which is about five hundred feet north of Highway 69. There are two cement road barriers pushed to the side to allow access. Send backup."

"We need to confirm your identity . . ."

"Shit," Raquel spat. She repeated her identification. "The silver Ford has turned left. No street sign but I see what might be a fire station on the right. I think she's headed into a chat pile."

"Ma'am, we need . . ."

"You need to get someone to that shed. The suspects have crates of what appear to be weapons and ammunition."

Raquel drew closer to the silver Ford. They passed two streets, neither with signs on their corners. Raquel could see that the chat pile loomed in front of the Ford, yet Rhonda kept going.

"Holy shit!" she yelped.

Rhonda missed the left turn and plowed straight into a pile of chat. The truck stopped awkwardly, as if it had run into a runaway truck ramp in the mountains, and then emerged onto rocks, one of which took out the oil pan and broke the differentials. The Built Ford Tough pickup came to a stop amid knee-high brush and streams of chat. Rhonda jumped out, ran around the open door, and headed across an empty lot that had once served as the foundation for a two-story home with a chicken coop and a cement pad for a carport.

Raquel exited the undamaged door of her modest truck, calmly locked her door, then sprinted after the blonde who seemed to have no plan other than to flee. Before Raquel could tackle Rhonda, the fugitive tripped over a metal bar that was once part of a teeter-totter and face-planted into the dry grass. Raquel was on her in a second. The Choctaw Lighthorseman officer spoke while she grabbed Rhonda's right hand and yanked it behind her back.

"Officer Raquel Hunter, Choctaw Nation Lighthorseman. Rhonda Paul, you're under arrest for the kidnapping of Dels Billy."

"No, no, NO!" Rhonda screamed. "I didn't do it. He made me go along with it."

Raquel didn't have her handcuffs or lights on her vehicle. She did, however, have her badge and ID. When the first Quapaw cruiser stopped next to her truck and the two officers jumped out, Raquel raised her hands, her badge in her left one. She still sat on Rhonda, who squirmed and cursed.

"Officer Raquel Hunter, Choctaw Nation," she said when the two men came closer. "This woman was fleeing. Did y'all get someone to that building?"

28

Perry knew that if she did not come up with a way to subdue Sean, this fight would end badly for her. The lacerations he inflicted stung and although she knew he had not hit a major vessel, all of his hits bled.

Sean was also breathing hard. He paced back and forth to catch his breath and to think about what to do next.

Perry had to hurry. Her left hand felt numb. That last slash had damaged a nerve.

Then, in the distance, a siren began wailing. Sean looked at her with wide eyes, then to the door. His truck was gone, but the big rig was still there. *Surely he is not thinking he could outrun the Quapaw police in an eighteen-wheeler,* she thought.

Sean glared at her and she knew he was going for broke now. He had to escape.

She visualized Dennis Archer, the high school wrestler who had won nationals. She and Troy had always followed Archer. Fast, never hesitating. Her breath quickened. Suddenly, she knew what to do.

Perry had earned her red belt in tae kwon do in college. In one of the tournaments she fought in Houston, she went up against a woman who had not lost a match in four years. Perry had stayed with Shirley Wiley until the last few seconds of the match, when her opponent suddenly executed a front kick that landed right between Perry's legs. The woman's instep hit Perry's genitals with such force that she lost her breath and fell to the mat. Such a simple yet devastating kick.

People unfamiliar with martial arts believe that the flashy roundhouse kicks to the jaw were the most effective moves. In reality, high kicks were chancy. They took too much time to execute if your opponent was a skilled fighter. They might kick your supporting leg out from under you, dislocate your knee, grab the elevated foot and break your ankle, or shift to avoid the kick and take one step forward, from where they would have a variety of options that could wreck your neck, face, and groin.

Perry's high roundhouse kick had always been effective while sparring in class and she'd racked up many tournament points with it, but there was no way she should attempt it in a street brawl when her opponent wanted her dead.

She thought as fast as her tired brain allowed. A kick to Sean's groin or knee would be most effective. He would expect the former.

When Sean approached her again, Perry feigned a kick to his abdomen. When Sean instinctively tried to block her foot with his arm, Perry quickly raised her foot without touching it to the floor and popped him in the nose with the toe of her shoe. Before he could fall, she lowered her leg and kicked him in the knee. Like the high school wrestler she so admired, she did not hesitate.

In shock, Sean dropped the knife, his hands going up to his broken nose. Before he could grow comfortable, she stepped in again and slammed his right temple with her left elbow. She yelped at the excruciating pain in her ulna.

Sean wailed, moving one hand from his ruined nose to his new agony.

Got him.

Perry's right hand drew back just six inches and she struck him in the throat with her middle knuckles.

As Sean croaked and gasped, Perry took hold of his hair with both hands and shoved his head down to meet her knee. His nose was already broken. Now it was crushed.

Sean slammed down on his back, hands over his face. He moaned as Perry fell on top of him, her legs astride his chest. She seized his right hand and dislocated his thumb. When he pulled that hand back to his face, she grabbed the left hand and broke two fingers. She was about to hit him again when she registered voices around her and strong hands grasped her lacerated forearm.

"Okay, enough," came the unfamiliar voice.

She tried again, but that strong grip restrained her downward strike.

"Detective!" boomed a male voice.

She turned her head to see two uniformed officers. The man's tag said ADAMS and in smaller letters underneath his name was QUAPAW MARSHAL. The tag of the tall, thin woman next to him read PORTIS.

Perry fell on her side next to Sean and pointed to her badge, which had somehow stayed attached to her belt. The energy she'd summoned to fight Sean had dissipated. Now she lay on the floor gasping like a fish on the bottom of a boat.

The male officer flipped Sean over while the woman took hold of his right arm and pulled it out from under him. Sean howled.

"Fuck that bitch," Sean said, although the words came out

"Fuh tha bitch." Perry thought he might have lost a couple of teeth.

"Quiet," Adams said as Portis handcuffed him.

Not that Sean could do much even without handcuffs. His ruined nose, battered TMJ, and assaulted throat caused tears to stream down his face. He was blind and in misery.

Marshal Adams knelt and assessed Perry. "You look like a walking rare steak," he said.

"Yakoke," she greeted. "You gonna kick me out?"

"Well," the young man began, "this isn't Quapaw land. So no."

The previous wounds on her face combined with the new lacerations that extended from her temple to her jawline—plus her sliced right ear, left forearm, and triceps—created an exquisite pain not unlike having barbed wire wrapped around her. She had endured a bout of shingles when she turned twenty-eight, but that string of activated nerves around her forehead and behind her ears felt like a gentle massage compared to these new aches.

"Get me up," she said. "Where's my partner?"

"She's okay," Adams said. "Hold still." The officer had a roll of gauze and began wrapping her arm. "This is all I had with me, but it'll help until the medics can tend to you."

She turned and saw Sophia sitting with her back against the south wall. Blood covered her face and she held her right arm with her left.

Another siren wailed in the distance.

The small gator man lay on his belly with his arms handcuffed behind his back. The man's face was turned toward Perry, his eyes unfocused. His face looked as bloody as Sophia's.

"Your partner took a fall and hit the back of her head on the concrete," Adams said. "And her elbow. That might be fractured. Ambulance is on the way."

"And him?" She pointed to the small man with her lips.

"Concussion at the very least. Your partner nailed him in the jaw. And the end of his nose is gone. There're a couple of teeth on the floor."

"Get me up," Perry said again. "Thank you Marshal Adams."

"At your service."

Perry thought he sounded like a man who was at her service until he wasn't.

"How'd you know we were here?"

"Raquel Hunter called. You should have called earlier."

Perry detected a hint of annoyance. She could not argue with that.

"This is not our jurisdiction. We are now in Kansas, so you'll have to deal with the Cherokee County sheriff's officers. We all work together. Still, it would have been a good idea to contact us before you, uh, barged through our land."

"I know."

Marshal Adams put his hand under her right armpit and lifted her. Perry stood and wobbled.

"Dels Billy," she said. "The missing woman. She's in the truck. The trailer." Her eyes watered. "She has to be," she said quietly.

"You're bleeding from, well, everywhere," he responded. Marshal Adams took her left arm and pulled apart the ripped shirt. "This is deep." He moved the hair that covered her left ear. "And so is that. You need stitches in both. And your jaw."

"I already took the pain meds." Impatient with his evaluation, she made her way to Sophia.

Her partner sat staring at the opposite wall. Perry knew that if she squatted she might not be able to stand again, so she bent over.

"Sophia," she said.

Sophia's gaze went to Perry's face. She studied Perry's cheeks, the long vertical laceration, her cut ear.

"Troy is not going to be happy about this, Perry."

"Ya think?" Perry pushed stray hairs from her partner's bloody face, then she heard more footsteps behind her and turned to see three more officers in different uniforms from the Quapaws'.

"Miami police will take them in," Adams said. "It's just a few miles south."

Sirens sounded.

"And here begin the jurisdictional debates," Sophia said.

"Yeah," Perry said. "I'm going to look in the truck."

"I know. Go."

Perry turned to Marshal Adams.

"Come on," she said.

"Are you kidding?" He gaped as he looked her up and down.

"Believe me," Sophia said in a loud voice, "if you want to have a happy life, just fricking do it."

Perry and Marshal Adams moved to the back of the rig. The red heavy-duty cargo lock lay on the bumper instead of linking the vertical locking bars.

"That means we can go in," Adams said, drawing his side-arm.

"It does." Perry put her hand on the rear bumper to steady herself. Adams noticed but did not comment.

"Here goes," he said. "Stand back."

Adams took hold of the right side of the door and pulled. A dim light poured out. So did cool air.

He looked inside. "What the . . ." He pulled down the short ladder with his left hand, climbed in, then put his weapon back in its holster and held out his hand to help Perry up the ladder.

They both stood at the edge, taking in the shocking scene.

"Oh my God," she whispered.

The two scanned the inside of the trailer. Chain-link dog kennels ran along one side and the back of the trailer. Two steps in and Perry realized that those were not four dogs sleeping on mattresses. They were people.

Marshal Adams hurried to the first enclosure. Perry limped to his side. They looked down at an unconscious black-haired woman lying on a thin, bare mattress.

They quickly moved to the second cage.

"Holy shit," said a voice behind them.

A man in a navy T-shirt and baseball cap had climbed the ladder. His shirt said MIAMI FIRE DEPARTMENT. "Jake Wilson," he said. "Paramedic." He eyed Perry. The blood was still running down her face and neck and drops hit the floor. The white gauze around her arm was already soaked with blood.

She turned back to the caged woman. "I'm okay," she said.

Jake eyed her with concern but decided against arguing. Instead, he went to the gate and found it padlocked. He squatted next to the fencing and watched the unconscious woman. Perry heard him speaking into his phone.

"Drugged," he said.

Perry limped to the next cage. This blond woman wore a plain homespun dress, something a grandma might wear. She looked to be in her early twenties.

"Where're the keys?" Jake asked.

The three glanced around but did not see any key chains hanging.

"Probably in the cab," Perry said. "Check there first."

Jake hopped out of the trailer and they heard his steps on the crunchy ground.

The third woman was dressed in tight jeans and a crop top. Her dark hair was a tangled mess and makeup streaked her tawny face. Like the other women, her chest rose and fell.

Alive, Perry thought.

She went to the fourth cage. This dark-haired young woman wore khaki pants and a black polo shirt with an insignia on her left breast.

"What's that say?" Adams asked as he moved around, trying to get a better look.

"Oklahoma Aquarium," Perry said.

The woman moaned.

"Can you hear me?" Perry asked loudly.

The woman moaned again. This time it sounded like a sob.

"Hopefully these are the right keys," Jake said as he jumped back into the trailer. He went to the first cage. Perry heard the keys jingle, but her eyes moved over the cages.

She stared down at the awakening woman, then put her forehead on the fencing and closed her eyes. Her energy flowed out of her along with her blood.

She turned to face the two men.

"Dels Billy isn't here."

29

"If they left Dels where I think they did, we're gonna need a ladder," Perry said.

"Where is that?"

"We saw the trucks backed into an empty lot in Picher. There would be no reason for them to be back in there other than to hide or to hide something. In a tunnel."

Marshal Adams paused before saying, "Oh man. I hope not. This whole place has the potential to become a sinkhole. No one's supposed to go back here." He thought for a moment, then opened the passenger door. "Get in," he said.

Perry limped to the side of his cruiser and put her left hand on top of the vehicle. She stopped and took a deep breath.

"You okay?"

"Yes," she snapped. She gingerly turned and sat on the seat, then slowly bent her knees and lifted her legs. "I'm in."

Marshal Adams shook his head but said nothing. She closed her door.

He turned on the lights and sirens as they led the two other patrol cars. They quickly realized that the road was too narrow to accommodate the number of Miami and Cherokee County police cars headed toward them.

"Let them park, then we'll go," Perry said. "My partner's truck fell in a sinkhole not too far from here."

"What? Where?"

"On the other side of those trees." She pointed to the west.

"This is not a safe place either," the marshal said as he picked up his radio to inform the Cherokee County dispatch that there was now a police truck underground in Treece. "None of it is safe."

Once the other vehicles parked, he proceeded to the road, then reached Highway 69.

"Turn right," Perry said.

"I know. This was downtown Picher," Marshal Adams said.

Perry dabbed her face with a Kleenex. The blood still seeped and the paper stuck to her. "Did you see it before, uh, all that happened?"

"Oh yeah. I played on the chat piles with my brothers and sisters. We used sleds."

She didn't know what to say to that. The blood oozing from her arm felt as if it were draining the life out of her. She saw that it had leaked through her bandage and colored the white gauze bright red. She wondered how pissed off Troy would be when he saw her. So far, Marshal Adams had not mentioned the reality that his passenger seat was now turning red.

Now that the sun had started to rise, she wondered if she would see any trace of the two trucks from last night. The thick trees blocked the sunrise, leaving the roads in shadows. Even if it were the middle of the day, she was not sure she could identify where they had parked without tracks. She rolled down the window and the heat rushed in.

"This all looks the same," she said.

"Pretty much," Marshal Adams agreed.

She leaned her head out and squinted at the side of the road. "Slow down."

He did. "See anything?"

She didn't respond for a few seconds. Then she said, "Here. I see indentations of the big rig." The vehicle moved past the old driveway. "And where they pulled out. Yeah. They were backed in right back there."

Marshal Adams stopped and turned off the siren. He kept the lights flashing, as did the two other drivers. A third patrol car marked MIAMI POLICE pulled up behind the others.

"And you think your girl is in here someplace?" Adams asked again.

Perry opened the door. "She has to be." Her knee buckled when her foot hit the dirt. She pitched forward and caught herself with her hands. Pain shot up her arms from her wrists. She gasped and quickly prayed that she had not fractured them as skateboarders often do when a rock gets caught under a wheel.

"Shit. Fuck. Damn," she muttered, then realized that she had adopted the phrase she'd heard Dels use in the video.

Adams jumped out and ran around the front of the car to her side. "You okay?"

Perry stood and shook her hands. Both palms were tender from her encounter with Sean's truck and the tunnel beam's splinters. Now they had little stones stuck into the flesh.

"She's here," Perry said.

He did not argue.

The four other officers quickly got out of their vehicles. All had flashlights except Perry, who'd left hers in the metal building.

"Hey," yelled Marshal Portis, who had been in the other Quapaw vehicle. "What're we doing?"

"Searching for a hole in the ground," Perry said. "I think those perps put a woman named Dels Billy somewhere around here."

She limped slightly ahead of Adams.

"Wait a sec!" the woman said. "Don't just rush in. This place is unstable."

"This is true," Adams agreed. "Hold on. Everyone look around you."

"Care to fill us in?" asked a gray-haired man in a Miami Police uniform.

Perry sighed. "Those perps back at the metal building are trafficking women and guns. We're trying to find a young Choctaw woman named Dels Billy," she said as she moved down the rutted dirt driveway.

"There's nothing here," the Miami officer said, his arms wide.

Perry ignored him. She could see the broken foundation where a house used to stand. A few bricks of a chimney remained, as did a broken pipe that stuck up through the fragmented concrete on the east side. Perry wondered if that pipe was for the clothes washer or a shower. Maybe a sink.

As the sun rose, she could see more detritus of the former home. Two clothes hangers lay amid the brown grass. Part of a buckled swing set leaned against the remains of a sagging garden fence. What might have been a teddy bear continued to deteriorate under a thirsty redbud tree. Perry knew that spending time in Picher would propel her imagination into working overtime. And not in a good way.

Behind the broken foundation lay another flat spot.

"What was that, I wonder?" asked Portis.

"Detached garage or maybe a barn," Adams offered.

"What's that to the right?" Perry limped to a round area of foliage that didn't match the brown grass around it. "You can see that the big rig backed up here." She pointed to the ground next to the foundation.

She limped closer to the round spot. "This isn't real grass," she said.

The others hurried over. Adams squatted and inspected the deep green grass that up close looked plastic. “This is fake,” he said.

Perry fought a wave of dizziness. She took a deep breath and said, “There’s a bunch of dried grass and little branches on top to try to conceal it.”

Adams took hold of some of the plastic grass and pulled up. “It’s heavy.”

The other officers walked the circumference of the ten-by-fifteen-foot anomaly.

Sunlight streaked through the treetops. Beams landed on the circular area.

A sunbeam hit Perry’s eyes and she winced.

The gray-haired officer glanced at Perry, back at the ground, then did a double take at her face. She thought he would ask if she was all right, but instead he said, “Let’s lift this.”

The officers took the eastern edge of the cover and lifted. They peered underneath.

“Oh my God,” said Adams. “It’s a pit.”

He shone his light into the darkness, then back up under the cover. “There’s a couple of two-by-fours supporting this cover so it won’t fall in. I think we can throw this back.”

Perry’s side ached where Sean had kicked her, more so than her other pains, though she hadn’t noticed it much until now. This pain was high on her side, maybe her floating rib. *What if he broke it?* Well, if he did, he did.

Her heartbeat was too fast just from walking, and Perry knew she had to hurry. Her combined injuries and fatigue might take her down no matter how hard she willed herself to stay alert.

The officers tossed back the cover and it lay doubled over, the underside revealed.

“The bottom is about fifteen feet down,” Perry said.

"I agree," said another Quapaw marshal.

Perry lay on her belly and peered into the pit as Adams shone the bright light all around the cavern. It seemed vast and smelled of cool earth.

"Dels Billy!" she screamed. "Law enforcement! Are you there?" Her voice cracked on the last word.

30

The first thing Dels felt was the cloying dampness. Then the sharp throbs in her ankles jolted her into coherence. Her nose felt stuffy, and when she tried to open her mouth something stuck to her lips.

Dels felt the prick of panic. She normally used Afrin at the first hint of congestion. She knew she needed to wean herself off it, but it worked so quickly that she carried a bottle with her everywhere. Her mother used the stuff ten times a day.

Dels tried again to get air through her mouth but realized that strong tape covered the lower half of her face. Also in those few seconds, she understood that her hands were tied behind her back and her ankles were tightly bound together as well.

Fear caused her to freeze before her brain surged to attention. If she didn't get the tape off her mouth she would suffocate. If she began crying . . . well. *Don't,* she thought.

Dels lay in darkness. Not on the mattress with the buttons. This surface was hard. A floor, maybe. Her fingers moved like a curious octopus, inspecting the surface. No, this was not a floor. No carpet, tile, or laminate. She was on dirt. It smelled of earth. Damp dirt.

She pondered what that meant. Dirt.

She looked up and around with her left eye. She knew that her right eyelid had swollen shut. No light at all. It was complete darkness. No sounds either.

Her memories flooded through her like water pushed downstream from a Montana spring thaw.

Uncle Poinsettia Sean.

Land's gonna be mine now.

He hit me. My uncle hit me.

She recalled slapping him first. No, that wasn't right. She'd *clawed* him.

Land's gonna be mine now. His refrain reverberated even louder in her head.

She had to get the tape off her mouth.

I need to sit up.

She bent her knees to her chest, then rolled to a sitting position, her legs in front of her, knees under her chin, hands behind her back.

Her nostrils flared as she tried to stay calm. As she thought about what it might be like to suffocate, she also wondered what might be in the dark with her. Snakes? A bear? Where was she? She had no idea how long she had been unconscious or where these men had taken her. Her right nostril seemed to be closing.

Hurry.

Dels didn't care for yoga or organized exercise like aerobics. She ran, lifted weights, and did a lot of stretching. Now she would see just how flexible her body could be.

She rounded her shoulders to sit on her hands, the wrists bent awkwardly. But she was stuck—she couldn't get her hands any farther. She let out a cry of anguish and panted through her nose.

Stop it.

Keep going.

She pushed her hips up as if doing a mini glute bridge and groaned as she struggled to get her hands past her ass and under her knees.

First she paused to calm herself. She knew that if she didn't hurry her nasal passages would close.

Dels squeezed her heels as close to her butt as she could manage in order to get her wrists under and in front of her feet. The problem was that the zip tie had been pulled so tight that her wrists had no wiggle room, and her ankles were bound as tightly as her wrists.

With a growl, she forced her hands past her large feet. Now her fingers went to the duct tape over her mouth. As she suspected, the strip wrapped around her head.

Assholes!

Her hands found the top of the strip. She tried to peel it off with her nails but the tape was adhered to her face and would not come off without tearing her skin.

She panted. She tried again with the bottom edge of the tape and this time managed to roll it upward over her bottom lip.

Air!

She rolled it over her top lip. She wanted the tape off her. She got a bit of it in her mouth and gnawed on the sticky tape until she tore it. Then her fingers tore the tape in half, taking skin with it. Now it hung down on both sides of her face to her collarbones. She would have to deal with her hair later. Maybe she could use olive oil. When Dels was a child, she once fell asleep with a wad of gum in her mouth, which ended up in the hair at the back of her head. Her mother had used a combination of selective snips and olive oil to remove it.

Sean P., you asshole.

Now that she could breathe, Dels sat and tried to figure out her predicament.

Darkness. No sounds except for a breeze. She knew that this cool, damp place was underground.

Dels felt a second wave of panic. She had to get out of here, but first she needed to untie her wrists and ankles. She knew how to get out of a zip tie around her wrists because Bake made her watch a video of zip-tie escape maneuvers. She had barely paid attention and had even asked Bake why in the world she needed to know this information.

He'd kissed her and said, "Watch it." She did.

It would be easier if there was space between her wrists, but her uncle had pulled the ties cruelly hard. So tight that her hands were crossed. She took a few deep breaths, then forced her hands to turn so that her inner wrists touched. Like the tape on her face, the zip ties took blood. She could feel it.

"Let's do this," she whispered.

She raised her arms to forehead level, then, in one quick movement, forced her elbows to either side of her torso. Sharp pain shot up her arms as the zip tie snapped.

"Fuck you, Sean," she yelled.

She waited for a response. There was only a brief echo. So she was in a *large* underground area.

Now for her ankles. As she lay back on the uneven dirt, she bent her knees so they were as close to her chest as she could get them. As quickly as she'd broken the wrist ties, she thrust her legs forward and forced her feet apart. She felt the sting on both ankles as the plastic gave way.

Now that she was free, Dels wasn't sure what to do. She didn't know where she was. Even without a swollen right eye, the area was pitch-black. She felt the ground around her and confirmed again that she was sitting on dirt.

Her right eye seemed to have puffed more after she awoke.

Now she felt that swelling in her right nostril and cheek. No doubt her uncle had hit her in retaliation for her raking his face. She smiled.

A deep breath caused her to cry out. She reached under her shirt and didn't feel any cuts, but her underarms, breasts, and scapulas ached. Had her uncle also hit her around her torso? Worse, with every heartbeat her feet and ankles throbbed from the zip-tie cuts.

Dels heard a distant squeal. Or maybe it was a bell. Then the cool, damp silence settled around her once more.

She moved her legs to the side and bent her knees. She placed her palms on the ground and put her right leg underneath her with the intention of pushing herself up to stand. Her body weight was too much for her injured right ankle to bear. What had happened to it?

Dels tried the same maneuver with her left leg. That foot withstood her weight, but it felt sprained. How could she walk? Maybe she could hop on one foot, but where was she supposed to go in the darkness?

She stood still, thinking that perhaps a breeze would tell her the way to the entrance. All remained quiet, with just a hint of moving air. Was this a cave? She knew of stories about underground passages, where her ancestors used to live. According to the old stories, Choctaws and Chickasaws were at one time the same group. They lived underground, then emerged from Nanih Waiya, a real site in Mississippi. Two leaders arose: the brothers Chahta and Chicksa. The people separated, following the two brothers, and eventually became the Choctaws and Chickasaws.

The underground world is vast, her mother told her, and stretches under the entire country. The Choctaw grasshopper goddess, Eskeilay, still rules there over her minions, the human-sized ants and crawfish. Dels shuddered at remembering that Eskeilay's other name is Mother Dead.

Surely, she was not underground where Mother Dead would find her.

Her good eye roamed the darkness, fearful that she might see glowing red eyes.

Sweat stung her face, which meant she had more broken skin than just her ripped lips. Like many other Choctaws who knew the old stories, she considered their truths. Sometimes when she heard the hooting of Ishkitini, the great horned owl, she panicked, because that meant a bad event was imminent. She had no ill feelings toward owls and had in fact once rescued a young barn owl that had been hit by a car. Nevertheless, the old stories passed down through the generations held meaning, and Dels believed she must be mindful of them. When thunder boomed that meant Heloba the Thunderbird had laid eggs and they were rolling around. Heloba's mate, Melatha, created lightning when he tried to keep the eggs from falling. Those sounds always caused her to look to the sky.

She put her right foot forward. For a second she thought she would walk, then the pain shot up to her knee and she dropped to her hands again. When she fell forward, her head hit something sharp. She quickly sat back and put her hands to her forehead. It burned as if a wasp had stung her.

She put her hands out in front of her and felt the same chain-link fencing that had held her in the back of the truck. She grasped the fencing and pulled herself up, then used it as a support as she hopped on her left foot until she reached a vertical bar. Then she felt another. Two vertical bars.

"A door," she said aloud.

She ran her fingers along the length of the metal until she reached the horseshoe-shaped latch. She tried to raise it but it would not move more than a quarter inch. Soon she realized why. It was padlocked.

Dels stifled a cry, then reached up. If this was a basic dog kennel she could just climb over, but the top of the kennel was another section of chain link and her exploration revealed that the horizontal section was chained to the rails of the vertical walls.

This was the same way that she and Bake secured their chickens from varmints.

Dels leaned against the fence and took several deep breaths. Last year she wanted the chicken pen under the shade of a cottonwood, so she and Bake put on gloves and stood on opposite sides of the four-sided fencing. Bake lifted and inched his side forward, then Dels did the same on her side. They had not wanted to remove the top because it was covered in bird netting, so that made the job heavier and more arduous. The fencing was heavy, but not impossible to lift.

Dels squatted and worked her fingers under the bottom horizontal rail. She took a deep breath, made sure her back was straight, and used her leg strength to stand. She managed to lift the fencing five inches before it stopped. She gave it another heave and heard the top thump against something. Dels dropped it with a clang.

She reached up and worked her right hand through a section of the fence. Her fingers felt a solid ceiling of rock above her.

Any idea she might have had about flipping the cage over was not going to work. And she had nothing to set the bottom horizontal rail on so she could crawl under. The dirt floor was too hard to dig through.

She began to cry.

31

"Dels!" Perry screamed again.

Marshal Adams shone the light around. Across the floor and back and forth across the walls. He brought the light back to the edge.

"There's a ladder," he said.

Perry pointed. "I see an indentation here in the ground. I think there was also a rope."

The other officers hurried over and shone their lights.

Perry looked behind her and saw a tree five feet from the hole. "The rope was attached to that," she said. She dropped to her belly again and screamed into the darkness. "Dels! Dels Billy!" Her voice had become hoarse. "The rope is hanging over the second rung," she said. "You might want to get it."

"I think they climbed down the ladder and maybe lowered something with the rope."

"We called the volunteer fire department," Portis said. "Their truck is smaller and can get in here with a ladder we can trust."

Perry squirmed back from the edge of the hole and turned over. "Where the hell is it?"

"They have our location," Marshal Portis said. "Shouldn't be long."

"Have any of you been underground here?" Perry asked. She lay on the ground, the position alleviating her pain a bit.

"I have," said one of the Quapaw marshals. Perry turned her head to look at him. He appeared to be about twenty-five. "I went into a hole searching for a kid about two years ago. Where the grocery store used to be."

"Was he there?"

"No. He was hiding at a friend's house after they found out his mother had reported him missing. Kids aren't supposed to ride their bikes around here."

"What's it like down there?"

"All the lights strung on wires overhead are out. A lot of them are down and on the dirt. It's dark and it just gets darker farther in. There's been a lot of deterioration from the ceiling, so the ground is uneven from falling dirt and rocks. Old zinc-mining cart tracks run all over the place. You have to wear a mask. Or you should. This place is still contaminated. All those chat piles you see came from underground."

"Also a few years ago there was a large-scale effort to find the missing Welch girls," Marshal Portis added. "One of the men who killed those girls lived right over there." She pointed to the west. "On College Street. Nothing's there anymore, by the way. That's where the girls were last seen. They drained the ponds across the road from where Phillip Welch lived, thinking they might be in there. Then they dug around a lot. Nothing."

"They could be anywhere under here, Eileen," Adams said.

"I know."

No one else said anything.

The unpleasant silence was broken by the roar of a large vehicle quickly approaching.

"They're here," Marshal Adams said.

Perry got to her feet and wobbled.

"You really should sit this one out, Detective," Eileen Portis said. "You're hurt worse than you think you are."

Perry ignored her and looked to the shiny red brush truck. Three men jumped out, all in T-shirts and jeans. Two started to retrieve their heavy coats.

"It's about fifteen feet deep," Perry yelled to them. She looked back into the hole. Marshals Portis and Adams went to the newcomers to explain the situation.

When the men arrived at the edge of the hole with the ladder, Perry said, "The woman I believe is down there is about my size. I weigh one thirty-five. Maybe the guy had her over his shoulder, but he's my height and maybe one ninety. I'm afraid that if he couldn't balance her, she might have been dropped in. If that's the case, we'll need a stretcher. Or maybe she was lowered with the rope."

"We got a rescue stretcher," one of the men said. "And the ambulance is coming."

"All right. Let's find her."

Two of the firefighters slowly lowered one end of the ladder and extended it until it reached the bottom.

"This is a collapsed spot," a man with bedhead and stubble said. "We can't bring the truck closer, so this is gonna have to do."

Perry registered more vehicles arriving. She was too intent on getting underground to see who was driving them. Instead, she focused on making her painful way down the ladder. She gritted her teeth with every step down as she stared at the dark wall in front of her and trusted that her feet would hit each rung. Her legs and arms held up until she reached the bottom. She would keep going until they found Dels Billy.

"I don't think you need to be doing this," Marshal Adams said once they had reached the tunnel floor.

The officers shone their lights into the dark tunnel. It seemed to be an endless channel. She tended to agree with Marshal Adams.

"You sound like my husband," Perry replied.

"Same," Marshal Portis added.

"You too, huh?"

"Not as much. But he would prefer that I do something else. We can go along for months or even years without something happening and then once it does, well, we start all over with the arguments about how dangerous law enforcement is."

Perry laughed. So did Marshal Portis.

Perry stepped on something hard and her ankle turned. She used the small penlight donated by Marshal Portis and saw an iron rail. The light followed the straight line in the dirt made by parallel metal tracks atop wood ties. The line was almost completely covered in dirt.

"Watch out above your head," Adams said.

She shone her light above her and saw a few strings of electrical line. Thirty feet ahead of the officers was the wooden post where the lines attached.

"I doubt if those lines are live," she said.

"Probably not, but this entire place has a way of biting when you least expect it."

The officers moved slowly through the tunnel, the two firefighters behind them.

"Quapaw Emergency Medical Service on the way," came a female voice.

"Is that you, Erin?" Marshal Adams asked.

"Sure is. Matt too. We're down."

Perry turned to see two lights coming toward them.

"Cool in here," Perry said. "Feels good on my face."

"I bet," Adams said. "You're cut up pretty good. After we find this woman, you're going to the hospital."

"Yeah." After a few seconds she said, "I wonder what it feels like down here in winter."

"Don't wonder. After we get out, just let it go."

Perry didn't know if that would be possible.

He continued: "What happened here was devastating. People got sick. They lost their homes. When one of the residents wants to show their kids or grandkids where they grew up, what will they see? Nothing. The tribe is trying to clean up the town, but it's always going to be polluted and dangerous. And no matter how many warnings are posted, there's always someone wanting to come in and explore and get their butt in trouble."

Perry grimaced. She had been one of those trespassers several times, but at least she'd had sense enough not to wander off the roads.

"This is a reminder of what people can do," Marshal Adams continued. "Money, profit. To hell with who gets hurt."

"Amen," said one of the firefighters behind them.

"Happens all over the world," Perry muttered. "Dels!" she yelled.

Marshal Adams chimed in louder. "Quapaw marshals!"

"Miami Fire Department!" yelled another man.

A few beats of silence, then "Here!" came a voice from deep in the tunnel.

Adams gasped.

"Dels!" Perry screamed again.

"I'm here," came the response.

"Oh my God," Perry said. She started forward. After a few paces, Adams said, "Hold on! If those guys got her in there, then maybe they have a surprise waiting for us."

"Like what?" Then she visualized a tripwire and a bunch of arrows or maybe an axe flying toward them.

"Dels Billy!" she yelled. "We're coming. Stay where you are."

A distant "Okay" echoed off the tunnel walls.

The six officers and the firefighters and medics continued another fifty feet on the uneven dirt floor.

Perry coughed as she followed. On top of her recent lacerations, the older cuts and scrapes burned and reminded her that her body had a long way to go to heal. She would not be running to the lake for a few weeks, if not months.

Everyone shone their lights ahead, and then they saw her. Dels Billy sat upright on a wooden rail tie on one side of the tunnel inside a chain-link cage. The lights illuminated two more cages on the other side of the tunnel. There were a dozen crates like the ones in the metal shed stacked next to the wall.

All of the responders could see Dels's swollen face. Silver duct tape hung on both sides of her cheeks to her shoulders. As they drew closer, they saw that her lips were bloody and she was covered in dirt.

Dels held up a hand to block the bright light. A red line encircled her left wrist. She wore no shoes and her ankles bore the same red line as her wrist. Perry shone her light to the ground. Broken zip ties lay around her.

Perry rushed to the gate of her cage. "This is locked," she said. "Get a bolt cutter."

She turned to Marshal Portis. "Come here," she said.

Perry fixed her gaze on Dels. "Dels," she said quickly, "I'm Detective Perry Antelope. This is Marshal Portis from the Quapaw Nation Marshal Service."

Before she could mention the others, one spoke up, "Miami fire department."

"Quapaw EMS here," shouted a woman. "There's more up top waiting to get you home."

The young female paramedic made her way to the front of the crowd, then squatted next to the chain link to get a better look at Dels.

"My name's Erin," she said. "My colleague here is Matt."

The thirtysomething Asian American man standing nearby gave her a big smile. "We'll take care of you," he said. "Promise."

Dels coughed. "Thank you," she whispered.

"Hang on, Dels," Perry said.

"Where's my uncle Sean P.?"

"In custody," Perry said calmly.

"Are you sure?"

"Very sure," Adams said.

"What about the other creepy guy? The little one?"

"Him too," Perry said.

Dels sat back on her perch in relief.

"Dels Billy," Perry said. "Your team is waiting for you. Bake, Vera, Lee, Benny, Sealy, Issi, Worf, Xena, Gomer, and, and . . ."

Dels smiled and then began to cry. "Jezie," she said.

Perry moved her light to the ground. "Hang on, honey," she said.

The firefighter took off his pack. He unzipped the large compartment and took out a bolt cutter with short handles. "This will cut the chain link," he said, and got to work on the bottom links by the tension bar. "The lock's too big for this."

"Where do you feel pain?" Erin the paramedic asked. She scrutinized Dels's swollen eye. It seemed obvious where she hurt, but Erin wanted to know what injuries lay hidden under her skin.

"Everywhere. My ankles."

Perry's light revealed her swollen ankles and the ligature marks. Her heels were skinned and bloody.

"Under my arms," she added. "And my chest."

"Hang on," Perry said. The firefighter was already halfway up the fence.

"What's your name?" Dels asked him.

He smiled. "I'm Miguel."

"Thanks, Miguel," she said quietly.

Another few seconds and Marshal Adams grabbed the flopping fencing and pulled it back. "Clip that tension wire at the bottom," he said.

Another second and the paramedics were inside the cage with Dels.

"Let me look at your back," Erin said. Dels raised her T-shirt. A red rash ran across her back and under her arms.

Perry looked to Adams, then back to Dels. "Do you know how you got down here?" Perry asked her.

Dels squinted in the bright lights.

"My uncle hit me and I . . . well . . ."

"He knocked you out," Perry said.

Dels nodded.

"And you got him across the cheek."

Dels looked up. "I recall fighting back. I think that he might have . . . might have . . ."

Perry interrupted. "He'll have permanent scars." Dels would need to discuss her assault with the physicians.

Dels sniffed.

"And that little guy also looks pretty rugged," Adams added.

"I bit him."

Marshal Adams chuckled. "Good for you. And you got out of the zip ties."

"Dels," Perry started, "I think he lowered you down here

with a rope tied under your arms. And you were dropped. You landed on your feet."

"That would account for your ankle injuries and the rash around your chest," Erin said.

"My right arm," Dels said.

"It's skinned," Erin said. "Maybe you fell to the side and landed on your arm."

"He dragged me. My heels are burning."

Perry felt her anger rising but kept it in check.

"My uncle meant for me to be stuck down here." She sniffed. "And to die."

Yes, he did, Perry thought, but she said, "Let's get you out of here."

After strapping Dels to the stretcher, four responders carried her down the long tunnel, their headlamps lighting the way. Perry trailed behind them.

Sunlight illuminated the cave-in spot. Silhouettes of half a dozen people stood around the edge above them.

Dels lay still as officers hoisted her to the surface.

Perry gripped a ladder rung and wondered if she could climb. She felt more fatigued than the time she and Troy did a rim-to rim hike of the Grand Canyon several years ago in late June. The worst time of year for that trek. The last part of the hike from the Three Mile House to the top of the Bright Angel Trail was especially brutal. She'd thought she wouldn't make it.

She wanted to lie down.

"Just go slow," Adams said. "Then we'll get you to the hospital."

Perry stopped and focused on her wounded hands. "This whole area needs to be explored and photographed. No telling who else has been held down here."

"I know. We'll do it."

She started up and then put her foot back on the ground.

"They were going to leave her in here," she said. "Tied up. With tape over her mouth. They thought she wouldn't get out of the zip ties." She closed her eyes. "But even if she did get free of the ties, she couldn't get out of the cage. You saw it. She couldn't get out."

Adams studied the right side of Perry's face. Blood seeped through the remaining smears of Vaseline. It ran from her lacerated ear and covered her shirt collar. His gaze went to where her hands grasped the ladder rungs. Both shook slightly.

She continued. "You read about that spelunker who got caught in the Nutty Putty Cave in Utah? Late 1990s, I think. He got stuck in a narrow passage and was so jammed that rescuers couldn't get him out and he died. His body is still in there. The cave entrance is sealed, and he's still there."

"Detective—" Adams began. He thought she might be on the verge of an exhaustion breakdown.

"That's what I thought of when I saw Dels in the cage." Perry looked back at him. He saw that her eyes were bloodshot. The left one was halfway swollen shut.

Perry feared being trapped in a dark space with no way out. She flashed back to the time she'd panicked when she'd turned onto her belly while sleeping in a mummy bag. She could have easily flipped over, but her adrenaline caused her to pull her knees to her chest, then rise up. She split the zipper and tore the bag. A small thing, but the thought of being confined could send her into a dark mental state.

"What happened to that caver was not the same thing," he said. "We saved this woman. It's not the same situation at all."

Perry sniffed. "But if we hadn't saved her she probably would have died and no one would know except those men who did it to her. And that caver's body is still in the cave. And the Welch girls are probably down here someplace."

He sighed. She didn't know that he was part of the team

that assisted in searching for the lost Welch girls. "Detective Antelope. We need to get out of here. One step at a time." He motioned with his hand to where people stood watching them.

Perry took one glance back into the gloom, then started climbing toward the light.

32

Perry stared at the curtain partition on the other side of the Integris Health Miami Hospital emergency room. A young man moaned and cursed as he attempted to pass a kidney stone. After one loud expletive, his wife said, "Hush. Everyone can hear you."

He responded with a high-pitched "Argh" and "I don't give a shit!"

Perry wondered what it must be like to pass a rock through a penis. It sounded worse than what she was dealing with, but not by much.

Dels Billy suffered from a bruised cheekbone, one fractured and one sprained ankle, and numerous cuts, bruises, and rashes. A nurse removed the duct tape from her hair with olive oil and treated her torn lips with petroleum jelly. Her uncle Poinsettia Sean and his miscreant partner, Reginald Louis Swanton of Branson, Missouri, had drugged her, although with what had not been determined. Doctors also determined that she had been sexually assaulted.

Perry knew it would take time to heal the trauma of being abused and kidnapped by her uncle and sexually assaulted by one or both men.

Swanton's injuries included a torn cheek and the amputation of the end of his nose, which was inflicted by Dels, four broken front teeth exacted by Sophia's fist, and a skull fracture that resulted in cerebrospinal fluid leakage and bleeding. He was in a coma and would probably never wake up.

Poinsettia Sean Billy's fate had not been determined. Surgeons were into hour two of repairing a severed brachial artery in his left arm, a laceration across his chest that required over one hundred stitches, a broken nose, a fractured cheekbone, a dislocated right patella, and two broken fingers on one hand and a dislocated thumb on the other. All courtesy of Perry, who had unleashed her rage on a man who had caused so much pain to others. Perry smiled at the thought of the murderer and kidnapper trying to use crutches.

Now she lay listening to the wailing man as she waited for Troy to arrive. The lacerations from Sean's knife required seventy-two stitches. Twenty-three along her jaw, twelve on her right hand, five over her right eye, two in her ear, and thirty along her right arm. The physician and two interns who assessed her many other wounds expressed shock that she could walk, much less engage in a knife fight and then be able to climb into the Picher underground to rescue a kidnapped rape victim.

Perry pondered what lay ahead as the doctor stitched her cuts. Marshal Adams and Raquel kept her talking to distract from her many aches. Deputy Chief Loretta Dickinson had wished her and Sophia a speedy recovery and lauded their success in saving Dels and dealing with the perps, but the detectives were not fooled. Dickinson would ream them out for overstepping their authority the next time they saw her.

When asked if she was allergic to any medications, Perry responded, "I don't do well with oxy. It gives me a migraine. I'm also sensitive to cephalexin. That makes me feel like I have salmonella poisoning. Other than that, I'm allergic to Russian thistle and Mr. Bubble bath soap."

The tall, blond, German-accented physician in his starched white shirt and coat stared at her. He stood ramrod straight and viewed her through round spectacles. He was a handsome young man who took his job and station seriously. He looked puzzled at the mention of Mr. Bubble.

"You're almost free to go, Detective," he said. "But you must rest. I will give you pain medication now, then prescriptions for more, plus a milder antibiotic. I also recommend a tetanus shot."

"I had one six years ago."

"Well, normally ten years is fine, but with your wounds six years is too long. Some of these lacerations are deep and dirty." He kept his gaze on her. "You should have another one since it has been a while," he repeated.

She had not forgotten that tetanus shots were not exactly butterfly kisses. On top of everything else that hurt, the injection site would be sore tomorrow.

He continued inspecting her.

"What?"

"I don't like that spot above your eye. I want to put in one more stitch. Then you can speak with a plastic surgeon about having that area sanded down once it heals."

"Wait. Sanded—"

A yelp sounded from behind the curtain where the man struggled with the kidney stone with his overly sensitive wife.

"See, there it is!" the woman said. "All that yelling for nothing."

"Rhonda's in the Quapaw jail," Raquel said to get her attention. "She's being obstinate and insists that Sean P. forced her to come with him."

"There are cameras all over the casino that will tell a different story," Perry said. "Of her interacting with Sean, Line Billy, and Teresa Bennett. And there's the video at the relay."

"Oh, I know," Raquel agreed.

"How is Lee?"

Raquel paused. "Conscious but confused. Stable."

Perry bowed her head. "That damned Sean."

"Yeah."

"You're not as perky as the last time I saw you," said a voice that came from behind them.

They turned to the door.

"Well, well, Lighthorseman Osceola Tiger," Perry said. "What are you doing here?"

"I heard this is where the action is."

"You're a bit late."

"The crime happened on Seminole land. We've been busy chasing every lead."

"How could I forget that?" Perry asked.

The doctor pushed the needle into her forehead and she yelped.

"Sorry," he said. "Let us get you more lidocaine." The nurse nodded and turned to the cabinet.

"We have recent reports of seven Seminoles missing," Osceola Tiger continued. "Five women between the ages of seventeen and twenty-three. One is thirty-eight. One juvenile male aged thirteen."

"It never ends," Marshal Adams said. He introduced himself to Osceola Tiger.

Tiger said to Perry and Raquel, "If you get word about anyone matching those skimpy descriptions I would appreciate hearing about it."

The new dose of pain medication had kicked in and Perry felt the ache subside. The tightness in her cheeks remained, however. That skin would hurt for some time. As did her heartache for the taken women and teen boy.

The room smelled of disinfectant, vomit, and blood. She really needed to go home.

"Here we are," Perry said. "Representatives from the Quapaw, Seminole, and Choctaw Nations. The other kidnapped women are Citizen Band Potawatomi and Sac and Fox. Those perps committed major crimes in these Nations, across the border in Kansas, probably in Missouri too, and no doubt more that we don't even know about yet."

"Two sergeants from Cherokee County, Kansas, are here somewhere," Quapaw Marshal Owens said. "They're waiting to see what happens with the two perps and they'll want to talk to you in a bit. Not only are both those perps involved in human trafficking, they're also gunrunners with ties across multiple states."

"And Sean thought he could just drop his niece into the mix," Raquel added.

Owens nodded.

Perry added, "And then there's me and Sophia, detectives outside the tribal Nations."

"Sounds like the beginnings of a jurisdictional shit storm," Raquel said.

33

Raquel rolled Perry to Dels Billy's room. A nurse followed, pushing Sophia. Both had balked about sitting in a wheelchair, arguing that they weren't that bad off.

But Raquel had given the detectives a visual once-over. "Could have fooled me. Both of you need to throw away your clothes, and it'll take a stack of washcloths to get you clean."

Perry waved her right hand in dismissal. "Raquel, you're a Marine. You've been through the mud."

"Yes. But not with a hundred fresh stitches and more road rash than the riders in the Tour de France."

The nurse added, "Besides, y'all have to stay in the wheelchairs until you leave the hospital."

They reached Dels's door, which stood ajar. Bake Folsom was sitting on her bed. Vera Spring and Benny Durant sat in the chairs under the television.

Raquel knocked. Vera jumped up to greet them.

"Officers!" She hugged Raquel, then turned to Perry and Sophia. "I hope you're okay." She reached out and touched Perry's knee, then Sophia's.

The two women entered the room. Perry started when she saw Sealy Billy next to one of the chairs. He appeared exhausted. His eyes were red and puffy.

Dels sat propped on the bed, her hair brushed back from her swollen left eye. Her arms were atop the sheet, both wrists bandaged. Her right hand held a Kleenex. A purple cast covered her elevated left leg from the knee down.

"Detective Antelope. Officer Durant," Dels said.

Perry didn't want to ask a trite question like "How are you doing?" She had a pretty good idea as to how Dels was doing. Instead, she asked, "Can you rest?"

"I think so." She squeezed Bake's hand. "When we get home."

"And we will," Bake said.

"Sealy Billy," Sophia said. "Where have you been?"

"With Benny."

"We went to your house after we went to the cemetery." Perry realized that was a bit abrupt. "I'm sorry about your father," she added.

"Sean P. is an asshole," Sealy said. "I hope he dies."

Dels took a deep breath through her nose. Perry realized that she must have only found out about her uncle Line's murder in the last few hours.

"He's right," Dels said. "Our uncle Sean has always been bad news. My parents knew he was. I hadn't seen him since I was a child and I hoped I never would again. My mother didn't like him and Dad never talked about him except for the time he said Sean was worthless as tits on a hen."

Perry chuckled.

"When I was in fifth grade, he came to visit. He insisted on everyone calling him Sean, or Sean P. I asked him to play Chinese checkers. We sat on the floor to play and my parents went outside to feed the horses. All I can remember with clarity was that at some point he was sitting on top of me and wouldn't stop tickling me even though I was crying. He stood up as soon as he heard the screen door slam. I thought that maybe I was just being a baby and never told my parents about it. But as the years went by I wondered if maybe more had happened and I repressed it."

Bake moved closer and grasped her right hand with both of his.

Dels continued: "He never sent Christmas or birthday cards and I rarely thought of him except when listening to MeToo survivors. He came back to Oklahoma about a month ago. Lee mentioned that my uncle was at Sealy's one day when Lee came to pick up a new bridle. Lee said that Sean sat in Line's big recliner with one leg crossed over the other and his hands dangling over the armrests like he was a king." Dels clenched her jaw but didn't cry.

The room was quiet, everyone waiting for Dels to continue.

"Before I was in the dark, you know, underground, I was in the truck. He opened my cage and said, 'Land's gonna be mine now.' Then a smaller man squatted next to him and said, 'Here's those zip ties and duct tape. Gotta wrap that tape around her head a few times so she can't rub it off. We need to hurry. Everything's ready. Just need to get her down there, then we leave.'

"I didn't know what he meant by that until I woke up in the dark place." She turned to Perry. "Then I saw the light and you."

"If it helps," Perry said, "the small man did indeed have severe facial wounds when we first saw him, and your uncle had been swiped across his face with a set of fingernails."

Dels stared at the IV needle in her arm. Her nostrils flared but still she did not cry. "I know what that little man did to me," she whispered. "And now I know my uncle did the same when I was a child. But I got both of them."

In that moment Perry wished she had killed Sean and she

hoped that karma had smacked Reginald Louis Swanton as hard as he deserved. Perry rolled forward and grasped Dels's arm. "You certainly did, Dels. Now you need to do what we're all doing right now and that is to rest. It's over." She knew that this wasn't true. Dels would have to live with her reality and she hoped that Bake had the fortitude to support her.

Sealy coughed and then let out a sob. "I didn't know about Sean until a few weeks ago. My dad never discussed him."

Sealy glanced at Perry, then back at his feet. Perry knew that Sealy depended on his father and the loss would settle around him like a cold, gray fog.

After a few seconds Dels added, "None of us wanted to discuss Sean." Sealy continued to look miserable.

"Sealy, you can take care of things and you'll get through this. Just like I had to after my parents died."

Her cousin sniffed and didn't speak.

"You can come stay with me and Bake if you need to." Then she added, "Our uncle wanted to take what's mine. You've now inherited your father's portion. But know that I'm not selling the land," she continued. "Ever."

Sealy nodded.

"What happened to Sean P.?" Vera asked.

"He's in surgery with multiple injuries," Raquel answered. "Detective Antelope made sure he won't bother anyone again. And the other one, well, Detective Burns dealt with him." She looked at Sophia. "He won't make it."

"Did you shoot him?" Bake asked.

"No," Sophia answered.

"Knife?"

Sophia shook her head.

Perry jumped in. "Her hands."

"Whoa," Vera exclaimed. "I knew you seemed heavy-duty, but damn."

Perry agreed.

Dels showed the beginning of a smile, then lost it. She asked, "What about the women in the truck? I talked to one of them. She said her name was Colleen. She's a Muscogee from Jay."

"We have them all," Raquel said. "They're woozy but they'll be fine." She didn't say anything about their mental states.

"My uncle planned to leave me down there," she said. "He wanted me to die underground in the dark where no one would find me."

"You don't know that for sure," Benny said.

Perry thought that was exactly what Sean had planned.

"I mean," Benny continued, "he probably intended to come back and get you and take you someplace else."

"And that's supposed to make me feel better?" Then she asked Perry, "Did my uncle try to run you down?"

"I believe so, yes."

"And you fought him in the middle of the night."

Perry thought about that for a few seconds. She glanced at the clock on the wall. It read 12:38. The encounter with Sean in the metal building happened around six o'clock that morning. Only six or seven hours ago.

"Something like that," Perry said. "Lighthorseman Hunter here chased down Rhonda and caught her in the chat piles someplace," Perry said. "She's in custody."

Sealy's head jerked up. "Rhonda?"

"You mean the Rhonda who came to the race?" Benny asked.

"Afraid so," Perry said. She nodded at Raquel to explain.

"It appears that Miss Rhonda may have used you, Sealy, and your father. She met Line at the casino, where she worked as a bartender."

"No," Sealy interrupted. "I introduced them. I met her at the feed store. She asked for my number and I gave it to her."

No one responded. Sealy took a moment to catch the thought he was chasing.

"Oh," he muttered.

"Yeah," Vera agreed. "Why was she in a feed store?"

Raquel continued. "We think that she latched on to your father, Sealy, but in reality Rhonda was making plans with his brother."

"Oh, man." Sealy rubbed a hand over his face.

Raquel said, "There was another person involved, who sabotaged your tires and your gas tank, Dels."

"Her name was Teresa Bennett," Perry added. "She was murdered the same day that you were taken. She was the person found at the bike track."

"So many people involved in this plot," said Bake.

"Apparently so," Perry said. "But we still have work to do."

Dels took a deep breath. "And what about you, Detective Burns?"

Perry felt the lovely calm of the medication. She wanted more of it.

"I'll be fine. My ulna isn't broken, but it's bruised enough that I'll use a sling for a couple of weeks."

"Miss Billy," Raquel started, "you need to take advantage of your situation here. You are protected, you are safe, and you have medications at your beck and call. Enjoy it while you can."

Perry interjected. "There's a jurisdictional puzzle we have to solve. Your uncle committed crimes in at least five tribal Nations and three states. But you don't have to worry about all of that. Just be prepared for a lot of questions. You too, Sealy."

"Vera says Lee is conscious," Dels whispered.

"He is," Raquel confirmed. "They're about to take him out of intensive care."

Perry noticed that everyone's attention was on the door. She turned her head and saw Troy, Olyve, and Nico standing there.

"Oh, hi, dear," she said. "Everyone, this is my husband, Troy, and my kids, Olyve and Nico."

Troy wore a white cotton T-shirt and running shorts with Teva sandals. His hair was in two braids but much of it had come undone. Perry tried to remember the last time she'd called him.

Vera gave Troy an appreciative up and down. The muscular Comanche could have been a construction worker or a Ralph Lauren underwear model.

Olyve and Nico hurried to their mother. "Mom," they said almost in unison. Olyve wore her blue lifeguard shorts and a gray swim team shirt. Her younger brother wore a Dune T-shirt featuring Chani and red shorts. His thick, dark curls bounced.

Perry knew that Troy probably sped the whole way to get here from Oklahoma City. *Where is my phone?* she wondered. She dreaded the inevitable grilling she would get from her spouse once they were away from everyone else.

Olyve gripped her mother's hand. "Mother." Olyve called her Mother when she was mad or concerned. "You look—are you— Mother, what the hell happened to you?"

"Yeah, Mommy," Nico agreed. "You got hurt."

Troy strode to her and squatted so he was eye level. He took in her cuts and bruises, her torn and bloody clothing, the dark circles under her eyes. Finally, he reached out and gently hugged her.

"Troy," Perry whispered into his neck, but loud enough for her children to hear. "I found her. We got the culprits. We found the abducted women. They're all here. Sophia will be fine. That's Dels in the bed."

Troy stood and wiped his eyes. "Sorry," he said in his deep voice.

Raquel stepped forward and cleared her throat, took this moment to introduce herself. "Lighthorseman Raquel Hunter. We met a few years ago."

"I know who you are." He took her offered hand and squeezed. His gaze returned to his wife, who sat slumped in her chair like an ill nonagenarian in a nursing home. Then back to Raquel. "You okay?"

"I'm great."

"No you're not. You seem just like my wife—someone who goes full-blast. You need to go home."

Raquel laughed. "Well, you sound just like my guy. We could have a heck of a night playing Hearts and drinking sangria. Then you guys could lecture us."

Troy snorted. "Are you two related?"

Off to the side, Olyve stepped toward the bed where Dels was resting but stayed a respectable three feet away. "You're Dels Billy?"

She nodded.

"My mom told us she wouldn't stop until she found you," Olyve said. "She means what she says."

Dels sighed. "And she did."

Perry coughed. "You know, Lee told us that he was attacked by a shampe," she said.

Dels's eyebrows shot up, as far as they could with her swollen face. Her unhurt eye went to Bake, then to Benny, Sealy, and Vera.

"A shampe?"

They all pondered that for a moment in silence and then burst out laughing.

34

Three weeks later

Dels Billy emerged from her barn leading a beautiful chestnut colt. His smooth coat and brushed mane and tail shone in the sun. A lock of mane fell between the horse's eyes, making it appear as if he had curtain bangs.

Dels now wore a walking boot on her left leg and a beige wrap on her right ankle. Her face had healed. The zip-tie marks were gone from her wrists. From the appearance of her arms, Dels had spent much time lifting weights. Perry understood. Weightlifting had gotten her past many stir-crazy moments when she could not run.

More importantly, Dels wore a huge smile.

"Beautiful horse," Perry said.

"Yeah," Dels said as she patted his neck. "My friend Yarda sent him to me."

"Yarda Red Plume," Perry said.

"The very one. Well, Yarda organized it all, I should say. The teams and the local rodeo association chipped in and she bought him."

The colt reared.

"Hey, hey." Dels held the lead rope firmly and kept her voice even.

"That's really generous," Sophia said. She had recently discarded her arm sling and had resumed lifting weights.

Dels sniffed. "You have no idea how generous. Every relay team is always after good horses. I mean, great horses aren't necessarily good racers. Some are incredibly beautiful like this one, but they don't like to run on a track. They'll run in a field, but when they're forced to do it they just don't want to. We'll see about this one."

"Can we pet him?" Nico asked.

"Of course."

Perry and Troy watched as Olyve and Nico greeted the horse with open palms under his nose and then gentle caresses along his cheek.

Dels cleared her throat. Her eyes glistened. "They didn't have to do that. We compete with one another. But we are together. You know?"

Perry understood. "Yeah. I think your friends are wonderful. I'm sorry you couldn't go to the world championships."

Dels glanced to her house and at Gomer, who lay next to the grill. "Some things are more important."

"They are indeed."

Dels looked at Sophia's arm. "How's the arm?"

"Good. I did twenty pushups today."

The horse snorted again.

"He's bored," Dels said.

"What's his name?" Perry asked.

"Perry. During a race I can yell 'Perr!' "

No one spoke for a few seconds. Perry's eyes burned with tears.

"Luckily your name is unisex. This is a colt. But, um, I

wanted to name him after you." She put a hand on the horse's nose. "You came underground and saved me. I thought Eskeilay was going to get me. She's there underground, you know. With her crawfish and ants. We just don't know where."

Perry felt Troy's hand on her hip. She knew what he was trying to impart.

"Dels," Perry started, "I don't know what to say."

"I have something else for you and Detective Burns." She handed a rolled-up black cloth to Perry and another to Sophia. Curious, they unrolled their gifts at the same time. The white capital letters on the black shirt read SHIT FUCK DAMN. "Bake told me your reactions when you heard me say that on the video."

Sophia laughed and before Perry could start crying they heard a whinny from the barn. They all turned to see Bake leading the prancing Issi and a stout, golden-brown horse with a white tail and mane that fell over its eyes like overgrown curtain bangs.

Dels beamed. "Like I said. Some things are more important."

Both horses wore saddles. They watched as the trio trotted to them.

Bake said, "Detective Antelope. You have already met Issi."

Perry stepped forward and put her hand on the mare's neck. Issi stilled and watched her. Perry leaned forward and breathed into the mare's nose. The horse's nostrils flared, but the filly did not move. Bake held the reins out to Perry.

"We also saddled a horse for you, Detective Burns. This is Gonzo. He's a Haflinger I got from an estate sale. The husband and wife were killed in a crash. He's older, very calm, and gets along with the racers. Sometimes he jogs with me."

"Oh," Sophia said, her eyebrows rising. "Well, that's nice, but I've never ridden a horse."

"That's fine."

Olyve grabbed her mother's arm.

Dels laughed. "You want to take him out?"

Olyve bit her lower lip and looked as if she was about to burst.

Dels held up a hand. "Let your mom go first. Then you'll go. Gonzo knows the way."

"Mother . . ." Olyve prodded. "Daddy? I'm half horse culture!"

Troy held up his hand. Perry knew that despite the Comanches being the historic Lords of the Plains who dominated the southwest, her husband had only been on a horse a few times. He said, "Let Mom go and then Dels will tell you what to do."

Olyve jumped with glee.

Dels turned and looked over her property. "There's a hundred and eighty acres out here. We created a trail next to the fence all the way around, plus a winding trail that does a figure eight. No rocks, no roots. It took our team a long time to do this."

Perry almost started to cry again at hearing that. Clearing land is no small feat.

Dels caught Perry's expression. "We don't always have access to a track. This has to do."

Perry considered that. Issi, a racehorse, would be used to running this land. She closed her eyes and told herself she could stay on her. But if she fell off, there were a lot of people who would rescue her if Issi came back riderless. Then self-doubt kicked in. It had been a long time since she had ridden a horse. She used to ride a lot with her childhood friends who kept horses. She had always wanted a horse, but her father said, "Buying a horse is one thing, but paying to take care of it is another."

Troy squeezed her butt. "Go," he said.

"Yeah," yelled Nico. "Go, Mom!" He jumped up and down.

Perry rubbed Issi's nose again, then went to the horse's left side. She grabbed the saddle horn and jumped on. It was like riding a bike.

"Whoa," Sophia exclaimed. "You're a jockey."

"It's been a while," Perry said.

"You could relay," Dels said.

Perry sat atop the fantastic horse and laughed. "I know how insane you relay riders are. I might be nuts but I'm not crazy."

She got her feet situated in the stirrups and looked down at Dels. "Thank you."

Dels smiled and pointed to the west. "Go through the gate and start by that cottonwood. The trail will take you all around the property."

Perry took the reins in her right hand and gently lay them over Issi's neck. The horse obeyed, turning.

Perry took a deep breath, clucked, then gave what she thought was a gentle kick. Issi took off like a rocket toward the road.

"Don't kick her!" Dels yelled.

Perry gasped, trying to make herself relax. If she fell off, it would hurt. Not only her body, but also her pride.

She pulled back on the reins a little and Issi slowed to a trot.

"Good girl," she said to Issi, then muttered "Damn" to herself. She knew not to kick. Horses usually interpreted that as a punishment.

"Sorry."

Issi flicked her ears.

Perry heard the colt, her namesake, whinnying behind her.

As they made their way along the fence line, Perry took in the dried grasses, the tall cottonwoods along the creek, the scissortail flycatchers perched on the barbed wire fence.

She gave Issi more lead, and the horse increased to a lope,

but Perry knew that she wanted to run. She gently but authoritatively pulled on the reins to show Issi she was in charge. She forced herself to relax.

After a half mile of loping, Perry saw a stand of wild plums. The fruits would be ripe soon. She wondered if Dels picked them and made jelly. A coyote streaked across the open area of buffalo grass and a mourning dove cooed from a redbud tree next to the fence.

Perry inhaled and then exhaled her tension.

Another eighth of a mile and Issi crossed a stream. Her hooves clicked on the river rocks. Perry felt the cool shade under the many cottonwoods.

They emerged into the bright light and a hawk screamed. Then another. Perry looked up and saw a pair. This was unusual. Hawks mated in spring. Maybe through May. But these two were either pissed at each other or happy they were streaking across the sky together. She liked to think these hawks were like her and Troy. Always mad about something and yet always happy enough to yell that they were still together.

Issi now galloped along the trail that bordered the east fence line and her speed increased as if she had been waiting for this final stretch. Perry eased into the gait and her ass did not bounce on the saddle as it had when they started.

Perry sensed that Issi knew that trauma had visited where she lived, but now the horse realized the worst was over.

"Okay, Issi," Perry said.

She relaxed her grip on the reins, leaned forward so she was low on Issi's neck, and squeezed with both feet.

"Let's go."

AUTHOR'S NOTE

Halito! (Hello!) And yakoke (thank you) for reading *Blood Relay*!

The issue of MMIW/P (missing and murdered Indigenous women and persons) is an epidemic-level human rights problem. In 2018, Oklahoma ranked among the top ten states with missing and murdered Indigenous peoples, and the majority of those trafficked, assaulted, and murdered victims were Native females. Many assaults in the northern United States and Canada occur near reservations or "man camps," which house male pipeline construction workers. Oklahoma has only a few man camps, but there are thirty-nine tribes.

Congress approved the Dawes Act in 1887 with the rationale that allotment would help Natives to become prosperous, "civilized" farmers and ranchers. The irony, of course, was that tribes in Oklahoma already were agriculturists and many were wealthy from ranching. Thousands of Natives adhered to their cultural mores, or at least were well aware of them, but they could also read and write in English, lived in houses with chimneys, and had adopted Christianity. Some had attended eastern schools, where they'd earned medical and law degrees in the 1880s. Despite the reality that many Natives were as knowledgeable as their white neighbors, they still had to relent to the allotment process in which tribes lost at least ninety million acres.

Like Perry Antelope, my father's mother was born in Red Oak. She sold her allotment for a pittance in the 1920s, but our family retained the mineral rights. Offers to buy the remaining rights arrive weekly. My husband, who is Comanche, continues to care for the Mihesuah allotment, known as the "home place," located outside of Duncan. Like Perry's and Dels's allotments, parcels purchased by white ranchers and farmers surround his. My great-grandfather created the blueprints for the town of North McAlester and his son was the boxing champion of the southwest in 1913, then later served as chief of police of McAlester. Like Perry's family, my grandparents are buried in the Oak Hill Cemetery in McAlester.

Perhaps you have read the novel *True Grit* by Charles Portis (or have seen the movies). That story takes place amid the violence of post–Civil War Indian Territory, specifically the Choctaw Nation. Tens of thousands of rapes, murders, thefts, and assaults occurred each year across the territory. There were so many crimes that the United States government established the Federal Court for the Western District of Arkansas at Fort Smith to handle the overwhelming caseload. Indians who committed crimes against other Indians in their Nations were tried in tribal courts, but if they transgressed against a non-Native they were tried at Fort Smith. So were the non-Natives who committed crimes on tribal lands. Violence continued after Oklahoma became a state in 1907.

Skip forward to 2020, when the Supreme Court ruled in *McGirt v. Oklahoma* that Oklahoma state courts have no civil or criminal jurisdiction over tribal affairs on reservations. Non-Natives who commit crimes against Native people, however, are under the criminal jurisdiction of state courts. This is why my characters Perry Antelope, Sophia Burns, and Raquel Hunter were concerned about who they called for assistance. Each tribe deals with their own issues. In this story, our heroic women could testify in multiple state and tribal courts. I chose to create Choctaw, Quapaw, Seminole, Miami, and Muskogee tribal police who cooperated with the women who were outside of their jurisdiction, but in reality, that does not always happen.

Picher is a real place, located two hours from my home. The destroyed town is as dangerous as I portray it. Admittedly, it is compelling and I have wandered around the backroads more than I should have. There are many short videos available online that chronicle the once-thriving community and how the residents were forced to leave because of overzealous mining and an F5 tornado.

Indian horse relays are just as exciting and potentially dangerous as I attempt to describe. Riders must possess strength, coordination, timing, determination, and a respect for horses and fellow competitors. There are indeed many women capable of making the horse-to-horse exchanges, but until there are more female participants the ladies' races are either once around the track or twice with just one horse exchange. There are many races each summer, culminating in the world championship, which awards significant prize money. If you want to see horses and Native power, beauty, and pride, make sure you attend a relay. I suggest that you visit the Fort Hall Relay Association's page on Facebook for a schedule of events as well as the Shoshone-Bannock Tribes website.

Although this novel is a work of fiction, I, like most other Native writers, focus on topics that concern me. I draw my themes from personal lived experiences, family stories, and histories. Those concerns are also reflected in my non-fiction books about genocide, violence, racism, boarding schools, repatriation of skeletal remains, stereotypes, Native women, and tribal justice. You read about some of those topics in this book.

The difference between writing about tribal realities and fiction is that with novels I can control the outcomes. I am more interested in problem-solving and solutions than I am in trauma. I believe that the way Native women are presented in art, movies, and literature has an impact on how they are treated. I feel that I have a responsibility to project female positivity and strength. In all my stories, I attempt to describe the resilience and intelligence of Native women. The characters of Dels Billy, Perry Antelope, Sophia Burns, Raquel Hunter, and Yarda Red Plume all exude characteristics of women I know and admire.

ACKNOWLEDGMENTS

I want to thank Robert Rome, master sergeant of the Wyandot Sheriff's Office; Chief Benjamin Barnes of the Shawnee Tribe; Brad Barnard, deputy chief of patrol of the Quapaw Nation Marshal Service; Alonzo "Punkin" Coby, the Shoshone-Bannock mountain sledding and Indian horse relay athlete extraordinaire; Julianna Brannum, movie producer, whose credits include the Picher documentary *The Creek Runs Red* (2006); Richard Godbeer, former director of the Hall Center for the Humanities; and Marcie Rendon, author of the Cash Black Bear series. I also thank my agent, Jacqui Lipton of the Tobias Literary Agency, for her support, enthusiasm, and spot-on suggestions. Much gratitude to Jenny Chen, the executive editor at Ballantine Bantam Dell; editorial assistant Ivanka Perez; editorial assistant Jean Slaughter; production editor Jennifer Rodriguez; managing editor Saige Francis; production manager Jane Haas Sanker; copy editor Melissa Churchill; and interior designer Caroline Cunningham.

I am especially grateful to my family, who are always

there—my husband, Joshua; my children, Toshaway and Ariana; my new children-in-law, Taylor and Austin; my mother, Olyve Hallmark Abbott; my sister, Taryn Wilson; and my sister-in-law, Adele Mihesuah. I also thank my indispensable confidants, the brave writers Trevino Brings Plenty, Gordon Henry, Tiffany Midge, and the indomitable Jacqueline Keeler. Finally, I am grateful for the support of the bighearted Carrie Cornelius, supervisory librarian at Haskell Indian Nations University, who never fails to make me smile. Your bossy chicken rules my backyard.

ABOUT THE AUTHOR

Devon Mihesuah, an enrolled citizen of the Choctaw Nation of Oklahoma, is the Cora Lee Beers Price Professor at the Hall Center for the Humanities at the University of Kansas and the former editor of *American Indian Quarterly* and the University of Nebraska Press book series Contemporary Indigenous Issues. A historian by training, Mihesuah is the author of numerous award-winning fiction and non-fiction books, including *Recovering Our Ancestors' Gardens: Indigenous Recipes and Guide to Diet and Fitness,* which was recently named Best Indigenous Book in the World by Gourmand International; *American Indigenous Women: Decolonization, Empowerment, Activism; Ned Christie: The Creation of an Outlaw and Cherokee Hero; Choctaw Crime and Punishment: 1884–1907;* and *American Indians: Stereotypes and Realities.* She also authored the novels *Roads of My Relations, Hatak Witches, Dance of the Returned,* and *The Bone Picker,* which are optioned for film and television. Mihesuah has been a lifeguard, distance runner, musher, and skijorer; a gun salesperson, line cook, and high school biology and physics teacher; a swimming, basketball, cross-country, and tennis coach; and she holds a black belt in tae kwon do. She was the first female athlete to receive an athletic scholarship under Title IX at the Division I NCAA institution TCU. She is an avid gardener and food photographer. She lives in Kansas with her husband, Joshua Mihesuah, a former university administrator and graduate of Oklahoma State University. His family is chronicled in *First to Fight: The Story of Henry Mihesuah*. Their son, Toshaway, earned his BA and MA degrees from Fort Lewis College in Durango and the University of Arizona, and their daughter, Ariana Taryn, is a graduate of Kansas State University.

devonmihesuah.ku.edu
Instagram: @devon_mihesuah
Bluesky: @dmihesuah.bsky.social

ABOUT THE TYPE

This book was set in Sabon, a typeface designed by the well-known German typographer Jan Tschichold (1902–74). Sabon's design is based upon the original letter forms of sixteenth-century French type designer Claude Garamond and was created specifically to be used for three sources: foundry type for hand composition, Linotype, and Monotype. Tschichold named his typeface for the famous Frankfurt typefounder Jacques Sabon (c. 1520–80).